Romance was the ⁣ ⁣ ⁣ ⁣ ⁣ ⁣ if it rolled in her directi ⁣ ⁣ ⁣ ⁣ ⁣ ⁣ ⁣l fling. But not with a ɪ

Mariko elbowed _ _ _ ⁣ ɔt older guys hang out on this side of the Atlantic," she murmured, eyeing another tall, juicy morsel passing by on his way out the door.

"Alex is married, in case you haven't noticed."

"Oh, I noticed. No law against enjoying eye-candy." Mariko grinned. "You should write a sidebar for your magazine article, 'How to Meet Cute Guys on a Beach.' Tessa would love it."

"Ha, that'd spice up my travel piece." Her editor would love it.

"Sprinkling a handsome guy with dead rose petals would be a fresh angle," suggested Mariko.

"You think?"

"You've had a sniper dot on Alex the whole time. You may as well write about him."

Alex strolled toward them, and Dayna fantasized a slow-motion movie scene: *Arms swinging, he moves toward me, wind teasing his hair, with an I-Want-You-So-Bad expression on his face. His arms scoop me up, and he plants a hot, moist kiss on my quivering lips, dissolving me—*

The seating hostess snapped Dayna back to reality. "This way, please."

"Oh!" In her haste to follow, Dayna's foot caught a chair leg and she tripped. After a sloppy recovery, she limped after the hostess with heated cheeks, to a table for three.

Mariko jerked her head toward Dayna, smiling sweetly at the hostess. "Her name's Grace."

Praise for LoLo Paige

"Hello Spain, Goodbye Heart" won the 2019 Romance Writers of America Tara Contest in Florida, under the working title, "Galicia Starlight." LoLo Paige's contemporary romance books garnered several awards in 2020 and 2021 for best romance, including the Next Generation Indie Award, an Eric Hoffer award, an Indie B.R.A.G. Medallion, and a Kindle Book Award. LoLo's books have been featured in Publishers Weekly, and her true story about escaping a runaway wildfire won a 2016 Alaska Press Club award. Her books have ranked No. 1 on Amazon Bestseller Lists in global markets, including the U.S., Canada, and Australia.

NYT bestselling author Cherry Adair endorsed Alaska Inferno: "Cinematically plotted in a spectacular, dangerous setting…smoldering passion where fire isn't the ONLY heat…"

Hello Spain, Goodbye Heart

by

LoLo Paige

The Wandering Hearts Series

Hello Spain, Goodbye Heart

COPYRIGHT © 2022 by LoLo Paige

Cover Art by *Diana Carlile*

The Wild Rose Press, Inc.
PO Box 708
Adams Basin, NY 14410-0708
Visit us at www.thewildrosepress.com

Publishing History
First Edition, 2023
Trade Paperback ISBN 978-1-5092-4603-8
Digital ISBN 978-1-5092-4604-5

The Wandering Hearts Series
Published in the United States of America

Dedication

To Marc,
The love of my life.

Chapter 1

Dayna

Dayna Benning eyed the ominous Portuguese sky hovering over the roiling sea. Glancing left across the expanse of empty beach, she raised a hand to shade her eyes. She squinted at two beefy guys next to a just-as-beefy Jeep with water rescue equipment; beach lifeguards: one pointed binoculars at her.

Ahead of Dayna, and intent on her mission, Mariko Waller ignored the lifeguards and strode toward the surf, clutching a small, plastic bag with its gray, gritty contents. Wind made a mainsail of her unzipped jacket and her bare feet scrunched sand as she tramped toward thundering surf, like a Viking warrior on a sea quest.

"Don't toss him on the sand, get him in the ocean!" Dayna called out to her best friend.

She zipped up her jacket and plunged bare toes into the warm, white sand, loving how it massaged every crevice and felt oh-so-good after walking around Nazaré all morning. The air had turned chilly, but the sand warmed her toes, like a soothing pedicure.

As Dayna straggled after Mariko, she eyed a yellow sign with two fluttering red flags: *Praia fechada surf perigoso*. Didn't take rocket science to figure it warned of dangerous surf conditions.

We shouldn't be out here.

Dayna quickened her pace with one eye on the brawny guys who had climbed into their Jeep and were now speeding toward them, no doubt to kick them off the beach.

"Hurry! Go-go-go!" yelled Dayna, the crashing waves eating her words. She spun around to see if anyone else might interrupt their mission. She caught sight of a tall guy striding toward them from the direction of the boardwalk.

Oh great, probably a cop or something.

"Come on, Mariko, get Harv into the ocean!" ordered Dayna. The lifeguards and the dude coming up from behind were gaining on them.

Mariko broke into a spasmodic run, opening her bag and holding it high.

Dayna sprinted, her Girls bouncing hard as she clutched an open gallon bag of meticulously preserved rose petals. "Hurry, my boobs are trying to kill me!"

The sound of a shrill whistle competed with the roaring sea as Mariko's legs spun like an Olympic sprinter. Dayna chuckled at seeing her friend run. Mariko detested exercise.

As the fast-approaching vehicle closed in on them, one lifeguard stood in the passenger side, pumping his whistle.

"Do it now!" Dayna barely heard herself against the pounding waves.

Mariko shook the bag as if shaking dice in a million-dollar bet on a craps table. "He's being stubborn—I can't get him out!"

"Oh, for crying out loud." Dayna snatched the bag and hurled the contents onto an emerald wave that curled and broke at the shoreline. "Come on, Harv, swim!"

The women watched with bated breath as the ocean swept his ashes away from the shore. "Goodbye, Harv," said Mariko, her hand on her heart.

Dayna slid an arm around Mariko's waist in a sideways hug, then pulled her arm away to dig into her bag of petals.

"Rest in peace, Brother." She flung a fistful of petals after Harv's ashes, but a powerful wind gust blew them back at her.

"What's this?" spluttered a deep voice, followed by spitting and coughing.

Dayna turned to behold the lofty guy who'd followed them out to the roaring surf. He swiped at the rose petals sticking to the stubble on his face. She jerked around like a chicken, then froze after showering this person with dead rose petals.

Dayna's hands flew to her mouth. "Oh, I'm so sorry! I mean *lo siento*."

The Jeep slid to a stop in the sand and a lifeguard jumped out, motioning them toward the boardwalk, traffic cop style. "*Saia da praia,* please leave the beach."

Mariko held up her strong, slim fingers. "Please sir, we were just leaving."

The lifeguards waited until all three dutifully headed toward the boardwalk before driving away.

Dayna shot a sideways glance at the gentleman with his salt-and-pepper hair, blue and white rose petals stuck to him like magnets.

"*Lo siento, lo siento,*" ventured Dayna, as she stepped through the white sand.

"I speak English," he said, picking a petal from his sleeve. "And it's *desculpa* in Portuguese."

An American. A rather *hot* American.

"Right...*desculpa.*" Dayna's cheeks heated. She berated herself for not studying her Portuguese language program before leaving California. Writing deadlines devoured her time up to the minute she'd boarded the plane. She'd clicked 'Submit' on her phone while scooting down the jetway, relieved she'd made her last deadline.

Hot American plucked another rose petal stuck to his fleece jacket. "What flowers are these? Do you want these petals back?" He held out his fist as the three of them moved away from the beach.

"Yes, but wait until we get out of this squall." Dayna's hair glommed to her face. "They are, or rather were, Blue Dragon roses. Harv grew them, and he started me growing them in my garden back home."

"Beautiful flowers. My auntie grows these." He strode briskly between Dayna and Mariko.

"They're my favorite," gushed Dayna, thrilled that this gentleman appreciated the pride and joy of her garden.

"At least we got Harvey into the sea, just like he wanted." Mariko glanced at Dayna as they stepped up onto the wooden boardwalk.

Dayna squeezed her friend's arm. "Yes. That was important."

Hot Guy pointed his sunglasses in Mariko's direction. "And Harv was...?"

Dayna motioned to her friend. "Mariko's husband. We had to scatter his ashes before the lifeguards chased us off. Honestly, I didn't know you were so close behind us. Sorry the petals blew into your face." The wind fluttered the sleeves of her gray and orange *San Francisco Giants* jacket.

His hair blew into a sexy, wild man vibe. "Blame it on this blustery weather." He turned to Mariko. "I'm Alex. So sorry for your loss." Sympathy crossed his face, despite the sunglasses hiding his eyes. Dayna suspected those peepers would be in happy agreement with the rest of his fine features.

"Pleased to meet you, Alex." Mariko tilted her head, dipping her chin. "I'm Mariko and this is Dayna." She retrieved her flip-flops from her small tote bag.

When Alex smiled at Dayna, the sun came out for her, despite the real one hiding behind purple storm clouds.

"Mariko, I'm sorry you didn't have time to say words for Harv." Dayna wished the lifeguards hadn't chased them away so fast. "I had my eulogy on the ready."

"We'll do it next time," said Mariko. "I'll light candles for him in the cathedrals on our tour."

"You're a good woman." Dayna admired Mariko's ability to conceal her grief, as if reserving it for her very own. Dayna couldn't hide her pain. Instead, she wore it like a sandwich board. All the money she'd spent on counseling after her divorce—what a waste.

The wind re-styled Mariko's short black hair. "Let's get out of this breezy weather. Besides, I've worked up an appetite. Alex, the least we can do for dousing you with dead roses is to buy you lunch."

Dayna noticed Mariko eyeballing him like she wanted *him* for lunch. Not if Dayna could help it. He'd appeared on *her* menu first.

"Yes, it's the least we can do," echoed Dayna. "We have a bus to catch, so it'll be a quickie."

"I have time for a quickie." He grinned at the two

women.

"We only have forty-five minutes." Mariko tapped her wristwatch as if this beach would combust if she didn't eat.

This guy could easily fit the mold for the article Dayna had written for Society Magazine, *The World's Ten Sexiest Men.*

Alex unzipped his jacket and more petals fell out. He bent and scooped them up before the wind seized them. He tucked the petals into his pocket.

Dayna sat on a nearby bench to strap on her sandals. Brushing sand from her toes, she squinted up at him. "So, what do Blue Dragon rose petals taste like? Sorry about that. Would it help to say *desculpa* again?"

Alex laughed. "Unnecessary. Here, I'll help you up." He offered his left hand, and she zeroed in on it.

Gold glinted on his finger. Married.

Damn.

Chapter 2

Dayna

Dayna let him pull her to her feet. His hand warmed her. She glanced around, expecting a woman to pop out of nowhere to claim her husband.

"Thank you. Are you a local?" She shocked herself with a fantasy of yanking him down and doing him on the boardwalk. She shook off the absurdly erotic thought.

"No, just vacationing." Regrettably, he let go of her hand. "Where do you want to eat? This place is full of seafood."

"We love seafood. Right Mariko?" said Dayna, despite the wedding band sting.

She figured eagle-eyed Mariko had noticed, along with the sexy widow's peak in the center of his hairline. Somewhere, Dayna had read a widow's peak was a sign that a person would outlive their spouse. If that included ex-spouses, she wanted one. She'd get a widow's peak implant.

"I eat anything from the sea, long as it's dead. Don't enjoy stabbing wiggling things," quipped Mariko.

Alex pointed to a low-key white building with a green awning. "The Maria Notella restaurant has great seafood stew and a clean rest room. I'd like to wash my hands."

"Me too. Let's go while we're still young." Mariko

flashed Dayna a fake smile and shot out ahead of her.

"Okay, I'll get us a table," Dayna called after her friend as Mariko scooted through the door.

Alex paused and moved in close, holding out his fist. "Here's your rose petals back."

Dayna's breath caught at his sudden nearness. She unzipped her bag and held it open as he dropped the petals inside.

"Thank you," Dayna said shyly, flicking her eyes up at his.

He dipped his chin in response and followed Mariko to the restrooms.

Dayna waited at the seating podium, watching Alex saunter to the rear of the restaurant. Where was his wife? Maybe they take separate vacations. Why would any wife not want to vacation with this guy? Romance was the last thing Dayna trolled for, but if it rolled in her direction, she wouldn't rule out a casual fling.

But not with a married guy. She wasn't a homewrecker, like He-Who-Would-Not-Be-Named.

Mariko appeared and waited with Dayna. "I've heard a lot of hot older guys hang out on this side of the Atlantic," murmured Mariko, eyeing another tall, juicy morsel passing by on his way out the door.

"Alex is married, in case you haven't noticed."

"Oh, I noticed. No law against enjoying eye-candy." Mariko grinned. "You should write a sidebar for your magazine article, 'How to Meet Cute Guys on a Beach.' Tessa would love it."

Dayna laughed, picturing her magazine editor's delight at the idea.

"Ha, it would spice up my travel piece." Tessa *would* love it. She loved Dayna's unique twists in her travel features.

"Sprinkling a handsome guy with wilted rose petals would be a fresh angle," suggested Mariko. "You should write it. If Tessa won't print it, *Cosmo* will."

"Ha, you think?"

"You've had a sniper dot on him the whole time. You may as well write about him." Mariko funneled words out of the corner of her mouth as Alex strolled toward them.

As he approached, Dayna fantasized a slow-motion movie scene: *Arms swinging, he moves toward me, a subtle breeze teasing his hair, with an I-Want-You-So-Bad expression. His arms gather me up and he plants a hot, moist kiss on my quivering lips, dissolving me, melting my...*

"*Senhora. Senhora!*" The seating hostess snapped Dayna back to reality. "This way."

"Oh!" In her haste to follow, Dayna's foot caught a chair leg, and she tripped. After a sloppy recovery with heated cheeks, she limped after the hostess to a table in the center.

Mariko jerked her head toward Dayna and smiled sweetly at the hostess. "Her name's Grace."

Dayna ignored her friend's sarcasm and turned to the hostess. "*Obrigada.*"

She'd remembered how to say thank you from the Portuguese cheat sheet she printed before hustling out the door of her bungalow in Cambria.

The hostess gave Dayna a disdainful once-over, handed her the menus, then sailed off to her podium.

Alex removed his fleece jacket and draped it over his chair.

Dayna glimpsed his sculpted chest and brawny

arms, outlined by his form-fitting, navy Henley shirt, *Denali Aviation* embroidered on one side.

He took a seat, and Dayna chose the chair across from him. He'd removed his sunglasses, revealing gray eyes, tinged violet, like the purple skies over the sea.

Mariko seated herself next to Dayna.

"Are you okay? Saw you trip back there." Humor glinted in Alex's eyes as he picked up a menu.

"Yep, I'm good." Dayna forced her sophomoric gaze down to her menu, like a high schooler sitting with the hottest guy in the school cafeteria. Never mind the fact that she was almost half a century old.

She glanced up. "Did you get the wilted flower smell washed off? Don't want you smelling like a funeral home."

Alex laughed. "Not to worry. Think I smell normal now."

Dayna wouldn't mind getting close to see how he normally smelled.

Mariko spoke up. "As Dayna explained, I'm scattering Harv at every stop on our tour. I started in Nazaré because we honeymooned here forty years ago. In case you're wondering why I carry my husband around in plastic sandwich bags."

"I'm sure your husband appreciates it." A slow smile stretched across Alex's face.

Hard to believe Harv had been gone five years, while Dayna's ex-husband still lived. Not that she'd wish ill will on her ex—well, yes, she did. Three years since the divorce and thinking of him still made her seethe. She hadn't come here to think about He-Who-Would-Not-Be-Named.

Mariko pointed her finger at him. "I knew I liked

you. You're good people. I thank you, and Harv thanks you for aiding our mission."

"I did nothing, except interrupt your ritual," said Alex with a modest smile.

Mariko gave him a solemn look. "You did more than you know."

Dayna meditated on her menu like it held the meaning of life, so she wouldn't gape at the well-packaged testosterone across from her.

Ask about his wife?

No, it would send the wrong message. Like she intended to hit on him.

"Everything here is delicious." Alex's voice tugged her from her menu.

"I take it you've eaten here before?"

"Last night, actually."

She casually lifted her gaze to him, casting aside lusty thoughts of passionate sex in her porn-infested brain. Her face heated, and she blew out a breath.

"Hot in here." *This isn't a hot flash. Only the heat of desire I haven't felt in a gazillion years.* Her inside voice sounded like the unfinished romance novel fermenting on her computer.

Alex retrieved reading glasses from a pocket. "The seafood stew is excellent."

"You've sold me." Dayna laid her menu on the table, noticing his tanned face and windblown mane garnishing his forehead.

"So, you're an airplane pilot from Alaska?"

"You must be a psychic."

"I was born in Sedona. We have psychic abilities." She gestured toward his chest, wrinkling her nose. "It says *Denali Aviation* on your shirt."

Alex glanced down and laughed. "That's right, it does. You're observant."

"It's what I do. I'm a travel writer."

"For Sunrise Magazine. And she's a good one." Mariko's hand smoothed over her short, black hair.

Dayna shot her a look. "That isn't what you said about my Napa Valley article."

"You emphasized the wrong wines." Mariko gave her an eye roll. She lowered her reading glasses and peered over them at Alex. "She clearly needs schooling on excellent wine."

"Hey, I know my way around wine." Dayna shot Mariko her resting snooty face, then turned to Alex. "My story emphasized the wine tours."

"Were you really born in Sedona? I've read about their electromagnetic vortex and spiritual healing with quartz crystals."

Dayna narrowed her eyes in a thoughtful assessment. This guy knew stuff, and he wasn't easily bullshitted.

She shook her head. "I apologize for being a smart-ass. I'm originally from Sacramento. No quartz crystals. Only hipsters, the state capital, and the Tower Cafe. Best breakfast on the planet."

He chortled, and his laugh reminded her of Christmas.

"Wine country. What's your favorite?" He studied her with those tempest eyes.

She feigned a blasé tone. "I liked Australian shiraz until the wildfires. Then theirs tasted smoke-tainted, so I switched back to California reds. Mostly merlot."

"California has their share of fires, too." He lifted a water glass and gulped.

Don't watch him swallow.

"If California wines become tainted, I'll switch to Malbec."

Alex chuckled. "Have you tried port? You're in the best country for it. Rich and full-bodied."

You're the one who's full-bodied.

"So, you're a *Giants* fan." He motioned to the jacket hanging on her chair.

"Never miss a game." She sent a decisive smile across the table. "Today, I'm drinking a white Portuguese varietal."

The server arrived to take their order. Dayna ordered seafood stew and Mariko asked for clam chowder.

Alex leaned back and turned to the server. "*Bacalhau à brás, por favor*. And whatever wine she's having." He gestured at Dayna with a sly wink, and she liked how his eyes crinkled on the sides, giving him a welcoming vibe.

He'd deferred to her wine choice, and her eyes darted to his gold wedding band. The blasted thing was like an irksome pop-up ad she couldn't click away from.

She'd tossed her wedding band into the Pacific Ocean.

Stop it. He's taken. Besides, we'll part ways and I'll never see him again.

She leaned forward to give Alex a shameless eyeful of her low-cut top. She may as well get whatever mileage she could from her new chest assets. "What did you order? In English this time."

His eyes indeed darted to her two reliable beauties. He snapped his gaze to hers.

"*Bacalhau à brás*. Shredded cod sautéed with onions and straw-fried potatoes, mixed with olives and parsley. We have lots of cod in Alaska, but I enjoy the delicious way it's prepared on this side of the Atlantic."

"You speak Portuguese well," Mariko commented.

"Yes, I'm impressed by your linguistic prowess." Dayna leaned back in her chair as glasses of wine appeared at their table.

"Sounds like what a travel writer would say." He fingered his wineglass and looked at Dayna, then Mariko. "My grandparents were Portuguese. I flew for a commercial airline and spent considerable time in Europe. Even married a French girl."

"Oh." So. There it was. Dayna swallowed hard. Of course, he had a sleek French supermodel, probably named Genevieve, same as her ex's trophy wife, she thought sourly. Aren't they *all* named Genevieve?

She glossed over the wife reference. "Do you still fly for the airline?"

"Retired five years ago. Still fly small planes. Why drive when you can fly?"

His eyes drifted to her Girls, and he jerked his gaze away.

"I completely agree," she simpered, relishing the attention. Her heart took off for who-knows-where. She'd find it later.

He lifted his glass. "Here's to Harv in the sea, with his Blue Dragon roses." He winked at Mariko and shot a smile at Dayna.

She wasn't sure why she blushed.

They all clinked glasses and sipped.

Alex sobered. "Honestly, Mariko, I'm so sorry for your loss."

"Thank you, my dear. It's been a good while now." Mariko dipped her chin in the elegant way Dayna had seen her do countless times with her Japanese family in San Francisco.

The server brought their food, and Dayna realized her stomach had been gurgling. She plucked out the clams, pulling the meat from the shells, then picked up a spicy shrimp and pulled off the legs and tail.

When everyone finished eating, Mariko glanced at her watch. "Time to go."

"Our bus to Lisbon will be at the mermaid statue in ten minutes." Dayna sounded like she had a date with the grim reaper.

Was that disappointment that crossed Alex's face as he leaned sideways to retrieve his wallet from his pants pocket?

"No, Alex, I've got this," said Mariko. "So nice meeting you."

She tapped Dayna's wrist and stood. "See you on the bus." She rushed off before anyone could protest.

"Thank you, Mariko. So long," Alex called after her. "She didn't have to pay for my lunch."

"Mariko has a generous heart."

Alex pulled out bills for a tip. "Where are you going next?"

"Lisbon, then Barcelona to begin our group tour with Wanderlust Travel. Mariko talked me into going on this tour, and my magazine editor thought it would make a great travel article. Northern Spain, southern France, then back to Portugal."

"Sounds fantastic. I hope you ladies enjoy yourselves." Alex finished his wine and stared off.

Dayna detected a hint of sadness in his eyes. He was too exquisite to be sad. "What about you?"

"I plan to walk part of the Camino de Santiago trail,

the Way of St. James, in Spain. Are you familiar?"

Her mind raced, ticking off the list of sights in her travel brochure. She remembered scribbling an asterisk next to this popular destination.

"Yes, it's on our group itinerary. When I read about why people walk it, I considered making it a sidebar for my travel piece." She thought for a moment. "I had a friend who walked it a few years ago to find herself. Is that why you're going? To find yourself?"

"Something along those lines. I'm walking from Burgos to Santiago de Compostela in Spain, about 250 miles. They say it takes about three weeks. I hope to average ten to twelve miles each day."

Her eyes roved him in a two-second evaluation. "You seem like you can manage it. I couldn't, possibly. Twenty years ago, maybe."

His eyes roved her right back, along with a million-dollar smile. "Sure, you could."

She couldn't remember how long it had been since a guy smiled at her that way. Goosebumps sprung up on her arms like daisies. "Are you walking alone?"

"Yes."

What about the French wife? Dayna wished she could walk the trail with him. What a wild and crazy thought.

"I have to go. Sorry you got rose petals in your face—but not sorry I met you." She feigned a lighthearted tone.

"A unique experience, for sure." He stood and pushed in his chair, gesturing for her to walk ahead of him. "Where's your bags?"

"On the bus. We're only here for the day." She drew a deep breath, hating the gold band on his finger—hating how the good ones are always taken. She wondered if anyone had ever thought the same about her, back when she wore her own wedding band.

They wandered out to the boardwalk as the bus pulled up. Mariko stood next to it, waving her to hurry.

"Dayna." Alex spoke her name in such a way, her gaze drifted to his.

He slanted a grin at her. "Maybe our paths will cross someplace in Spain. You never know."

She knew darn well she'd never see him again. "Wouldn't that be something?" She extended her hand and wished he would press it to his lips. "Nice meeting you, Alex. I hope you find answers on your trail walk."

He squeezed her hand. "Thanks. It was fun meeting you. Tell Mariko thanks for the delightful meal. And what a humbling experience it was to witness her scattering her husband's ashes." A sad expression crossed his face.

Alex fixed his eyes on Dayna's as if he could see into her soul.

She wanted to bare it for him. If things were different, she'd bare a heck of a lot more than her soul. She couldn't look away.

Apparently, he couldn't either.

Time suspended, as if every air molecule had stilled. *Did he feel it too?*

If he wasn't married, she would have asked for his email address. If her schedule wasn't so rushed, she would have hung out with him…which made no sense for someone she could never have.

Life sucked sometimes.

"Dayna, get the lead out!" Mariko called to her.

Dayna glanced at Mariko, then back at Alex.

17

"Good luck to you. Have a safe trip." She donned her sunglasses and turned away.

Everything slid to slow motion. An impossible tide rolled toward her as she stepped to the bus. She couldn't dispel the feeling of walking away from something wonderful. Her chest clenched and a familiar heaviness anchored her heart. Similar to when her ex had walked out on her for the last time.

Alex is married. Don't do to his marriage what your ex's mistress did to yours—don't be a homewrecker.

Then why did she feel like Meryl Streep in the truck behind Clint Eastwood at the end of *Bridges of Madison County*? Meryl was torn between staying in the truck with her husband or jumping out to run after Clint, knowing if she didn't, she would lose him forever.

Wait, this is insane. She'd only known this guy for a couple of hours and didn't even know his last name. Her heart mashed up in a roiling mix of confusion. The romantic notion of being on a European vacation had clouded her mind with impossible fantasies.

Then again, how often during her forty-nine years had she made a choice, that if chosen otherwise, her life would have been on a different trajectory? If she hadn't turned left that one time when she did, she would have been T-boned. If she hadn't forgotten her birth control pills on her trip to Tahoe, or hadn't married He-Who-Would-Not-Be-Named, then she wouldn't have her son, Josh.

A hole opened in her heart and Mariko and the bus blurred. Choices, choices. Which were the right ones? She reminded herself of the wonderful people she had yet to meet on this trip.

Alex was only the first of many. He stood on the

boardwalk as the bus pulled away, smiling and waving as if he'd known her all her life.

She pressed her palm to the window, watching him grow smaller.

The bottom fell out of her.

If only.

Chapter 3

Alex

Alexander Mendes thought he'd had it all figured out. His daughter, Zoey, had talked him into walking the El Camino de Santiago trail when he couldn't shake the continuous funk he'd fallen into. Zoey's husband, Ethan, had hiked the trail two years ago, from St. Jean Pied de Port on the French side of the Pyrenees to Santiago de Compostela, in northwest Spain—all four-hundred eighty miles.

He'd be lucky to walk half that distance.

His phone vibrated and Zoey's photo appeared. He picked it up and tapped it.

"Hey Z, what's up?"

"How's Spain, Dad?" Her voice sounded warbled. Another bad cell connection to Anchorage.

"The weather is nice, but chilly. Glad I brought a warm jacket."

"Are you stoked for the El Camino?" She sounded chipper.

"Yeah. I'm—stoked."

He honestly wasn't, but he wouldn't let her know that. Zoey had purchased his airfare for Father's Day and insisted he do this. He paced the small room, then looked out the window at the picturesque lights of Burgos.

"Ethan said his phoenix had risen from the ashes

after walking the El Camino. I'm glad I convinced you to do it. Your phoenix needs a serious kick start, Dad," she said in a cheerful voice. "This walk will help you figure things out. Everyone who does this pilgrimage says they saw things more clearly after doing it."

"Right, honey, I'm sure it will."

Silence hung between them as Alex stared at a neon light for San Miguel beer across the street from his hotel. He could sure use one right now.

Alex had shouldered his grief for so long he couldn't remember what normal felt like. He'd tried to piece his shattered life together after becoming a widower.

Widower. He hated that word. It sounded portentous, like he'd lacked for something.

Zoey let out a sigh. "You don't sound convinced. Where are you and what are you doing?"

He sat on his bed and tapped his phone speaker icon. "In my hotel room in Burgos, rearranging my backpack." He set down his phone and picked up his wallet.

Abrielle's memorial card fell out, her beguiling headshot on one side, a flying gull on the other. His heart ripped in half.

"I wanted to wish you safe travels before you set out tomorrow."

"Thanks, honey. I appreciate it." He picked up the card and studied it, rubbed his thumb over Abrielle's face.

Zoey paused. "You'll meet some wonderful people along the way. I hope you find peace and it helps."

"Me too, honey." He'd give it his best shot to satisfy his only daughter.

"When do you plan to visit Aunt Mara?"

"A few days after I finish the El Camino. I reserved

21

one of our Mendes villas at the Santa Maria."

Zoey squealed. "Oh my gosh, the new Mendes village development! I finished the bookkeeping to pay the contractors and sub-contractors at your end, as you'd requested. I love the brochures Aunt Mara uploaded on the company website. Wish I could see the villas in person."

"You and Ethan can stay in one sometime." He gazed out at the twinkling lights in the square. "Write it off on your taxes."

Zoey giggled. "Love how you work the angles, Dad. Congratulate Aunt Mara for the profit windfall from the Santa Maria development. She is truly a visionary and a savvy businesswoman. I miss her so much."

Alex smiled into the phone. "I know, honey. I'm looking forward to seeing her."

"You haven't seen her in a long time either. You've been stuck for so long. I hope you can move on with your life after you walk the El Camino trail."

Alex hoped he could, too. It felt like he was ready to move on. He just had to convince his grieving heart to do it.

"Your partnership with Aunt Mara and Mendes Enterprises has done well, Dad. You two make a stellar team. You should treat yourself. Replace your antiquated plane and buy yourself a Lear jet."

"Well, I know how to fly one." He laughed. "I love that about you. Always thinking ahead. I love my Beechcraft Bonanza. We've shared lots of hours together."

"Old habits die hard, Dad." He appreciated her teasing sentiment and concern for his well-being.

"Right." He sighed at her subtle truth.

A door slammed on the Anchorage end. "Ethan's home. Got to go, Dad. Take it easy on your knee. Got your knee brace?"

"Yep. Love you too, honey. I'll call you from Aunt Mara's."

"Sounds good. Love you, Dad. Bye."

Sighing, he plugged in his phone and set his alarm for the morning.

He spoke to Ellie's photo as he always did. "Best friends and lovers aren't supposed to die young," he mumbled to the photo, setting the card on the silky comforter. "We were supposed to grow old together. Sit on our rockers and play with the grandkids."

Alex didn't have grandkids yet, but the thought of it in a future without Ellie was unthinkable. Try as he might, he couldn't get past the finality of Abrielle's death. She would always be the love of his life.

He brushed his fingers across her face and lifted his hand to study his distorted reflection in the gold wedding band. Alex couldn't bring himself to take it off yet. He wasn't sure how these things went, but he couldn't bring himself to remove it. Removing it would be disloyal, a betrayal to his marriage vows.

Maybe he'd take it off after walking the El Camino. *How the hell do people get through losing a spouse they love more than life itself? How is this supposed to go?* He tried grief counseling but stopped going—didn't enjoy spilling his guts to a group of strangers.

He'd welcomed the break from Alaska, only because everything there had reminded him of Ellie; skiing and snow-machining at Resurrection Pass, and spending summers at Ptarmigan Lake when he'd fly them to their cabin in his float plane. They'd cherished

23

their gorgeous home at the top of Potter's Marsh overlooking Turnagain Arm, south of Anchorage. And their wonderful daughter, Zoey. Life had been spectacular.

Until the damn cancer.

Walking the El Camino was legendary for resurrecting the spirit. His trampled spirit needed resurrecting, all right. Ellie died two years after he'd retired. They'd made so many plans.

Three years later, he felt no better off than before. Time had dulled the pain but not ended it. He'd tried dating other women but had never gone beyond the first or second date. No one measured up to Ellie. Part of him wanted to let go of her, but the other part thought loving another would be a betrayal, as if his precious wife had never existed.

Here he sat on the eve of his big walk, hoping to quash the pain. His knee bothered him again. An old football injury had become arthritic, and he'd had to pamper it these past few months as he'd worked out and ran his laps to prepare for this long trek.

He leaned back, assessing the usual pain relievers, hot and cold compresses, and the elastic knee brace.

He laid his clothes out for the morning, planning to rise before daybreak for an early start. Wincing at his arthritic knee, he stripped and crawled into bed. He'd planned every trip aspect—how many miles per day and where he'd stay. If his knee didn't give him fits, he figured he could manage the trail distance in twenty-three days.

A strip of pink neon nudged between the window drapes, and he stared at it, willing himself to sleep. His thoughts drifted to Dayna, the animated travel writer from California. What had she asked him—was he walking the trail to find himself?

He chuckled. Hadn't heard that one since the 1970s, when it was trendy to search for yourself.

Images of the brown-haired, free-spirited writer cycled through his brain. He wished he'd had more time with her. They seemed to hit it off, and she'd made him laugh. He liked her zest for life and vibrant energy. What a flipping idiot—he hadn't asked for her last name. He'd find out from Sunrise Magazine once he returned to the States.

Too bad they couldn't meet up on this side of the Atlantic since they were both here.

He hadn't intended to follow Dayna and Mariko that day on the beach, but something had drawn him to Dayna. Even from a distance, she'd reminded him of Ellie—her walk, the way she carried herself, and her spirited verve. Or maybe her impish grin after covering him with rose petals had attracted him.

He'd enjoyed her feisty personality. An image of *San Francisco Giants* on her savory, latitudinal chest scrolled across his brain like a news ticker. He became aroused and let out a slow breath to relax himself.

Get some sleep. He had a long walk ahead. Three weeks' worth. Sighing, he rolled over to dream about free-spirited travel writers on white sandy beaches.

Chapter 4

Dayna

"Where is Burgos?" Dayna asked Mariko as they settled into their comfortable hotel room in Barcelona.

"In the middle of northern Spain." Mariko tossed her a tour map, then whipped a toothbrush from her carry-on and ducked into the tiny bathroom.

She popped her head out, brushing like her mouth was on fire. "So, what did you think about our beach boy, Alex? Mister Sex-on-a-Stick?"

"I know, right?" Dayna made a face as she sat on her bed, studying the tour map. "You *would* have to bring him up. I've been trying to wipe him from my brain ever since yesterday. He talked about starting his trail walk in Burgos."

Dayna ran her finger along the map and squinted at it.

Mariko yelled from the bathroom. "Your hot Alaskan pilot will be long gone by the time we get there. We're on a motor coach. We won't be zooming down the road like back home on the 405."

Dayna gave her a pained look. "Did I say I wanted to see him? No. I didn't. And he's not *my* hot Alaskan pilot. Besides, he's *married*." She said it like it was the scourge of the universe.

"Why don't you Google him?" Mariko sucked in

water from a cup and swished it from one cheek to the other.

"What do I type in? 'Alex, hot pilot from Alaska?' He didn't tell us his last name. I didn't ask once I saw Fort Knox on his finger."

Mariko rolled her eyes and ducked into the bathroom to spit. "It frosts your corn flakes that he's married, doesn't it?"

She came out holding a towel. "Ever since Paul left, you've buried yourself with work, hiding away in your cozy little bungalow in artsy-fartsy Cambria. Talking you into this trip was like yanking out your incisors."

"What's your point?"

Mariko sat on Dayna's bed. "So, we begin our vacation and right off, you meet a nice American guy. And not bad on the eyes, either. It's too bad he's married because it's time you got laid. No more cheap thrills with your poor, overworked phone vibrating between your legs."

Dayna guffawed. "I'm not a homewrecker like He-Who-Will-Not-Be-Named. When and if I get laid, it'll only be to satisfy my carnal needs. I've never had sex with a random guy simply for the thrill. I want to see if sex with hot strangers is everything it is cracked up to be. Get it on, then go our separate ways." She swished her hands together and held them up.

"By the way, I don't masturbate with my phone. I have more sophisticated vibration equipment."

"We'll be in France, the perfect place for you to sow your loose oats." Mariko shot her a suggestive look.

"Remember when menopause hijacked my libido and locked it in solitary confinement? Now it's out on parole, and I plan to get as much mileage out of it as I can in case it violates me again."

"You shouldn't rule anything out because of the past," chided Mariko.

Dayna frowned at the map. "I don't care about the past anymore. Only the present."

"They call that memory loss," quipped Mariko.

"Sunrise Magazine might be paying for this trip, but that doesn't mean I can't fool around while working on my travel piece. I consider it research. I can even write off condoms." Dayna flashed a smug smile.

She folded the map and tossed it aside. "The whole love thing is overrated. From what I remember, when you're in love, you lose perspective. Even stinky cheese tastes yummy. Won't make that mistake again."

"Who said anything about love?" Mariko said dryly. "Let me know how this casual sex thing works, stinky cheese notwithstanding."

Dayna stuck her tongue out at her friend.

Mariko stood. "Since you want to loosen up, start with a Sangria and a hot Flamenco dancer. Our tour group has dinner and a show tonight, remember? Come on, old lady."

"Hey, watch it. I'm in good shape for an almost fifty-year-old." Dayna straightened and lifted the two sculpted girls that lived on her chest.

Mariko pursed her lips. "You think you've scored a home run with those fake boobs? I'm sorry they weren't enough to keep He-Who-Will-Not-Be-Named, but no one can compete with a supermodel."

"Who says I plan to let these babies go to waste? Paul paid for them before the divorce, so I'll use them to get my revenge." She sent her friend a wicked grin.

"Your real ones were just fine." Mariko scowled.

"The real ones weren't enough. Neither was I."

Dayna recalled how devastated she was when Paul had asked for the divorce after she'd unveiled her New Girls for their twenty-eighth wedding anniversary. His infidelity and abandonment had turned her into an embittered mess. It'd take a miracle to rid herself of her anger and resentment toward Paul, and a bigger miracle to convince herself her failed marriage wasn't her fault.

Mariko's face changed to apologetic. "I didn't mean you only did it to hang onto Paul."

"We both know that's exactly why I did it," grumbled Dayna. "I wasn't lucky like you. Harvey loved you, no matter how you looked."

"Looks aren't everything."

"Tell it to He-Who-Will-Not-Be-Named."

Dayna cupped her Girls. "Now that I'm here in the land of anything goes, maybe I'll test-drive these beauties. They've stuck with me like two reliable pals. They haven't turned traitor and gone south on me yet."

"Give it time. Those things have their own zip codes. Took forever to get them through airport security. They enter a room before you do." Mariko pulled on a light jacket. "Come on, let's go. And stop playing with yourself."

Dayna liked that when she let go of her Girls, they didn't drop far.

"And bring that map," ordered Mariko. "Maybe we can track down your Alaskan pilot."

****

"Wake up, we're in France." Mariko tapped Dayna's arm.

Dayna's lids fluttered open to a large, vertical sign, *St. Margarita Hotel*. Hung over, she'd slept through the drive to Lourdes. Last night, she'd flirted with the sizzling Flamenco dancer after too much Sangria at the tour group dinner theater in Barcelona. The male dancer, Merche, had kicked toward her in the sassy way Flamenco dancers did with their don't-screw-with-me attitude. The female dancer had practically spit fire at Dayna as she sat in front row center.

Probably because Dayna had flirted with Merche and kept whistling at him.

Afterward, she and Mariko had walked the La Rambla, a tree-lined promenade famous for shopping, restaurants, and people-watching. Their group had toured Antoni Gaudi's architectural masterpiece, the *Sagrada Familia* cathedral, and ambled through the congested *La Boqueria* market. They'd gaped at the rows of pork legs with hooves still attached and squiggly slimy things Dayna figured belonged on an *Addams Family* dinner plate.

Barcelona had been incredible, and she'd wanted to stay longer than their three days; the downside to being on a group tour. She vowed to come back on her own someday.

Dayna glimpsed the glistening river across the street from the hotel in their new France location. The bus crossed a quaint, decorative bridge, and Dayna noticed the snow-topped Pyrenees mountains looming in the background.

"Isn't this beautiful?" Dayna squeezed Mariko's arm.

"Welcome to France, ladies and gents," said Rachel, the Wanderlust Tour director, over the PA system. "Get checked in. Lunch is in one hour in the hotel dining room."

Dayna trudged in behind Mariko, and they settled into their hotel room. The rest of the afternoon was free until their tour group met for evening dinner at the hotel.

"Feel like walking around Lourdes? You need to help me scatter more of Harv." Mariko pulled out her toothbrush and set to work with her frenetic brushing, as she always did when they arrived somewhere.

She finished brushing and tapped her mouth with a hand towel. "Don't forget to take your blood pressure."

Dayna's head still pounded after the morning drive to Lourdes.

"I know, I know. Took it before we left California and it had skyrocketed." She opened her bag and pulled out her portable blood pressure cuff and wrapped it around her bare bicep, then pumped it tight. Her doctor told her if it didn't come down after her trip, she'd put her on blood pressure medication.

"I'm too young for this," grumbled Dayna. "Damn genetics."

"Better keep a close eye on it. Think happy thoughts. Think about Alex, the hot Alaskan pilot."

"Uh-huh, right? Thinking of him would explode my arteries."

Dayna sighed at her BP of one-forty-eight over ninety-three. Hypertension ran in her family and her parents had passed away because of it. She jotted her numbers down in her dog-eared journal with the rest of her high BP numbers.

After their scrumptious meal of croissants and cream cheese, Dayna and Mariko strolled through the historical, picturesque village of Lourdes.

"Walk slow, on account of I had too much Sangria and made googly eyes at Merche." Dayna lagged behind her friend.

Mariko gave her an eyeroll. "You're such a flirt."

The two women entered a wide stone walkway shared by pedestrians and small vehicles. It led to the outdoor Grotto, the shrine to Our Lady of Lourdes, where the Mother Mary had appeared to St. Bernadette in 1858. The Grotto was nestled at the base of a huge cathedral, built to honor what had happened there. The apparition events had precipitated a worldwide pilgrimage, where people from all walks of life and religions visited, many desperate for mental or physical healing.

Dayna tapped these notes into the note-taking app on her phone.

Mariko pointed at a metal pedestrian bridge over a calm river that paralleled the wide walkway.

"Our tour map says this is the Gave de Pau River. Let's sprinkle Harv from the bridge."

"There's people everywhere. You don't want to get caught scattering him, do you? And get arrested? Unless it's a handsome *gendarme*." Dayna craned her neck to see if she could spot a French police officer.

"We'll hang out on the bridge until no one is around," said Mariko in her matter-of-fact tone.

Dayna glanced at people strolling by. "Good. I'm not up for getting arrested. I don't speak French."

"Ye of little faith. Come on, Miss Skeptic." Mariko lifted a plastic snack bag from her pocket, holding more of her husband. She charged ahead to the bridge.

Dayna followed, hoping they could pull this off.

Mariko waved her to hurry. "The coast is clear!"

Dayna made a covert glance left, then right. "Do it now," she said out the side of her mouth, sliding her hand inside her purse to grasp a handful of dried rose petals.

Mariko slipped her hand over the metal railing and turned her snack bag upside down. Harv's ashes streamed down to the water's surface. She peeked over as Harv hit the lazy river and floated into the current. She blew him a kiss and waved goodbye.

Dayna opened her hand to release the Blue Dragon petals. As she watched them drift to the river, a twinge twisted her heart, recalling this was how she'd met Alex on the beach; and she wished things could be different.

"Rest in peace, Harv," Dayna said to the river, then crooned the first few lines of *Amazing Grace*.

Mariko put up her hand. "Enough already. You're always off key."

"Then *you* sing it. You're the music teacher," groused Dayna.

Mariko taught violin and piano to music majors. "I said a prayer instead."

Dayna hollered at the river. "She won't let me sing to you, Harv! Don't worry, I'll keep an eye on her for you."

She shot Mariko a wink as the current swept him downstream.

Mariko gave her a dour look. "You're such a smartass."

"What are friends for?" Dayna slid her arm around her friend's waist and hugged her. "I expect you to do the same for me when the time comes. How much of Harv do you have left?"

"Two more bags. One for the Cape of Finisterre and one for Lisbon. Harv loved those two places."

"You're a good wife." Dayna patted Mariko's back. "Harv would get a kick out of all this. He was the brother

I never had."

"He loved you, Dayna." Mariko stared off. "The first time we did this trip, he said if he died first, to please scatter him in the rivers and ocean shores along the way."

Dayna and Mariko left the bridge and approached the grotto. A continuous line of wheelchairs and people with canes and crutches mingled with people from all over the world. All stood in single file to pass the shrine. Some dipped fingers in a small pool of clear water near the back of the grotto and rubbed it on their faces as they passed. Several blew kisses to the statue of Mary, then stepped through with folded hands. Others rubbed their hands on the cliff face as they moved past.

Dayna marveled at the grotto's polished sheen from countless hands, having rubbed it for well over a hundred years. The number of people visiting this site and their displays of devotion awed her.

"What's that?" Dayna tapped Mariko's shoulder and pointed beyond the grotto to a long, gray stone wall with people spread along it, holding plastic containers under bronzed faucets.

"Holy water from the grotto," said Mariko. "Thought to have healing powers. People come from around the world to drink and bathe, believing they'll be cured of what ails them. The holy baths are right beyond it."

Dayna hung back, dubious. Her cynical nature prevented her from buying into what it promised.

"I've heard about this—but not sure it's my thing. You know I'm not religious."

"Come on, Miss Prove-It-To-Me-Or-I-Won't-Believe-it, do the holy baths with me."

"Yeah, right? Lightning will strike me." An idea

occurred to Dayna. "Will it fix my blood pressure?"

"I'm not the miracle worker on duty today, so I can't guarantee a BP fix. Come on, what can it hurt?" prodded Mariko, stepping ahead of Dayna.

"This is your thing, not mine. I agreed to come with you, but not to do all this other stuff." Dayna waved her arm around, then caught Mariko's disappointed face. She let out a resigned sigh. "I suppose it'd be grist for my magazine story. Oh, what the hell."

"You'll wind up there if you don't stop swearing." Mariko marched off toward the holy baths.

Dayna knew her friend took her faith seriously, while her own had muddied these past few years—okay, over the past decade—well, all right, two decades. It still didn't give her the right to disrespect Mariko's devotion to her faith.

She and Mariko took a seat alongside two hundred other women waiting for the baths. It was a long, chilly wait, but they had a roof over them to keep off occasional rain. Soft hymn singing broke out as they waited. After two hours of shivering, Dayna stood.

"Stick an ice pick in me, I'm frozen. I'm so not up for this."

Mariko stepped in front of her. "You've waited this long. Don't bail now. If anyone could use a healing bath, you could. Trust me, you'll be glad you did. Maybe it'll get your nose back in joint and you can forgive He-Who-Shall-Not-Be-Named."

"And why would I ever consider forgiving that piece of—"

Mariko's forefinger sprang to her face. "No cussing," she hissed.

Dayna let out an impatient sigh. "I heard someone

say we have to get naked. Of course, this is France. I don't want to go skinny-dipping in holy water—it'll sizzle when it hits my skin. You know what? This is a bad idea. I'm out of here."

She turned to go when a short, gray-haired nun with soft eyes emerged from a narrow wood door in the wall of gray brick. She motioned Dayna and four women to follow.

"Too late now," murmured Mariko, shoving Dayna forward.

The group of five entered an area where people sat in chairs along a wall, facing what resembled department store changing rooms, with blue-and-white striped curtains. Dayna sat next to Mariko, listening to women's voices murmuring prayers behind the curtains. Every so often a kerplunk and a whoosh sounded like someone had cannon-balled into a pool.

Dayna leaned toward Mariko. "Sounds like they're baptizing Loch Ness monsters in there," she whispered. "They can't force me to strip, can they?"

"Course they can. They're nuns."

"They can't make me. No way." Dayna shook her head. "It's too cold. I'm out of here."

She stood to go when the little nun laid a firm hand on her shoulder.

"Madame, *viens avec moi, s'il vous plaît. Anglais or Francais?*"

Dayna went deer in the headlights and stared at her, translating in her head. "Um, English, please—I mean *s'il vous plaît.*"

She towered over the little nun like a Lakers point guard. The nun took Dayna by the hand and led her to the mysterious curtain. Dayna shot Mariko a crazed look as the nun whisked the curtain open and motioned her inside.

Dayna stepped into a small space enclosed by gray stone.

"Remove your clothes, please," the nun said in perfect, accented English. She held up a blue square of cotton with Velcro, reminding Dayna of a swimsuit cover-up.

"Put this on, then sit until I come for you." The little nun darted out again.

Mariko stood a few feet away, doing the same. Dayna trembled with cold, annoyed with herself for letting her friend talk her into this. She was still easily swayed, thanks to He-Who-Would-Not-Be-Named, who'd controlled her like a Stepford wife.

Dayna thought back over things while she waited. She despised her ex for abandoning their decades-long marriage for a cutie-pie half his age. What was the deal with men, having to get a glamorous trophy wife to have and to hold from mid-life on?

Her only solace would be knowing that Genevieve would be Paul's caregiver when he reached the drool stage. Then his sweet, young squeeze would tire of it and leave him as he'd left Dayna.

Payback. The thought of it warmed her shivering heart.

The little nun appeared and held out her hand.

"Come, madame." Dayna took her hand and followed her beyond another mysterious curtain into a small enclosure encased by the same gray stone as the wall outside. A six by four-foot pool full of foreboding, green water occupied the middle of the space.

Dayna must have appeared nervous because the

37

little nun cupped her cheek. "Don't be afraid. Open your heart to forgiveness, of yourself and others. Let the soothing water wash your anger and bitterness away. Heal your heart, *ma chère.*"

Dayna drew back, startled, as if the nun had a window into the most private part of herself. How did this person know what lived in Dayna's heart? She'd hit the proverbial nail on the head. Dayna shook as if hypothermic.

Two nuns stood, one on each side of the rectangular pool, two stone steps leading into the dark green water. The little nun prodded Dayna to stand on the edge of the steps. The wet stones were cold and slick. Her toes curled under, searching for stability, so she wouldn't slip.

Dayna glanced anxiously at the taller nuns, one on each side. Each took her hand and nodded. Her stomach cramped from nerves.

What am I supposed to do?

"State your intention, madame," said the little nun, whispering behind her. "The healing bath is your personal sacred act."

Dayna cast a furtive look over her bare shoulder. "I—I don't—oh shit. I mean, I'm sorry—" she shook her head. Her mind blanked, and she hoped no lightning bolt would zap her for her 'shit' slip.

"*C'est bon.* Don't be afraid. We'll pray over you."

The icy water shocked Dayna's system as she cautiously stepped into the bath. Another step, and the water rose to her thighs. Shivering, she braced herself.

"Relax, madame. Sit down," the first nun instructed.

Her body stayed rigid. The three nuns took hold of her and rocked her backward, so the back of her head touched frigid water. They then stood her up, all in one fluid motion, while murmuring in French.

The little nun shielded her with the blue wrap, then folded it around her. "Get dressed now. Let the water dry naturally. It dries fast. Do not wipe it off."

Before Dayna knew it, the moisture had indeed evaporated from her skin, and she dressed. She no longer shivered. Instead, a warm feeling permeated her. No lightning bolt had struck.

Dayna stepped out of the bath area into the cloistered stone walkway outside.

Mariko came from behind and touched her shoulder. "How was it?"

"I feel good, actually."

Mariko studied her. "I know. But do you feel different?"

"What does different feel like? I'm warm, if that's what you mean."

The nun's forgiveness comment had been spot on, but maybe it was a universal thing she said to everyone. Who hadn't been hurt by others? Still, the nun's comment had hit a soft spot in Dayna's underbelly.

Forgive He-Who-Would-Not-Be-Named? *Yeah, that'll happen when the moon falls into the ocean.* She hadn't the faintest desire to think about her past while on vacation. There were places to go and people to meet.

And where there's one fine-looking guy, there'll be more.

She'd brush up on her Spanish. And buy a couple of low-cut, flirtatious tops.

Chapter 5

Dayna

Dayna fell into bed early and sank back on her pillow, comfy and warm. She dreamed she was looking down into the ocean at Alex. He stared up at her as he sank into the deep, reaching for help. She tried to help him but couldn't.

He sank lower and lower until he disappeared.

She woke, gasping for breath, and pushed herself to sit.

What was that all about? Why was she dreaming about a guy she'd never see again?

Mariko slept in the twin bed across from her. Dayna tried going back to sleep but tossed and turned. She got up and stepped to the window, peering into the dark, four stories down. The peaceful river sparkled under the streetlights.

Inspired for a closer look, she pulled on her jeans and zipped up a hoodie. Grabbing her phone and writing notebook, she quietly let herself out into the dim-lit hallway and took the elevator to the lobby. She stepped to the front doors of the hotel.

"Madame, the doors are locked. You won't get back in," called out a hotel clerk.

Dayna turned in surprise. "I can't use my room key card?"

"No, madame," said the clerk, busy with her keyboard.

"*Merci beaucoup.*" Dayna spotted a neon turquoise light leading to a narrow hallway. She followed it to an intimate sitting area with plush, overstuffed chairs and a small TV mounted on the wall. She let a chair swallow her and picked up the remote. Clicking, she settled on a local newscast and picked up her phone to check her email.

She glanced at the TV, back at her phone, then shot her gaze back to the TV. Incredulous, she sprang from the chair and ran up close to the flat screen, fumbling her pocket for her cheaters.

I know that fine-looking face!

A French newswoman interviewed Alex, the Alaskan pilot she'd met on the beach in Nazaré, Portugal.

She rushed to the chair and groped for the clicker to turn it up. When she turned back, he'd gone offscreen, and the newswoman talked.

"Oh, come on, put the camera back on *him*," she hollered at the TV, like when the San Francisco Giants missed a play.

Local news aired a story about people walking the El Camino trail. She squinted at the newsprint. "*Peregrinos en Ponferrada.*" *Peregrinos* meant pilgrims, as Rachel had explained on their motor coach ride to Burgos.

"Where's Ponferrada?" she mumbled.

Fixed on the screen, she stepped back, groping for her pen and notebook. She scribbled the location, then tossed the notebook and grabbed her phone to Google it. She danced her thumbs at record pace, found Ponferrada on the map, and tapped a screenshot.

This is crazy wrong to track down a married man.

As Dayna lifted herself up the four flights of stairs to her room, she couldn't believe the coincidence of seeing Alex on a French newscast. She'd only intended to walk by the river when she couldn't sleep. If the hotel doors hadn't been locked, she wouldn't have seen him.

She flicked her eyes upward and spoke out loud. "Okay, I'm getting these messages, but what am I supposed to do with them?"

Would she see him again? But how could she?

Before Dayna crawled back into bed, she thought of checking her blood pressure. Her cynical side figured the numbers hadn't changed. She quietly extracted her blood pressure cuff from her bag and took her pressure, waiting for the reading to settle. One hundred thirty over eighty.

It *had* lowered.

It had been years since it was this low. Whether her low numbers were because of Alex the pilot or the holy bath, it didn't matter. *I'll take it!*

After she tucked herself in bed, she couldn't stop thinking about Alex. Why couldn't she get him out of her head? What was it about him that had her tracking him like the CIA?

He was married, and she was broken.

Who was she fooling? She'd never see Alex again, anyway. All these things were random coincidences. Flukes. None of it meant anything.

Stop fantasizing and focus on reality. You have a trip to write about. Pay attention to your travel story.

Chapter 6

Alex

Alex read the placard outside the church. "The Church of Santiago Villafranca was built in the 12th century. The northern door is called the Door of Forgiveness. Pilgrims who can't continue their journey because of injury or illness are granted the same indulgences as if they'd reached the Cathedral in Santiago."

He looked up at George, a guy from Montana he'd met on the trail. "It wouldn't hurt to go in through the Northern Door. I need all the help I can get right now." His knee had bothered him for the past several miles.

"Yeah, me too. My shoulder's been bugging me." George removed his pack and rested it on the cobblestone. "Should have done this thirty years ago."

"The first fifty miles were okay as long as I stopped to rest. But the last ten miles..." Alex shook his head. Their next pit stop was the high mountain village of O Cebreiro, but his knee pain had seriously increased.

The thought of climbing any incline didn't appeal to him.

All he had to do was make it to O Cebreiro and spend the night before continuing to Santiago de Compostela, his destination. Another fifty miles. He'd walked two hundred miles before his knee gave him serious fits. Compresses, wraps, the brace, his meds—none of it helped now. His knee swelled and stayed swollen at the end of each day.

The two men walked through the Northern Door, admiring the beautifully appointed stained-glass windows.

"Dude, take a load off," said George. "You're limping pretty good."

"Good idea." Alex took a seat on a wood bench along a frescoed wall.

George sank down next to him, his long, gray ponytail draped over his shoulder. "Think you'll be able to finish?"

"I'll decide once I get to O Cebreiro." Alex felt his fifty-two years, even though he'd worked out and stayed in shape most of his life. He'd known all along his knee would be a wild card.

After resting about twenty minutes, they rose and walked outside, back to the dirt trail. They sat on a large shelf rock, sipping water, and enjoying George's beef jerky while nodding hello to other *peregrinos.*

"It's about nine days to Santiago from O Cebreiro. But it's mostly level. Not mountainous, like this." George motioned at the surrounding slopes.

Alex glanced around. "I know. Maybe I should have started and ended in Galicia, from Sarria to Santiago de Compostela." Quitting or giving up wasn't his thing.

"Okay, let's do this. O Cebreiro by dark."

George flicked his eyes at him. "You sure?"

"Yeah, let's go."

Alex focused on what he'd seen so far, to take his mind off his knee. He'd begun in Burgos, where he'd enjoyed eating tapas and found his favorite beer, San

Miguel, in an out-of-the-way bar across from his hotel.

He wished he would have started his walk in Pamplona. He'd missed the beautiful La Rioja wine region and their wine harvest festival.

His mind switched to Dayna and her comment about California reds. Where was she right now? He should have exchanged information with her.

Dammit, why didn't I get her last name?

After Villafranca, the men climbed a steep incline leading to the high mountain town of O Cebreiro. They passed five brown cows lying in a meadow next to the trail. A farmer passed them, leading a line of cows with cowbells clanging.

Alex and George ambled along a steep paved road and passed a stone marker with yellow paint and an arrow pointing to O Cebreiro. Alex tossed a small pebble on top of the stone marker. Zoey had told him to bring a handful of small pebbles from Alaska and set them on the stone trail markers along the way, for good luck. He chuckled at what TSA must have thought when he'd passed his plastic bag of pebbles through airport security.

A muddy path led up another steep incline. Rain fell, soft at first, then picked up momentum, turning the trail of dirt into slick mud.

For every step forward, Alex slid back, his boots refusing to grip. His blisters were killing him.

They came to the border of the Spanish province of Galicia, marked on the trail with a gray stone sign. Not far now to the village of O Cebreiro, situated over the crest of the next hill. A chilly breeze hit Alex's neck and face. He zipped his jacket to the top.

Cowbells sounded and another cow line plunked behind him. Alex stepped to the right to get out of the way and his right foot slid. He overcompensated and tripped himself, falling hard on his bad knee.

"Ow, dammit!"

George, who had walked a few hundred feet ahead, turned around.

Alex rolled to his side in the mud, holding his injured knee, rain soaking him. He prayed he hadn't cracked his kneecap. Excruciating pain rocketed through his leg, tingling his body and making him lightheaded.

George hurried back and kneeled next to him. "Can you sit?"

"Think so."

George helped Alex to a sitting position.

"Mate, need a lift?" An Australian voice called out and two guys on horseback came up from behind and stopped alongside the two men. The horses pawed at the mud.

"Not sure I can straddle a horse." Alex winced as he pushed to stand, saturated mud glistening his clothes.

"Got a two-wheeler." The Aussie pointed at his buddy, whose horse pulled a sizeable two-wheeled cart with bicycles and gear. "We can get you to O Cebreiro."

Alex sighed with relief. "Are you sure it's no bother?"

"No worries." The Australian jumped off his horse and helped George load Alex into the cart, where he sat on their pile of gear. He rested his bad leg across the top, and the other dangled off the side of the cart.

"Hold on, mate," said the more talkative Aussie. "Don't want you falling off. These horses sometimes get frisky."

George waved him on ahead. "See you at the bunkhouse in O Cebreiro, dude."

"Sounds good. Sorry to bail on you." Alex gripped the edge of the cart as the horses started forward. "See you later." His knee had swollen even larger than before. He couldn't walk on it for any more long distances.

He'd have to find a ride to Santiago de Compostela, then Lisbon, where he'd stay a while before catching a flight home to Alaska.

The horses plodded the final kilometers up the trail incline until Alex heard them clip-clop on pavement, as a cluster of gray stone buildings came into view. A sign appeared: O Cebreiro, population fifty. The views were breathtaking as they rolled through the quaint village, surrounded by mountains, green with patches of orange-red, where the colors had turned in the early fall.

Galicia reminded him of Alaska with trees giving off pungent scents and the air smelling of manure and wood fires.

"Where to, mate?" the Aussie called over his shoulder.

"The *peregrino* bunkhouse," Alex hollered back. He'd planned to stay there, anyway.

They passed a stone building with wood-trimmed windows and silver disks of art. A moss-covered stone statue stood guard out front, boxes of large scallop seashells at its feet. The scallop shell symbolized the El Camino trail, appearing on all the trail markers, to show *peregrinos* the way.

The horses stopped in front of a rectangular brick building, and the Aussies unloaded Alex's pack and helped him inside the mostly empty bunkhouse. He thanked them, then chose a single lower bunk in a corner. The men left to tend to their horses.

Alex dug through his pack for his knee brace, then

removed his cargo pants to assess the damage. He figured he'd either torn cartilage or had sprained his knee. He found his wrap and wound it around his knee. The toe blisters bothered him, so he wrapped them in moleskin, as he'd done on his marathon runs in Alaska. He fastened on his knee brace to immobilize the joint, then popped a couple of pain caplets.

He attached his phone cord to the voltage converter and plugged it into an outlet. Too tired for food, he flopped back onto the bed and dug under the covers.

At least he'd made it to O Cebreiro.

Chapter 7

Dayna

Rachel made an announcement on the motor coach PA system in her elegant Welsh accent.

"Ladies and gents, since we've had such an early, efficient start this morning, we'll have time for a brief stop in the small village of *O-theh-BRAY-roh*, in the beautiful Spanish province of Ga-LEE-cee-a on our way to Santiago de Compostela. It's a quaint hamlet perched high on a mountain ridge."

Dayna hadn't heard of O Cebreiro, but she found it on her tour map. After spending a few nights in Burgos, she'd taken in the sights as the motor coach rolled west on the highway that paralleled the El Camino Trail.

Mariko sat next to her. "Say, where did you go yesterday while I napped? Didn't have time to talk to you last night. I hit the hay hard. Being on the go finally caught up to me."

Dayna thought back to the past few days in Burgos. "I took a walk around our hotel. Spotted a bookstore and bought a few novels, one in Portuguese, one in Spanish." She reached into her purse and produced a sack. "Then I saw a sign on a window for San Miguel beer, so I went in and had one. You know it's my favorite, but I can never find it in the States."

She didn't say that while she'd sipped her beer in the

tiny bar with beer decals from around the world, she'd noticed one for Alaska Amber and had commented on it. The bartender said a guy from Alaska had been in a while ago and gave him the decal for his collection. He'd remembered him because he talked about flying planes in Alaska.

Dayna asked what the guy looked like and what beer he drank.

"Tall guy, older, drank San Miguel," said the bartender.

Her neck had prickled at seeing Alex on TV but prickled more after this karmic development. She kept it to herself, or she'd suffer the never-ending ribbing from Mariko.

The motor coach climbed a series of narrow, curved roads and Dayna marveled at the patchwork of fall colors and the beauty of Galicia. The sun hung high in the sky as they slowed on a narrow, two-lane road around the edge of the tiny village. It reminded her of Hobbiton meets Ireland, with the curved stone buildings and thatched roofs.

Dayna couldn't wait to write about it. She wanted to walk around and get a feel for this beautiful, isolated village.

"Only an hour and a half here, folks," announced Rachel as the driver parked their coach and turned off the engine. "It's noon, so be back by one-thirty."

Everyone stood and filed out the front and rear doors.

Dayna gathered her day pack and stepped out of the coach, inhaling the moist mountain air. She loved the smell after a rain. Everything smelled so clean. The fresh smell mingled with the scent of wood fires and a dash of cow and pig manure. She took in the expanse of never-ending mountains, reminding her of Northern California.

"I'm hungry, so step lively to beat the crowd," Mariko ordered, setting a fast pace along the gravel walkway leading to the center of the old-world village.

"You're always hungry." Dayna followed her, yawning. She knew better than to get in Mariko's way during her friend's ravenous prowls for food.

Stepping along the cobblestone, they found a quaint deli with enticing smells. Mariko ducked inside and Dayna stepped in after her. The place was impossibly tiny and maybe fit twenty people at the most.

Her eyes took a minute to adjust to the dark interior. She spotted a short bar on the left and a few tables on the right. Rachel recommended they try the *caldo galego*, a traditional soup referred to as pilgrim stew, made from stock with cabbage and potatoes. Dayna ordered two bowls for her and Mariko and a bottle of San Miguel. Somewhere in the world, it must be after five P.M.

The stew hit the spot, and Dayna downed her beer. She glanced at her watch. Forty minutes left. She wanted to explore and take photos.

"Mariko, see you back at the coach. I want to walk around a bit."

"Go do your thing." Mariko waved her off, turning to chat with a young woman who had seated herself at their table.

Dayna hurried out of the dark, cozy restaurant and veered left along a cobblestone road curving around town. As she walked down the road, she noticed a group of people sitting on a wide stone wall next to a bright green pilgrim statue. Two men stood, each holding horse's reins, talking to a couple of guys sitting on the stone ledge. All wore brimmed hats, except for one.

A taller one with a baseball cap—with *Alaska* across the front.

"Oh. My. God."

She walked fast as if drawn by a magnet toward the man in tan long-shorts and a dark blue Henley, sitting on the ledge, with one leg propped up on it. A black knee brace encased his knee as he engaged in an animated conversation with two men who sounded Australian.

Her breath came fast, and her heart knocked around, same as the last time she saw him.

Not wanting to interrupt, she stopped, hovering behind the Aussies. One horse whinnied and shook its head as if to say hello. She stood there, all smiles.

Alex's eyes widened, and his jaw dropped as if she'd risen from the dead.

"Look who breezed in! Miss California Travel Writer." He broke out in a grin that lit up the mountain.

The men turned to see who'd captured Alex's rapt attention and did the requisite head-to-toe once-over. Their expressions showed Dayna they approved, and she noted Alex caught it.

Excitement shot through her, but she tamped it back to appear casual.

"Well, if it isn't Alex from Alaska," Dayna said smoothly. She high-fived herself for the scoop-necked top she'd hastily pulled on that morning.

He laughed. "Fancy seeing you way up here in the back of nowhere. But then, that's your job, isn't it, Travel Writer?"

Dayna couldn't stop smiling. "I can't believe this. Our tour director stopped only because we had an early start this morning."

Oh God, he's here!

She wanted to throw her arms around him. Instead, she hung shyly back.

"Guys, this is Dayna. We met in Nazaré, when she covered me with—" He sent her a mischievous grin. "Dare I say it?"

She shrugged. "Sure, why not?"

The Aussies looked at Alex expectantly.

"Rose petals." Alex seemed to get a kick out of it.

Dayna liked how he told the story with humor, making everyone laugh.

"That's how you two met, huh?" The dark-haired Aussie grinned. "And on that note, it's time we hit the trail. See you, mate," he said to Alex, extending his hand.

"Can't thank you enough for helping me out," said Alex, shaking each of their hands. "Come to Alaska and I'll take you halibut fishing. Good luck, *peregrinos*."

"I'll take you up on it, mate," said the shorter guy. The two Aussies mounted their horses and guided them down a trail leading to the El Camino.

Dayna watched the horses sway down the mountain. *Ask him!*

She took a step closer. "I don't mean to pry—well okay, yes I do—what's your last name?"

"Mendes. Alexander Mendes." He took off his sunglasses, folded them into his shirt pocket, and flashed his toothy smile.

"Hm, Alexander. The Great." She held out her hand, wanting him to touch her like that day on the beach. "Pleased to meet you again, Mr. Mendes."

"Good to see you." He slid his hand around hers and took his time letting go.

She pointed at his knee brace. "What happened?"

"My knee crapped out after Villafranca, about seventeen miles back. The Aussies gave me a ride in their horse cart."

"I'll bet you're glad they happened by." *I know, I am.* Dayna warmed inside.

"Yes, a lucky break, for sure." He ran a hand over his knee brace.

"Saw you on the news at our hotel in Lourdes," Dayna ventured, enjoying how easy he was on the eyes.

Alex laughed. "Yeah, some French reporters did a story. Must have been a slow news day. I happened by, and an amiable woman interviewed me."

Of course, she did.

"You looked good on TV." Her gaze roamed his face. His eyes matched the purple-gray of the mountains.

He chortled. "Good thing you couldn't smell me. Did you notice how the reporter kept her distance?"

She leaned in and inhaled pine. "You don't smell bad."

"Took a shower this morning. First one in weeks." He lifted his arm and made a comical sniff.

"Here's a coffee." A man with a long, gray ponytail moseyed up and handed Alex a steaming cardboard cup.

Alex gestured at him. "Dayna, meet George from Montana. We met on the trail."

"George, this is Dayna..." He shrugged at her. "I don't know your last name."

"Benning. Dayna Benning." She pronounced it slowly, as if talking to a phone computer, so he'd remember.

"I know some Bennings in Alaska," drawled Alex, sipping his coffee.

"Could be related. We get around." Goosebumps

sprang up like dandelions at his deep, smoky tone.

George raised his coffee at her. "Pleased to meet you, Dayna. I've heard about you. Don't worry, it was all good," he hastened to add. "Except how you showered Alaska Boy with dried flowers."

Alex had talked about her.

And it kicked her heart up a notch. She laughed, recalling the surprise on his face. "Not my fault. The wind did it." She caught his eyes smiling at her.

"Sit down and take a load off." Alex patted the space next to him. "Unless you have more sightseeing."

Screw sightseeing.

She accepted his invitation and sat on the low concrete wall, her insides playing hockey with a wild puck.

"Hey George, take our photo." Alex held out his phone.

"Sure, buddy." George took it and stood back, positioning himself.

Dayna fidgeted and an uncomfortable feeling pitted her stomach. She couldn't contain herself any longer. She removed her sunglasses and leaned away from Alex.

"Are you sure this is okay?"

Alex did a quizzical double take. "Why wouldn't it be?"

"What'll your wife say when she sees photos of you with random women in Spain?" She pointed at his wedding band.

Alex's face changed. He stared at her as if she'd turned into a scallop shell. He glanced at his finger and chuckled.

"Ah, I see why you thought that. My wife passed away. Haven't gotten around to taking off the ring." He

55

turned his hand over and rubbed his ring with his thumb.

The familiar way he did it reminded her of how she used to do the same with her engagement ring and matching wedding band for twenty-eight years.

"I'm so sorry. How long ago?" She did her darndest to sound sincere while her brain screamed, *he's single!*

He stared off at the distant mountains. "Three years ago."

Dayna waited for further explanation, but there was none.

"I'm sorry." She hated herself for not meaning it.

He nodded. "Hasn't been easy, for sure."

An avalanche of possibility flooded Dayna, drowning all logical thought. Save for one: *Get his contact information before we part again.*

She beamed at the phone camera as the entire Montserrat choir chorused a jubilant hallelujah inside her head.

The bag of anvils tethered to her heart for so long suddenly released its grip.

Her heart floated up into the blue Galician sky.

Chapter 8

Alex

Alex noted relief flooding Dayna's face. *The ring.* Of course, she'd thought he'd been off limits. Served him right. What had he expected her to think? He'd noticed no wedding band on *her* finger when he'd taken her hand that first day on the beach.

"Okay, smile you two," said George, squinting at Alex's phone.

Thankfully, Alex had showered earlier at the *peregrino* bunkhouse. He and George had traded barbs about their stench when bath or shower facilities weren't available on the trail.

Alex gently pressed his shoulder against hers, wanting his hands on her. He instinctively lifted an arm to put around her shoulders but stopped himself. He didn't know her well enough, and he planned to remedy that, for darn sure. He hadn't felt an attraction like this in a long time.

When Dayna had grasped his hand that first day on the beach, she'd affected him in a big way. He'd spent much of the trail time thinking about second chances, and whether he should try to find her.

Now, here she was, like a miracle.

"I took a bunch of photos," said George, handing Alex's phone back to him. Alex tapped to view them.

LoLo Paige

God, what a beauty. It thrilled him to see her. This time he'd get her contact info. This time he wouldn't stand there and wave goodbye, like a doofus.

"What will you do now, since you injured your knee?" Dayna asked him.

He liked her genial smile and sparkling eyes. "I'm trying to find a ride to Santiago de Compostela."

"Have you had any luck?"

"Not yet." The breeze brought her citrus scent straight into him and he inhaled it.

Her face lit up. "Maybe our coach driver will give you a ride to Santiago. We have empty seats. I can talk to Rachel, our tour director. What do you think?"

"She doesn't know me from Adam. I'm sure Wanderlust Travel has policies about taking on passengers." Alex was familiar with the rigidity of company policy after years in the travel business.

Dayna beamed at him. "I'll say I've flown with you in the States and knew you were walking the El Camino. Do you still have your commercial pilot ID? I'm a travel writer, so it stands to reason we'd know each other. Wait here, I'll be right back."

She took off jogging up to the parked motor coach, then turned around, stepping backward. "And whatever I say, agree with it."

"Yes, ma'am." He gaped at her lovely receding backside, her fine hips, and shapely thighs. Alex couldn't believe the luck of running into her.

He turned to George. "Help me up to the parking lot, will you, buddy?"

"Dude, it'd be great if you could catch a ride with them," said George, helping Alex uphill to the bus. "I can tell you want to go with her."

"It's that obvious?" He should probably cool his enthusiasm.

"The way you look at her—um, yeah, it's pretty obvious. And you mentioned her quite a bit on the trail."

Dayna appeared, accompanied by a tall, lively blonde woman with a cheerful grin.

"Alex, this is Rachel, our travel director," said Dayna.

Rachel extended her hand. "Good day, gents. Dayna tells me you need a lift. I can't let you onboard without checking a few things. Passport, proof of travel insurance, and ID."

"Sure." Alex tugged a cord around his neck and lifted a flat nylon wallet from under his shirt. He handed Rachel a fistful of IDs.

She studied his passport, checked the rest, and handed them back. "Dayna mentioned you used to pilot long hauls between Europe and the U.S."

Dayna interjected. "I can vouch for Alex. I've known him from flying around the U.S. and overseas for my work." Her eyes prompted him to rally support.

Alex quickly agreed. "Yes, I flew long hauls. Dayna's right. We've been friends a long time." His brain gonged with the notion he'd go to hell for lying.

Rachel gave Alex another once-over. "Company policy is, normally we don't pick up passengers because of insurance concerns. But since you're in need, and you have the proper IDs and travel insurance, we'll make an exception. We'll settle cost onboard the coach."

"I'm happy to pay whatever," Alex assured her.

"Good enough. Time to hit the road." Rachel turned and hastened to the motor coach.

"Dayna, I really appreciate this," said Alex.

She reached up to take the weighty pack from his back and George helped her ease it from Alex's shoulders. Dayna hefted it up the stairs to the motor coach, and several hands reached for the pack to stow it. Her strength impressed him, not only lifting the bulky thing, but hoisting it high for others to grasp.

Dayna stayed onboard and waited while George helped Alex up the steps.

Once on board, Alex turned to his friend. "Hey buddy, thanks for your help. Let's meet up in Santiago." He gave George a man hug and slapped his back.

"I have your number. I'll text you. Good to meet you, Dayna." George raised a hand in farewell, stepped off the motor coach, and took off down the road.

Alex let out a long sigh of relief as he followed Dayna down the center aisle to the back of the coach. He gripped the tops of the seats as he limped along. She turned and sent him her infectious smile.

No way in hell would he let her get away from him this time.

****

Dayna

Dayna rocketed over the moon as she steered Alex to the last seat. Everyone gaped at the tall, silver fox making his way down the center aisle. A swan among the ducklings.

Dayna couldn't wipe the silly grin from her face.

"Well, look what the trail dragged in," said Mariko, as they passed her seat. She grinned at Alex, then Dayna. "You found him, after all."

Dayna glared at Mariko in a thanks-for-outing me look.

Alex lifted a hand in greeting. "Mariko. Good to see

you again."

She gave him a thumbs up. "Welcome aboard, Rose Petal Man."

He laughed. "Thanks."

The motor coach passengers craned their necks to check out the new person joining their tour.

Dayna's heart boomeranged; she was thunderstruck at seeing him. Too bad he'd injured his knee, but if he hadn't, their paths may not have crossed.

"I'll help you get situated." She led him to the last row of empty seats.

"Thanks." Alex lowered himself into a seat, propping his leg across the bench row.

Dayna carefully folded her jacket and lifted his knee to ease it under him for support. Touching him sent currents whipping through her. She was giddy with the notion he turned out to be single.

"I have a travel pillow in the overhead. I'll go get it." She moved to the bin over her shared seat with Mariko and retrieved the small pillow.

Mariko had sprawled over both seats and gave Dayna a cat-ate-canary grin.

Dayna leaned in. "He's not married—to anyone alive, anyway," she whispered.

"See what happens when you open yourself up to possibility?" Mariko's eyes gleamed. "You have a lucky second chance. Don't blow it."

"I don't plan on it." Dayna winked at her bestie and ducked into the aisle.

He was a widower but still wore his ring. She'd known people who hadn't removed their wedding bands for years after their spouse's deaths. Mariko still wore hers but planned to take it off once she finished

LoLo Paige

distributing Harv. Dayna had tossed hers into the Pacific. With any luck, it was now trapped under ice in Antarctica.

Dayna made her way to the back. "Here Alex, put this under your knee."

"Thanks. Appreciate it." He lifted his hard-muscled leg, and she replaced her jacket with the pillow.

"You can lean against the window and sleep." She turned to go to her seat.

"Wait—aren't you going to sit with me?" He motioned at the space between himself and the window.

"Figured you needed to rest."

"I have all night to rest. Want to hear about your trip. Come on, sit." He shot her his million-dollar smile.

Twist my arm.

"Okay." She stepped over his good leg and sank into the seat next to him. His shoulder touched hers, warming her.

The doors closed, and the motor coach made its way down the winding mountain road to the highway. They had two hours to chat on the way to Santiago de Compostela. Dayna loved telling him where they'd traveled on the tour and the sights they'd seen so far.

When she mentioned Montserrat, outside of Barcelona, his eyes grew wide.

"Isn't it magnificent, with all the sculptures and artwork, especially the Black Madonna?" He seemed excited about it. "One of my favorite places in Spain."

Talking to Alex was like talking to an old friend. Anyone listening would have thought they'd known each other all their lives.

For the first time in a long while, hope crept into Dayna's heart. She wouldn't expect anything other than

62

to go with the flow and enjoy the moment.

After all, isn't that what traveling was all about? New experiences.

And second chances.

Chapter 9

Alex

Alex crawled out of bed the next morning in the Santiago de Compostela hotel, took a shower, and put himself together for breakfast. After the motor coach had delivered him to the hotel last night, he'd been lucky to get a room after a cancellation.

He'd worry about getting to Lisbon to visit Aunt Mara later, before heading back to Alaska. He still couldn't believe his good fortune of bumping into Dayna Benning.

His knee felt better after icing it. He could get around okay, as long as he didn't overdo it. Upon entering the hotel restaurant, Alex spotted Dayna at a table with Mariko. He ambled over, doing his best to minimize his limp.

"Good morning, ladies."

Dayna's face lit up. "Good morning. How's the knee?" She broke into that infectious smile he first noticed on the beach.

"Not too bad. Iced it last night, so swelling's gone down." He lowered himself into a chair, noticing how lovely she looked this morning. All fresh and bright-eyed. "What's on the menu?"

"A help yourself Spanish buffet," said Mariko, pointing across the room to two long rows of colorful food. "Try the *Pulpa a Feira.* It's delicious. Octopus with drizzled butter and smoked paprika, served on a scallop shell. I made sure it was dead before I ate it."

Dayna chimed in, blue eyes sparkling. "I tried it. It's okay if you don't mind staring down a tentacle. The Santiago almond cake is also delicious." She'd developed a healthy Mediterranean glow from the sun since the last time he saw her.

Alex stood to get food, but Dayna motioned him to sit. "Stay put and prop your knee up. I'll get whatever you like."

Before he could protest, she'd started for the buffet. She lurched to a stop, spun around, and walked back to him. "What is it you like?"

"Coffee, for starters. I'll leave the rest to you since you've test-driven the buffet."

"You got it." She took off again, and he watched her sweet ass move across the restaurant.

Mariko stood to go. "I'm going with Rachel for the guided tour. I told Dayna I'd see her later. You two have fun today." She issued the order, drill sergeant style, then left him to his own devices.

"Will do." He hadn't talked to Dayna about her plans for the day, but gauging from what Mariko said, her plans must include him. He poured water from a pitcher into a tall glass and sipped, watching the lively, attractive woman across the room. He hadn't intended for her to get his breakfast.

While he waited for Dayna, he thought of the night before, on the motor coach. He'd been thankful she'd gotten him onboard, but curious why Mariko said Dayna had 'found him after all.'

Had she been looking for him? He hadn't wanted to

put her on the spot by asking.

On the ride to Santiago, they'd shared their experiences. She told him where they'd traveled so far, and he'd filled her in on the towns and villages along the El Camino. Next thing he knew, he'd awakened with his head on her shoulder. It must have been okay—she'd leaned into him—and he'd welcomed her body heat. He'd left his head on her shoulder and went back to sleep.

"Here you go." Dayna interrupted his thoughts, resting a tray of colorful, exotic food on the table. She presented it to him with a grand gesture. "How do you say, 'breakfast is served' in Galician?"

"*O almorzo sérvese.*" He caught her appreciative look in response and snuck a peek at her cleavage. *Thank you, God, for inventing low-cut tops. Am I that shallow? Yeah. I am.*

"I love it when you talk Galician." A corner of her sexy mouth raised.

"You've done so much for me. I appreciate it." He reached for a cup of coffee and emptied a creamer into it.

"I accessorized you with flower petals like you were a bridal wedding aisle," she teased, taking the seat across from him. She leaned back, scrutinizing his gorgeous, beat-the-wall peepers. "What are your plans for today?"

He stabbed a slice of octopus with his fork and studied it. "Was about to ask the same." He pulled it off with his teeth. "You were right about the octopus. It's good."

"I take pride in my culinary adventures when I travel." She popped a grape in her mouth, then swiped her phone. "According to the tour schedule, we have a free day, except for the guided tour of the cathedral. Care to team up and do our own tour?"

He tilted his head. "If you don't mind moving at sloth speed."

"I suppose I could slow down," she teased. "Don't worry, I'll get us around with minimum effort. How long will you be staying in Santiago?" She shoved in a forkful of food.

He shrugged. "I'm not on a schedule."

She touched a napkin to her lips, and he could tell her wheels were spinning.

"How about after breakfast, we go to our rooms, then meet in the lobby in half an hour?"

"Sounds good," he replied. Her food choices had been excellent.

They finished their meal, and Dayna rose to leave. She tap-tapped the table. "See you in thirty."

"Got it, ETA in thirty."

As he headed to his room, he fished out his phone. He'd call Zoey to let her know he was okay, then he'd call Aunt Mara in Lisbon to say he'd see her in a few days.

A familiar twist in his stomach niggled about Ellie. Walking the El Camino had helped with his grief. But he had to stop believing he'd mated for life. For the longest time, it had felt wrong to seek female companionship. But something that day on the beach in Nazaré had propelled him toward Dayna Benning, like a plane bent on trajectory.

She'd entered his life—twice—and he had to find out whether she was meant to stay in it.

He only hoped Ellie would somehow understand and forgive him.

Chapter 10

Dayna

As Dayna blew by the hotel lobby desk, she grabbed a handful of brochures to help plan their day. She hoped to impress Alex with her ability to scope out the best things to do in Santiago. In her hotel room, she'd Googled the best options.

She looked forward to spending the day with Alex Mendes. So far, this trip had exceeded her expectations. The added perk of seeing Alex again thrilled her. So many coincidences.

Is this a meant-to-be kind of thing? Don't overthink it. Be in the moment.

Alex seemed right at home in an overstuffed chair in the center of the lobby. He chatted with a young couple who hung on his every word, especially the woman.

Dayna slowed to watch him. She didn't know Alex yet—his likes and dislikes. Did he like to read? She knew he liked excellent wine and good-tasting beer. By the end of today, if nothing else, she'd know his favorite color and what music he liked. She couldn't wait to peel this onion.

She needed to be honest with herself. A powerful attraction to someone was one thing—as long as she didn't move beyond it. She'd been out of the dating game for so long the most she could handle might be a light fling. No commitment.

Been there, done that, don't want a redo.

What's not to love about a casual fling in Spain? It struck her as dangerous and erotic. She pictured the subtitle for her magazine story: *Two Americans meet on a windblown beach in Portugal, when a woman showers a man with rose petals...then bumps into him again—in Spain!*

Tessa might like it. If not, Dayna could pop it into her romance novel waiting in her computer back home.

After the divorce, Dayna had set out to reclaim the self-identity her ex had controlled throughout their marriage. She liked who she was now, but his leaving her for a younger version still stung. No one would do it to her again.

No one. Ever.

Alex glanced up to see Dayna walk toward him. The young wife fluttered her fake eyelashes, but his gaze fixed on Dayna. The pretty woman stopped in mid-sentence and turned to see who had Alex's rapt attention.

"Yes, sweetie, the hunk you're flirting with is looking at *me*, stretch marks and all," muttered Dayna, under her breath. She straightened, set her shoulders, and tucked one side of her hair behind her ear as she flashed Alex a movie-star smile.

She wore the tight, scoop-necked top she'd purchased in a Barcelona designer shop. And she'd topped it with a form-fitting waist jacket and skinny jeans that still looked good on her, despite the pounds she'd picked up on her trip to New Orleans for her foodie article. She'd fixed her shoulder-length hair, and it framed her face. She'd also applied light makeup around her eyes.

Alex stood as she approached, and she liked his up and down scan, his expression appreciating what he saw. "You look terrific."

"Thanks." She moved in close enough to inhale his scent, the same hotel bodywash from her own shower. "You clean up pretty good, too."

And how.

His brown leather jacket gave him a rock star vibe, and the faded blue jeans hugged each lanky leg and sexed his sweet derriere. He stood, leaning on his good leg, hands tucked in his pockets.

"Ready to see the sights?" She waved the folded city map she'd inspected earlier.

"Let's do it." Alex turned to the couple and spoke French, then exchanged goodbyes.

Dayna recalled that first day on the beach when he'd mentioned marrying a French woman. Of course, he spoke French...and Portuguese...and Galician.

"What were you saying to them?"

"I told them you're my exclusive travel guide." He motioned her ahead of him through the front door of the hotel. "They're headed to Lisbon for their honeymoon. I told them what to see and do."

"That was nice of you. You're familiar with Lisbon?"

He nodded. "I've been there a time or two."

"I can't wait to see it. Our tour ends in Lisbon."

"Yes, that's what Rachel said." His mouth lifted in a quick grin.

Dayna pointed at a bus slowing to a stop in front of the hotel.

"Here's our ride to Old Town." She motioned him

to follow and stepped onto the bus, taking a seat at a window. "How about the Santiago Cathedral, for starters? I read when pilgrims finish the El Camino trail, they visit there to give thanks for their safe journey. I hear you qualify."

"Don't know about that. I didn't finish." He eased into the seat next to her, stretching his outside leg into the center aisle. He let out a feel-good breath as he unfolded his knee.

"Don't worry, lightning bolts won't zap you. They didn't zap me."

"Why would lightning strike you?" He seemed genuinely curious.

Oops. Why did I say that?

She didn't want to talk about her Lourdes experience. She glanced at his outstretched leg with the knee brace. His other one barely fit in the tight space. "We'll mostly ride. I have an app for the bus schedules."

"Sounds like a plan," he said as the bus pulled away from the curb.

So much she wanted to know about him, but where to start? "How many languages do you speak?"

He shot her a lopsided grin. "Is this an interview for your magazine?"

"I'm a writer. It's my job to ask questions."

He tilted his head. "You're including me in your travel article?"

"If you grant me an interview." She hadn't thought of it, but since he'd brought it up, it was a great idea. Why hadn't *she* thought of it? A *peregrino* perspective after hiking the El Camino. Tessa would love it. She'd love his photo even more.

"Where do you want to start? When you tossed rose

petals on me?" He grinned.

"Hold that thought." She pawed through her satchel for her trusty spiral tablet and flipped it open. Pulling the pen from the spiral, she simulated a TV news reporter.

"Hello, travelers. This is Alex Mendes from Alaska. He braved the El Camino from Burgos to Villlafranca, and almost made it to O Cebreiro, before injuring himself…"

She paused, gauging his reaction. "I figured we'd start there."

He seemed amused. "What, no rose petals on the beach?"

She wrinkled her nose. "Dead flowers might not resonate with my travel readers. But they would with *Cosmo* readers. How about this? 'Ten Ways to Meet Guys on a Beach.'"

Alex threw back his head and laughed. People turned to gape at them. She loved making him laugh.

"But seriously, get a *Compostela*, the certificate of completion, for walking part of the El Camino."

He shook his head. "You have to walk the last hundred kilometers, or sixty-two miles, with two stamps per day to get the certificate from the Pilgrim's Reception Office here in Santiago. I read a plaque in Villafranca that said if I walk through the Northern Door of Forgiveness, and couldn't continue because of injury or illness, it'd be considered a completion."

She leaned back, staring. "Wait, back up. What's the Northern Door of Forgiveness?"

"The Door of Forgiveness at the church in Villafranca. I walked through it, then later on I hurt my knee. Why are you looking at me that way?"

"Everywhere I go on this trip, people mention

forgiveness," she mumbled. "Feels like a cosmic conspiracy."

"And this bothers you because?" He waited, but she let it hang in the air and turned toward the window.

She took a quick breath. "A nun in Lourdes. She said…" Dayna trailed off, then decided not to go down the rabbit hole. It had absolutely nothing to do with this guy, and he didn't need to know her excess baggage.

He gave her a curious look. "She said what? If you don't mind my asking?"

Dayna glanced at him, then down at her lap. "It's nothing. Forget it." No real-life reminders. She was sightseeing in Spain, for cripes' sake.

"Is something wrong?" He seemed genuinely concerned.

The last thing she wanted was him thinking she was a hot mess. "Nope. Everything's fine. Really."

The bus lurched to a stop, rescuing her from the awkward moment. "We're here," she said cheerfully. "Let's go see the *Botafumeiro*, the world's largest incense burner. It swings back and forth from one end of the church to the other. Guaranteed to make every stoned hippie envious for not owning one."

He laughed and waited for her to exit the bus, insisting she go first. She liked that and loved his laugh even more.

And she liked him.

A lot.

Chapter 11

Dayna

The day had sped by for Dayna. It was dark as she
and Alex rode a horse carriage back to their hotel. Alex
had insisted on paying for it. She loved the sound of the
hooves clip-clopping on the cobblestone and viewing the
beautifully lit buildings from inside their enclosed
carriage.

Sitting next to Alex, his body heat triggered
electricity in hers, even though they stayed a polite
distance from one another.

They'd toured the city, using hop-on, hop-off
double-decker buses, after browsing museums and art
galleries. They'd gone to the Cathedral and sat through a
mass in Spanish for the *peregrinos*. Dayna's jaw dropped
at the spectacle of the *Botafumeiro* being lit, smoke
billowing as three monks hoisted the enormous metal
incense burner high into the air, tugging on thick ropes.
Each time they pulled the rope, it had swung gracefully
to one side of the cathedral, then to the other, like a slow
pendulum, taking their breaths away and leaving the
pungent scent of incense behind.

Afterward, Alex and Dayna wandered down narrow
cobblestone streets to a restaurant Dayna chose for the
diverse seafood offering. They'd laughed through
dinner, comparing notes between California and Alaska,

from earthquakes to politics and everything in between. They shared a bottle of white Spanish wine, while Alex schooled her on Portuguese Porto.

No talk of real life, families, or past relationships. Their chatter stayed on light subjects, with jokes and laughter. Dayna made sure of it. They were on vacation.

The horses clopped to a halt outside their hotel. As usual, Alex waited for her to exit first. She could tell his knee bothered him. He kept rubbing it and wincing. She'd tried hard to minimize their walking, but sometimes it couldn't be helped.

"Thank you for the lovely carriage ride," she said as they ambled into the hotel elevator. She pressed the button for the fifteenth floor, keenly aware of Alex's gaze on her. An uneasy vulnerability made her feel self-conscious and insecure.

She stepped back and leaned on the railing, watching the numbers tick by.

He leaned on the railing next to her, hands in his pockets. "I had fun today. Thanks for hanging out with me."

The elevator stopped, and the doors slid open.

She glanced at him. "I enjoyed hanging out and walking slow with you." Either the wine had kicked in or he'd buried the arrow on the sexy-guy meter somewhere between the lobby and the fifteenth floor.

"In that case, I'll walk slow with you to your room. You never know who may lurk in these halls," he said in a low, southern drawl, slanting a smile down at her.

"This isn't America. We don't have to worry about that," she said in a low voice, raking in all six-foot-whatever of him. She leaned her back on one side of the elevator door to hold it open.

Her eyes drifted to his lips.

She smoldered.

Evidently, he noticed. "If you don't want me to escort you to your room, I have another idea."

He switched places with her to place his back on the door to hold it open. He gently pulled her toward him and bent his head to kiss her, soft and gentle.

Her lips and tongue were tentative, almost shy. Well, *this* was a new one. She'd always fantasized about making out in an elevator—in this case, half-in and half-out of one.

His tongue explored her mouth, slow and smooth, his kiss inviting her to explore his. She tasted Porto. She hadn't kissed like this in a long time and loved French kissing someone who knew how and did it well. And Alex knew how. Boy, did he. She pressed against him, loving the feel of him. She loved the give and take of their kisses.

The elevator door insisted on closing, and he shoved it back with an artful, back-assed motion. Each time the door pushed his back, he'd force it back with his hips, then press against her until the door caught up with him again.

The sensation electrified her each time the door nudged him into her.

"This is turning me on," Dayna mumbled against his lips. She pulled back and giggled. "You'll break the elevator."

"Charge it to my room." He pressed his lips to hers again.

She broke the kiss. "Other people need to use it, you know."

"I don't care," he breathed, covering her mouth with

his own.

Something about the way he said it rocketed a feral surge through her veins. Still in a lip lock, Dayna grasped the lapels of his leather jacket and tugged him away from the elevator and pressed him up against a wall in the hallway.

Turned on by her ability to steer his six-foot-plus frame wherever she wanted, she unzipped his jacket and slipped her hands inside to rub his solid back.

He moaned. And she moaned.

Oh, God.

Her touch amped him and he slid his lips down the side of her neck. Her breath shortened as he slipped his hands inside her open jacket and ran them lightly over her breasts. As he moved his mouth across the base of her throat, she dimly sensed the elevator door closing.

"Ooh—"

She eased her head back to allow him access. The want of him and what he might do with those hands— hands that had piloted the controls of a 747 and countless passengers around the world—made her ache down low. Dayna became oblivious to everything around her.

The elevator opened and a group of young people entered the hallway, talking and laughing. Alex lifted his head.

No, don't stop, don't stop.

He backed away and traded 'we're busted' expressions with Dayna. They burst out laughing. The group of people casually glanced back, then continued down the dim-lit hallway, chattering and laughing with phones in their hands.

"Feels like I got caught humping in a Chevy." Alex rubbed his mouth, giving her a close-mouthed grin. He backed into a hallway plant stand and tipped a fern over. He caught it before it fell, with an expression like a kid caught stealing candy.

Dayna laughed at the goofy look on his face. "Nice catch in the infield, Sporto. Do people still hump in Chevies?"

"Probably not. Maybe in a Prius. Or a Tesla. Why do I have this feeling my parents will ground me?" He straightened and cleared his throat.

She chortled, longing to pick up where they'd left off. Instead, her practical side made her glance at her watch. "We'd better go to our rooms."

"And waste all this foreplay?" He ran his hands over his hair with a comical expression. "Foreplay is scarce at our age."

She appreciated the blunt honesty of mid-life. "I know, right? Tell me about it."

They stood like awkward teens after a busted-up make-out session. Dayna didn't know what to say, so she stood there, smiling at him.

"I have a room all to myself. If you want this 'to be continued'… isn't that what you writers say?" He offered his hand.

Whoa, Nellie, shouldn't we slow down? Shouldn't I know him better first?

Momentary panic seized her, and she shook her head.

"I think—we should call it a night. Our tour is going to Finisterre early in the morning."

Three years of celibacy and she'd turned down a roll in the hay with the hottest American on this side of the Atlantic.

Am I insane? No. Only scared.

"Okay, I understand." He sounded disappointed.

She was inexperienced at this fling thing, so she gushed at him. "Come with us on the motor coach tour tomorrow. Rachel won't care."

He gave her a slow smile. "All right. I'll talk to her in the morning." He took a step toward her. "Kiss good night?"

She thought about it. "Uh—we better not. You know what could happen—"

"That's the idea," he drawled, hands in pockets as he remained fixed on her.

Dang it. He wasn't making this any easier. "Good night, Alex. Breakfast at seven. See you there." She tore her gaze from him and turned around. *Walk fast before you cave.*

Remembering her resolve from earlier, she stopped and faced him. He hadn't moved. "What's your favorite color?"

He shot her a curious look. "Pacific Ocean blue. Why?"

"Favorite song?"

"Is this for the article?"

"Answer the question."

"You writers. All you do is ask questions. *Jet Airliner,* Steve Miller Band."

"No surprise there." She smirked at him. "You realize that dates you?"

He pulled his hands from his pockets, shifting his lovely frame to the side. "And you want to know because?"

"Research. You're my interview subject for the travel piece, remember?"

It took every ounce of self-discipline to turn from

him and move her legs toward her room, but practicality overrode her lust. She needed time to know him better. She lifted her arm to wave. "Good night."

"Sweet dreams," he called after her.

The elevator door opened, and she glanced back to see him get on and the doors closed again.

Holy hell! He was so flipping hot! Did that really happen?

She reached into the back pocket of her jeans for her key card. Her hand trembled as she fished it out and swiped it over the lock to blink the light green. She opened the door and closed it quietly. Mariko's gentle snores were the only sounds in the room. She tiptoed to her bed, tugged off her clothes, and tossed them in a chair.

What the heck happened back there? They'd plundered each other like their elevator was on its last ride. But maybe she should slow things down...or not.

Pacific Ocean blue, he said. Not only blue, but *Pacific Ocean* blue. It's what an artist would say—or an airplane pilot.

It made her desire him all over again.

Remember, no emotional involvement.

She'd keep this fling on the down low and nobody would get hurt. They'd walk away in a mutual parting at the end of vacation. Between now and then, what the hell?

She'd sleep in the nude tonight...with her phone on vibrate.

Just because.

Chapter 12

Alex

Early the next morning, Alex rose to talk to Rachel. He inquired about finishing the tour with Wanderlust Travel and Rachel cleared it through her home office after sending his information. She ran his credit card to pay for the rest of the tour to their destination. This would take care of his transportation to Lisbon.

He'd decided after he closed the door to his room last night, this is what he wanted to do. A beacon of light had lifted his weary heart. And that beacon was Dayna. He hoped his continuing with the tour wasn't a reckless decision.

Alex boarded the motor coach and swung into the second seat next to a window. He liked the unfettered view out of the massive windshield. Seating changed daily, and Rachel graciously rotated him in. Others weren't onboard yet.

His knee had swollen from all the walking yesterday, and he'd iced it before bed. It hadn't bothered him yet today, and he planned to go easy on it. He had to get this knee taken care of when he returned to Anchorage.

He leaned against the window, watching people straggle from the hotel to board the motor coach. Last night had taken a surprising turn with Dayna. He'd lost his willpower on the elevator like an adolescent in heat. Dayna was as turned on as he was, but he respected her decision not to go to his room.

A hand on his shoulder caused him to look up.

"Ready for Finisterre, *peregrino*?" Dayna beamed down at him. "How's the knee?"

"Much better. Slept like the dead." Alex's eyes were even with Dayna's chest, so he snapped his gaze to hers. The last thing he wanted was her thinking he was only after sex. He wasn't all that sure what he was after. All he knew was that she attracted him like no other.

"Rachel rotated us to the middle today. See you when we get to Finisterre." Dayna moved past him to take her seat, followed by Mariko.

"Glad you're joining us, Captain. Excellent decision." Mariko winked with a thumbs up.

He responded with a wave, appreciating how Mariko and Dayna's upbeat natures lifted his spirits.

What a fortuitous thing to say after he'd questioned his decision to stay with the tour. He liked Mariko. She always wore a peaceful, uplifted expression. Or maybe it was the way her narrow eyebrows arched over her eyes in a perfect rainbow shape, giving her an inquisitive appearance.

Rain poured as the motor coach left Santiago and pulled onto a two-lane highway. It worsened as they neared the coast, sheets of rain slapping the windows as they passed seaside villages. The surf crashed rocks along the tide line, sending spray upward. Alex appreciated the beautiful Galician landscape despite the miserable weather. He admired the homes with red-tiled roofs nestled in small, tidy vineyards.

The Cape of Finisterre came into view behind a

copse of trees, and the road narrowed, winding uphill. Alex eyed the guardrail as water smeared the windshield. The wipers struggled to keep up.

The motor coach slowed, then stopped in a small parking area. The driver cut the engine, and everyone rose, retrieving raincoats and umbrellas from the overhead bins.

Alex tugged on his rain jacket and stepped out the front door, pulling his hood over his head. The wind blew it off. Dayna and Mariko soon joined him, and droplets dotted Dayna's sunglasses as she pulled her own hood up.

Mariko fought an umbrella the wind intended to steal.

Dayna motioned toward a couple of one-story wood buildings perched on a bluff overlooking the stormy Atlantic.

"I'm heading to the ladies' room." She resembled The Unabomber, a domestic terrorist from the 1970s, with her dark hood and rain-covered shades.

He grinned. "Lead the way. I brought the rest of my pebbles to place on the trail marker, even though I didn't finish the trail here." He patted his pocket.

"What a great idea. You're all over this trail tradition thing. Good on ya, mate." She imitated the Aussies from two days ago.

Alex laughed. "I do my best."

The wind tortured Mariko's umbrella until it flipped inside out. "Screw this. I'm going to the souvenir shop." Mariko veered left and entered the larger building, wrestling her rebellious umbrella.

"Hey Mary Poppins, forget about staying dry," Dayna called after her.

"I don't know about you, Mendes, but I have to visit the restroom." Dayna squinted at a water closet sign with an arrow. "There they are." She disappeared around a corner.

Alex took his time, babying his knee.

Shrieking erupted, followed by laughter. When he rounded the corner, eight large goats leaned against the rain-whipped building, with WC—water closet—in large black letters on the front. Two brown goats stood guard outside the restroom. One shook like a dog, droplets flying and ears flopping back and forth.

Dayna laughed. "Maybe they want to use the facilities."

"Nah, they want to snack on the toilet paper." Alex stepped toward the goats, waving his arms. "Shoo, get out of here!"

They didn't budge, merely flicked their ears at him with comical, inquisitive looks. Muffled bleats came from inside the restroom.

"They're so cute!" Dayna stepped around the goats and edged the door open. "Apparently, one is using the facilities."

A black-and-white speckled snout poked through the crack. Dayna pushed the door wide, but instead of one goat rushing out, two brown goats rushed in.

"When you've got to go, you've got to go," remarked Alex.

"Anyone in here?" Dayna bent to peek under both stalls. No answer. "Alex, help me get this herd out of here."

He stepped in behind Dayna, and she held the door while he herded the three goats out of the restroom. "There. It's all yours," he grinned, standing inside the

WC, water dripping from his jacket. He pushed back his hood and ran a hand over his hair.

"It's a lot easier than shooing bears in Alaska."

"You've done that?" Dayna's eyes widened, windblown ringlets spiraling over her forehead from the rain. She was pretty, all wild and dripping wet.

He had the impulse to finish what they'd started last night. Take her in his arms and lay one on her right here in the restroom. As he stepped toward her, the door opened and a familiar, made-up face with painted eyebrows peeked in, eyes wide upon seeing him.

"Oh goodness, what are *you* doing in here, Mr. Mendes?"

Alex recognized the woman from their tour group. "Don't mind me, I'm the lonely goatherd." He grinned, flinging the door open.

A line of womenfolk chortled and beamed at him.

"You can herd my goats any day," smirked a white-haired woman in a purple-flowered raincoat, stepping past him into the restroom.

Alex winked at Dayna, then stepped out, nodding at the line of ladies eyeing him with radiant smiles.

"You don't have to rush off, darlin'," murmured a buxom redhead with a Southern accent as he moved past. He'd become used to such comments when the ladies flirted shamelessly with him in his pilot uniform, back when he flew for the airline. Being happily married, he hadn't acted on it as some of his co-workers had.

Dayna followed him out and caught up with him. "You sure made *their* day, Mr. Mendes."

"Goats in a restroom on the coast of Spain. Who-da thunk it?" He braced himself against the pelting rain.

"Hey, the zero marker for the El Camino trail is up

the hill." Dayna pointed at a wide concrete walkway leading up to a gray stone lighthouse. "Want to check it out? You can put the rest of your pebbles on it."

"Let's do it." Alex zipped up his rain jacket, wind whipping droplets on his face. He tugged on his hood.

The horizontal rain stung their faces as the storm intensified. He and Dayna tucked their chins and pushed against it, moving slowly up the walkway. He needed a reason to touch her, so he put his arm around her shoulder. "I'd better hang onto you, or you'll blow away."

She didn't seem to mind. In fact, to his delight, she moved in closer.

"Rachel called this a gale, but it's more hurricaney to me," shouted Dayna into the saturated air.

"Hurricaney? Is that a travel writer's term?" he teased. "Gales are thirty-four to forty-seven knots. This wind is about forty-five."

"How often have you flown in stuff like this?"

"All the time. You get used to it." Alex took in the foaming, stormy seas. One lone rock jutted out of the water like a breaching whale, white surf pounding it. A few brave souls with phone cameras came toward them, taking photos.

Alex tapped Dayna's shoulder and pointed at the rock. "They considered this area as the end of the world in the Middle Ages," he said loudly, competing with the howling wind.

"I read about it. They named it The End of the World." She removed her sunglasses and tried to wipe them dry, then gave up and shoved them into the pocket of her raincoat.

Dayna pointed at three white buildings further up

the long hill. "I wish we had more time to go up there. Someday, I want to come back and stay at the Hotel O Semaforo. A converted lighthouse. Can't you picture this on a clear day when a gale isn't trying to blow us into the sea?"

She had a dreamy look on her face, an oasis to him in this hellacious squall, as he gazed at the stormy Atlantic. If that was an invitation, he'd be down for it.

"Yes. I can picture it," he responded.

A four-foot stone marker appeared to the left on the walkway, with the scallop shell and the familiar yellow arrow noting the end of the El Camino trail. Alex strode up to it, quietly interpreting a Galician quote welcoming *peregrinos* at the end of the trail, etched on a plaque mounted on the stone.

"Glad we walked up here. Thanks for suggesting it." Too bad his knee had crapped out. But then he wouldn't have chanced into Dayna. Life was a series of tradeoffs.

Dayna held up her phone, trying to shield it from the horizontal rain. "Stand next to the marker, and I'll take your photo."

"Technically, I didn't finish the walk. I'm not worthy," he teased.

"Yes, you are. You went as far as you could, plus you made it out here. Stand still," she instructed, waving him to stand next to the marker.

Dayna was right. He'd walked a good portion of the El Camino and visited this trail-ending site, and that was good enough for him. He glanced at the churning Atlantic, thinking he'd rather fly any day than be in a boat in this mess.

A deep puddle surrounded the marker like a moat around a castle. Alex straddled the mini moat, with one foot next to the marker, and the other outside of the puddle. His knee twinged, but he ignored it. Rain pelted his face, and wind whipped his jacket as he gripped the gray stone with one hand.

"Hurry, before I'm shark bait." He liked how the wind whipped color into her cheeks.

Dayna laughed and took the photos. She wiped her phone on the inside lining of her jacket and shoved it back in her pocket.

He stepped over the mini-moat and took out his phone. "Now let me get yours."

Her shorter legs didn't stretch across the puddle as easily, but she still managed the precarious position with her legs spread. His brain waterlogged at her sexy stance. The last place he expected a hard-on was in a badass gale. He was glad for the longer jacket as he tapped the photo burst button on his phone.

"Must be nice to have stork legs." Dayna tried to leap over the puddle.

"Wait. Give me your hand. Better yet…" Alex shifted his weight to his good leg. He lifted her over the puddle; her hands grasping his biceps.

"Why thanks, Captain Mendes." Her welcoming reaction didn't help his erection.

This time, he didn't resist the impulse. He leaned down and kissed her. Rainwater ran into their mouths, and he tasted cinnamon and rain.

"Who knew a hurricane could be so romantic?" called out a male voice.

Alex broke the kiss and glanced up. George from Montana strolled up the walkway wearing his transparent rain poncho.

"Hey, buddy! Fancy meeting you here."

Dayna broke into a smile. "George, you made it."

"Yep. Got to Santiago, then caught a ride here. Didn't have the energy to walk it, though I saw a few poor bastards slogging through this mess. Sometimes you gotta know when to hang it up," he said, grinning.

Mariko had moved up along the walkway and plucked the phone from Alex's hand. "Let me get you and Dayna in a photo." She glanced at George. "Hello."

"Mariko, this is George. We walked part of the El Camino together." Alex had grown fond of her and felt a kinship since they'd both lost spouses.

George flipped his soggy ponytail over his shoulder and grinned. "Pleased to meet you."

"Mariko, hurry and take a photo of us." Alex stepped behind Dayna and straddled the large puddle, his hands on her shoulders. He felt like the steadfast guys on *The Weather Channel*, trying not to get blown off camera.

He leaned into Dayna to stabilize himself and squinted as rain pelted his eyeballs. "Criminy, this is a powerful storm."

"Hope they turn out. It's a shitstorm out here." Mariko handed back his drenched phone. "Hey, you two, come help me scatter more of Harvey." She motioned to George. "You come too."

Alex raised his brows. "Seriously? It's blowing pretty hard."

"This is one place he wanted me to put him. Harv always liked the sea," insisted Mariko.

Dayna pointed up the walkway. "How about up there? No one is around." She motioned Alex to step back. "You'd better stay upwind."

"Don't have to tell me twice." Alex backed away to

let the two women scatter Harv's ashes. He motioned for George to follow.

A whistle caused Alex to squint at the parking lot. Rachel waved at them to get their butts in gear.

"Hurry ladies, we have to go," Alex called out to Dayna and Mariko.

The two friends stood at the edge of the bluff overlooking the roiling Atlantic, and Mariko emptied her bag. A fierce gust seized the ashes and carried them out to sea. Mariko blew a kiss and pressed her palm to her heart.

Alex clapped. "Good job, Mariko. He made it out to sea."

Mariko nodded and turned to go.

Dayna followed, her fingers brushing under her chin in a *Godfather* imitation. "He's sleeping with the fishes now."

Alex fell in step beside her and bumped her shoulder. "You're so irreverent."

"Harv knows I love him," she said fondly. "Besides, we did an abbreviated eulogy for him in Lourdes."

Another whistle sounded, with Rachel motioning them to hurry.

All four hustled down to the parking lot where the motor coach waited, engine running.

Alex noted Mariko eyeing his friend. "Mariko, George is from Montana."

He winked at George. "Mariko is an ash distributor."

Mariko poked Alex. "Haha, Funny Guy." She turned to George. "I remember you from O Cebreiro." Her eyes twinkled at him, his ponytail dangling down the back of his rain poncho like a wet rattail.

Rachel popped her head out the front door of the motor coach. "All aboard, ladies and gents."

"George, come to our hotel for dinner," suggested Alex, as George opened the door of a small Fiat. "We're staying at the Compostela."

"Sure, see you later." George winked at Mariko and ducked inside the vehicle.

Mariko gave him a flirtatious wave.

How about that? Alex chuckled to himself.

Dayna climbed on board, and he followed.

"See you back at the ranch," Alex murmured in her ear as she moved to the middle of the motor coach.

Her sultry look shot straight to his loins as he swung into his seat.

He wanted time alone with Dayna, and not in a hallway with security cameras and hotel guests. Last night, he'd wanted her badly. How soon was too soon? He didn't know and didn't care. They were on vacation in Spain…where anything goes.

He'd talked himself into letting go of Ellie as he'd walked the El Camino trail. Time to get on with his life and stop fearing relationships with other women.

Yeah, right? Easier said than done.

Chapter 13

Dayna

Dayna's shower worked wonders, ridding herself of perspiration mixed with rain. Her disheveled hair no longer glommed onto her head. Until now, she hadn't had time to process the past forty-eight hours with Alex.

Where do you park your feelings when having a casual vacation fling?

She had to figure out how to separate her sentiment from the desire that made her want to climb him like a stripper pole whenever she was with him. Why did he still wear his wedding band? She'd not asked him because she wasn't sure she wanted to know.

Dayna valued her newfound freedom and self-identity. She didn't want to give those things up for anyone. They hadn't been easy to achieve after the divorce.

So far, she and Alex had avoided discussion about their lives and marriages. They were enjoying each other, and neither wanted to ruin it. She liked Alex's kind, easy-going personality. He was a masculine blend of tough, gentle, smart, witty, and fun. Not to mention the eye-candy factor that had her fantasizing doing things to him that would make a hooker blush.

Dinner was in the hotel dining room, and the restaurant had gone all out with the ambiance. Simulated candlelight inside stained-glass vases flickered at tables, and dim lights of back-lit water slid down turquoise and royal blue glass along one wall. Dayna and Mariko found a table next to a gas fireplace in the center of the restaurant.

Alex and George showed up and joined them. Dayna smelled fresh showers. Alex had arranged for George to stay in his hotel room. Mariko and George talked most of the time through dinner. Now and then Dayna locked gazes with Alex, pulsing voltage through her veins. She inhaled deeply to slow the current. Alex's eyes traveled over her, and she pretended not to notice.

Mariko evidently caught it and kicked her under the table.

Dayna was familiar with the pheromone dance of attraction. She may have been out of the game for a while, but she wasn't too old to remember how things worked. Wearing her skinny jeans and tight top was a segue into that dance.

"Anyone up for dancing?" asked Mariko, glancing around the table after everyone finished dinner. "Rachel said there's good music downstairs."

"Sure," said George, rising to his feet.

Dayna gave Alex a questioning look, and he nodded. She didn't know if dancing was something he did. Or even if he could with his bum knee.

All four stood and pushed in their chairs, then Mariko led the way across the lobby and down the stairs. A lively Spanish beat pulsed louder as they neared the lounge.

After ordering drinks, George stood and extended a hand to Mariko. "Let's trip the light fantastic."

"You're dating yourself." Mariko laughed and

scrambled to her feet. She let George escort her to the dance floor.

Alex jerked his head at the dance floor. "How about it?"

Dayna shrugged. "I haven't danced in a while."

"Me neither. Hang onto me and go with the flow. I have to move slowly anyway, because of my knee."

She'd hang onto him, all right. Her heart thumped across the dance floor ahead of her as she followed him out.

A slow song played, and she rested her palms on his solid shoulders. He lifted one hand off and entwined her fingers, then pulled her in close. He floated her around with grace, and she loved the feel of their bodies pressed together.

It had been a long time since she'd danced like this, and she loved it.

Another slow song played. She placed her hand behind his neck and rested her head on his chest, cocooning into his heat. He leisurely rubbed her back as they danced, sending sparks to her every nerve ending.

Last night's wine-infused make-out session flashed. Well, she'd wanted a casual Mediterranean fling, and it appeared she had herself one. She wasn't sure about the timing of things. Keeping their relationship on a here-today-gone-tomorrow basis could be trickier than she first thought.

If she wasn't careful, she'd find her heart at the bottom of an Atlantic trench, where a pressurized dive suit wouldn't even save it.

Don't fall for him. No sentimentality. He'd be leaving soon and, most likely, she'd never see him again. She confused herself by not knowing how to feel about it. No way would she allow her heart to be another pincushion.

The music ended, and she hesitated before pushing away from him. She put a hand to her forehead. "I'm feeling warm."

Alex appeared concerned. "Want some fresh air?"

She glanced at their table. Mariko and George had gone. "Sure. Lead the way."

"Let's walk outside." He placed his hand on the small of her back.

His touch felt wonderful. She enjoyed being with him. But that's what scared her. Maybe this wasn't a good idea. Maybe they should part ways sooner than later.

She had cold feet. Second thoughts. Feeling panicky, her breath came up short, and her insides churned.

Her practical side took charge. "I'm tired from today. Think I'll go to my room."

He looked startled. "Are you sure?"

"Yes."

No, I'm not sure, dammit. I want to spend time with you, but I'm scared to death!

"Okay." His disappointed tone hollowed her chest, and she kicked herself.

This fling thing was harder than she thought. She didn't want to invest in a relationship with someone she'd never see again. Having sex was one thing but having feelings for him was another.

Go to your room, she ordered herself. It's the best decision.

When it came right down to it, could she make love with him, sweep her feelings into a dustpan, and dispose of them?

Maybe I'm not wired for casual sex after all.

They walked in silence to the elevator. He didn't try what he had the night before. She didn't know whether to be glad or disappointed. When the elevator doors closed, an elephant crowded in with them as Dayna thought of last night's lusty make-out session. She groped for something to say.

"Are you leaving tomorrow?"

"Leaving…here?"

"Yes. Are you flying back to Alaska?"

"When we returned from Finisterre, I arranged with Rachel to finish with your tour in Lisbon."

Her heart pounded at his news. "You have? Why didn't you say something?" She took a moment to digest it.

"We haven't had time to talk much since then."

The elevator stopped, and the doors opened.

It's go time.

Which way should she go? Should she keep her foot on the gas with this terrific guy or stomp on the brakes before she regrets it? If she puts on the brakes, no harm done. But if she continues—she'd be hanging her heart out like a paper target at a shooting range, flapping in the breeze.

She stood in a fog of indecision, staring blankly at the long hotel hallway.

The elevator doors began to close, and Dayna pushed them open.

"Would you like to come up to my room? We can watch *Big Bang Theory* in Spanish and eat almond cake. And I have wine." Alex said it like a little kid inviting a girl to his house for milk and cookies.

His innocent sounding invitation amused her.

"I like *Big Bang Theory*." She hesitated. "As much as I adore Galician almond cake and wine, I don't know. We—we hardly know each other…" Her words sounded lame.

"I won't persuade you if you're not comfortable. I really enjoy your company," he intoned. "The invitation is open, should you change your mind?"

"Thanks. It's just that—I haven't—it's been—"

He held up his hand. "Listen, no pressure. I won't do anything you don't want me to—the invitation stands."

She knew what he alluded to. "Thanks, Alex, I appreciate that. Good night." She left the elevator and hurried down the hall to her room.

Don't turn around. Don't get swept into something you can't control.

"If you change your mind, I'm in seventeen-fifty," he called out after her. The finality of the closing elevator stabbed her chest.

Was she out of her mind? Any other sane, single woman would have done this gorgeous man in the elevator.

She reached the door to her room, and her hand trembled as she swiped her key card. It opened, then jammed in place.

"What the—" she muttered, noticing the chain lock on the door.

"Mariko?"

"Dayna! Can you please go somewhere for a while?" Mariko stage whispered.

It took a moment to register. Then George's voice. "There's a single occupant in room seventeen-fifty. I'm sure he wouldn't mind a visitor."

"Oh. Uh—sure, yeah. Okay." Dayna pulled the door closed, dumbfounded. Mariko hadn't given a second thought to bedding down Alex's buddy. How had Mariko and George made it up here so fast from the hotel lounge?

And how'd they make it so fast into the sack?

Dayna mulled over her situation all the way back to the elevator. Why was she fearful about taking the sex plunge with Alex? She hadn't hesitated to make out with him last night.

I jumped in those cold holy baths, didn't I? I was nervous about it, and, afterward, I was glad I did it. If I go to Alex's room, will I be glad I did?

Flummoxed, Dayna stood in the hall, thinking of a million reasons she shouldn't go to room seventeen-fifty. She could return to the lounge, listen to music, or find a quiet place and write. She wished Mariko would have given her a heads up on her plan to frolic with Alex's buddy.

She thought back to the past few days. Dayna thought back over the sequence of events since Alex had joined their tour. They'd moved at warp speed— kissing when he'd made the first move—then again in today's storm on the bluff...an erotic *Wuthering Heights* moment that had electrified her. Holding him close tonight when they danced only intensified her want of him.

Was it wrong to be impulsive? No, she reasoned...not after the karmic coincidences that led to her seeing Alex again.

So what if it was impulsive? She'd done nothing on impulse since she hurled her wedding band into the

Pacific after Paul left her. The thing about Alex was, she was comfortable with him and enjoyed his company. And he was movie star sexy.

It slammed her like a tsunami.

It's too late—I've already fallen for Alex Mendes.

She'd tumbled into an ocean trench that first day on the beach, and she'd been trying to claw her way out ever since.

Chapter 14

Dayna

Dayna plodded along the plush hallway carpet toward Room 1750, smoothing her hair. She made sure her Girls were properly positioned, then slid a shade of fuchsia lipstick along her lower and upper lip for a hint of color.

She pressed her ear to the door. The television was on, so Alex must still be awake. She knocked softly but didn't hear movement.

This is a bad idea.

Heart thudding, the impulse to run spun her around and sent her down the hall.

The door opened and Alex peeked out. "Dayna? Leaving so soon?"

"Oh." She stopped in her tracks and turned to move toward him. "Didn't think you were awake."

"Sure am. Figured you'd be stopping by."

"Oh, you did, did you?" She narrowed her eyes at him. "Why do I have the feeling you and George orchestrated this?"

"Orchestrated?" His to-die-for gray eyes grew big, and he shook his head. "Uh no—you got the wrong idea here."

"I'm listening." Dayna folded her arms across her chest, handbag dangling from her wrist. She waited for him to stick his foot in his mouth.

He gave her a doofus grin and shrugged. "George told me after dinner that Mariko invited him to her room."

She looked at him, dumbfounded. "Why didn't you say something?"

"Why do you think I invited you up?" He swung the door wide, filling the doorway in his white hotel bathrobe, loosely tied at the waist. "You may as well come in and make yourself at home. It could be a while."

Seeing the amusement in his eyes, she laughed at the handy little situation Mariko so slyly created for the two of them. "Silly me. And here I thought you invited me because you enjoyed my company."

"I did—I do," he spluttered and hastened to add, "Honestly, I enjoy spending time with you. Do you—do you feel the same way?"

Aha, the moment of truth.

She delayed her response, for no other reason than payback for his not telling her Mariko wanted to get laid.

Finally, she said, "If I didn't, why would I be here?"

"Then why are you standing in the hallway?" He stepped aside, making a grand gesture for her to enter. "*Entrez, mon cher.*"

She stepped inside. *Big Bang Theory* was on TV and Sheldon spoke Spanish.

"Or maybe the real reason you asked me up here…" She let it hang there for effect, fastening her gaze to his. "Was to pick up where we left off last night?"

He appeared casually amused. "It might've had something to do with it."

"I like your honesty." She stood still with folded arms, feeling like a noob. Sit on the bed? Sit on a chair?

Seduce him? Tear off her clothes?

Why wasn't there a step-by-step manual on how to have a fling?

"Glad you changed your mind." He crossed his arms and leaned against a wall, scrutinizing her. "Is the only reason you're here because your room is busy at the moment?"

How in God's name am I supposed to resist him like this? One tug on his robe and he's naked. She snapped her gaze away from where she estimated his crotch was.

Her eyes met his, her head moving side to side.

He pushed off the wall and stepped to her, grasping her hands. "Dayna, it's okay. I'm glad you're here with me."

Her breathing shallowed, and she glanced at the TV. "I don't want…I mean, I do want…oh God, I don't know what I want." Her head swam with fear of all the what-ifs out of her control.

"Tell you what. Let's just enjoy each other's company. No strings attached. How about some Port?"

She sighed with relief. "Sounds good. You read my mind."

"Which part?"

"The Port for sure, and—the no-strings-attached part."

He nodded. "Fair enough. Have a seat and make yourself comfortable." He gestured to an armchair, then moved to the round table next to it and poured a bottle of Porto into two small glasses, filling them a quarter full.

She took a seat, and he offered her a glass. "Thanks, Captain."

She noted the salt-and-pepper chest hair poking out of his robe. She envisaged what was underneath, and a libido rush tackled her girl parts.

"Here's to finishing the tour in Galicia." She clinked her glass with his.

"And to us meeting up again in O Cebreiro." He sipped, then moved to a nightstand next to the king-size bed and picked up the remote. He settled for a music channel, Norah Jones, singing *Come Away with Me*. He sat on the edge of the bed across from her.

"Tell me, Travel Writer, have you enjoyed your time in Portugal, France, and Spain so far?"

She took a hefty sip, loving the Port surging through her veins, warming her.

"I truly have. I'm looking forward to going back to Portugal." Her eyes flashed to his. "Where I first met you."

His eyes smiled at her as he finished his wine. He set his glass down and held out his hand. "Come sit with me. I won't bite. I promise."

She finished her wine, took his hand, and sat on the edge of the bed.

"I need to know something—are you as attracted to me as I am to you? And don't bullshit me, we're both adults. And older adults at that." His thumb rubbed the top of her hand.

A corner of her mouth twitched. "Why else would I be here?"

She wanted to make the first move, let him know she wanted this. She scooted closer, leaned in, and kissed him. Her pulse raced as he deepened the kiss, his tongue seeking hers. She loved being back on familiar ground, picking up where they'd left off last night. She slipped her arms around him.

He smelled like eucalyptus and a fresh shower,

intoxicating her.

A rush of excitement reeled her senses in every direction, and she loved the soft, kissing sounds they made.

"Can I touch you?" he whispered.

He made her feel young and beautiful. "I want you to."

"Stand up," he breathed, lifting himself from the bed.

She stood, and he slid his hands under her top, leaving a trail of fire on her skin. He covered her mouth and she let him have control.

Her breath hitched when he skimmed his hands down her sides, took the bottom of her shirt, and lifted it over her head as if unwrapping a fragile gift. A flood of anxiety welled as she stood before him in her bra and jeans. She palmed his chest and looked up at him.

"Alex, I'm nervous. I can't help it. Haven't done this in a while."

"Would you feel any better if I said it's been several years since I've done this?"

His admission surprised her. "Honestly? Uh, well— with your looks and everything, I assumed—"

He laughed softly. "I'd say we're about even. It'll come back to us, like riding a bike."

"Or flying a plane?" She chuckled. "I've never learned to fly."

"Yes, you have. You just don't know it."

She felt more at ease. No, she didn't know him well, but it no longer mattered. She wanted to be all the way in this moment with him.

Standing before him, she realized the rise and fall of her breasts as her breathing sped. She hoped he would focus on her Girls instead of the rest of her midlife body.

"Please—can we turn off the lights? My half a century of stretch marks, cellulite, and C-section scar makes me self-conscious—"

He lifted her chin. "I don't care about that. Don't you see how beautiful you are?" He led her to the foot of his bed and turned her toward a mirror. He sat down on the edge of the bed behind her, his hands on her waist.

She avoided her reflection and turned to him. "You're just saying that to be nice."

He chuckled. "I wouldn't say it if it weren't true." His hands slid down her arms and grasped hers. "Look, I don't want you to be nervous. We won't do anything you aren't comfortable with, okay?"

A shiver waved over her, pebbling her nipples under the white lace. "Okay."

"Anything else for our pre-flight checklist?" He gave her a lopsided grin.

"Nope. I'm buckled in and ready for liftoff." She readied herself for him to take her.

He rose from the bed. "Then sit back, relax, and enjoy your flight. I'll take you up to altitude."

He rubbed her lower back and bent to kiss her stomach...kissed his way up and over the swell of her breasts...slid his mouth up the side of her neck. Nibbled her ear as he tugged on her hair.

Sensation shot through her, and her breath came fast. "See, that's the problem with celibacy. I'll drop my landing gear before you even do anything."

"Not before I fly you to zero gravity," he breathed in her ear, then swirled his tongue around it, driving her wild.

"So, this is what making love with a pilot is like."

She started for the lamp on his nightstand.

He held out his arm, stopping her. "I want to see you."

"I'm older. Everything's droopy."

"We're both older." His eyes roamed her body. "From what I've seen so far, you're anything but droopy."

"Alex, please. Okay, I'll make you a deal. The light can stay on for the top, but it goes out for the rest."

"Deal." He reached behind her and unhooked her bra. She tensed as he tugged one strap from her shoulder, kissing it as he did. Then the other. He freed her and beheld what he'd unwrapped.

His eyes raked over her chest. "You're so lovely." He slid his palms over her breasts.

"Please don't ask if they're real."

His voice was low and husky. "I don't care."

She gasped as he caught her nipple between his tongue and his teeth, giving it a nip, sending a scorching jolt of sensation straight to her loins. Her breathing became ragged as she gave herself over to it.

Dayna undid the belt on his robe and eased the robe from his shoulders, letting it fall behind him on the bed. She hadn't seen a naked man since Mariko and her girlfriends took her to a male strip show in Vegas.

Alex would have no problem fitting in with those boys, even at twice their age.

Her breath caught as she ran her fingers through the scant hair on his chest, then her fingers traced a scar that once confined an appendix. He was tanned, except for the lines where he'd worn shorts and shoes. No six-pack, but a flat, firm stomach and a slim waist. His biceps bunched when he moved his arms. Not bad for an older model.

He moved his hands to her jeans and undid them. He tugged but didn't get far.

"Are these things painted on?"

"They're stretchy skinny jeans." She reached down to help, and they laughed that it took two for this operation.

"Let me do this. I flew 747s for cripes' sakes." He peeled her jeans from each leg and tugged them to her ankles, being methodical about it. He must have been a good airline pilot. Visualizing him in his uniform only heightened her want of him.

She stepped out of her jeans, and they puddled on the floor. All she had left was her undies. She sucked in her stomach to mask her forty-nine years of mileage. She clicked off the lamp, and he protested.

"I said no lights. This isn't negotiable," she said firmly in a low voice.

She left on the dim flicker of the TV, then settled on the bed. He was already there, waiting, and eased off her undies. When he kissed where they'd been, he brought her to the edge.

Oh God, there goes my landing gear. Not yet!

"Alex, hurry," she whispered. "Please." Her breaths turned into jagged gasps.

He sped through her green light, moving his body over hers. "Should I worry about birth control or anything else?"

"Done with all that," she panted as his erection nudged her. A lifetime of pregnancy worries suddenly seemed absurd. Early menopause had its good points, now that she was on the other side of the tunnel. Her ovaries had permanently retired.

His smoky eyes were heavy-lidded. "You aren't old enough."

"Knew I liked you for a reason. Rev your engines, Captain."

She pulled his face to hers and massaged his tongue with her own.

Chapter 15

Alex

Alex had to be inside her, or he'd burst. He eased in gently. Once he moved, it wasn't long before she cried out his name.

Wow, that was fast! True to his promise, he'd flown her to altitude, and he enjoyed the wave of ecstasy that had crashed over her. She felt warm and delectable, triggering his nirvana, like a perfect plane landing…like a homecoming.

Her legs stayed wrapped around him, and she dug her fingers into the crest of his back. It didn't take him long to reach his own altitude, and he spent himself with a loud groan.

Best. Flight. Ever.

Breathing heavily, he collapsed on her, and they stayed quiet and entwined while their breathing slowed.

Smooth jazz played on the TV as Alex rested on her. He didn't want to leave her cozy warmth. Reluctantly, he eased himself from her and rolled to her side.

She curled into him and lifted her leg over his.

"How old are you?" he whispered.

She chuckled. "What a thing to ask, right after we just—"

He cut in. "I'm sorry, but you're so *youthful*."

Dayna stifled a laugh and made a playful swipe at

his chest. "Aww, get out of here. Don't worry, you didn't rob the cradle—though I wish that were the case."

He propped his head on an elbow. "I have you pegged in your early forties."

"Oh, you're just sucking up," she simpered. "But you saying that turns me on."

"You said you were 'done with all that.' What did you mean?" He slid his hand along her side and rested it on her hip.

She brushed his hair back from his sweaty forehead. "I'm forty-nine. On the other side of the menopausal abyss. Can't get pregnant unless it's immaculate conception."

His brows shot up. "No way. A decade older than I thought. Wow."

"Why? How old are you?"

"Fifty-two."

"I had *you* pegged in your 40s. You're ridiculously gorgeous for someone in midlife." She jabbed him with her elbow. "Don't let it go to your head."

He laughed. "Thanks for stroking my ego. I knew I liked *you* for a reason." He planted a quick kiss on her mouth. "What's a menopausal abyss?"

"The other end of menopause is where life is rosy again. No more monthlies. I save a fortune in feminine products, but I still get hot flashes now and then." She cupped his chin. "You're the first one I've been intimate with since my divorce."

"You've not been with anyone since your husband?"

"Not like this." She moved her hand down to caress him.

He'd barely recovered from their first time, but he had to wait. Age was cruel. He didn't want to stop making love to her, but he had to wait until he could recharge. The harsh realization he'd reached the Age of Little Blue Pills hit him like a bolt. Since he'd not been sexually active in recent years, he hadn't given it much thought—until now.

Shit.

He wanted to make love again. Wait—love? *Is that what this is?*

The thought jarred his psyche, and he tensed a little. His mind spun to Ellie, framing her front and center like the unveiling of a portrait she'd restored.

Had making love to Dayna been a betrayal?

"Alex, you're frowning." Dayna propped herself on an elbow. "Feel okay?"

"Yeah, yeah. I'm just tired." Confusion gripped him by the balls.

"I feel bad. We've been on the go and here you're trying to mend your knee." She sat up. "You're such a good sport after I walked you around all day. And then the dancing."

His hand flew to his forehead, feigning exhaustion. "You wore me out, woman."

She patted his chest. "We both need sleep. Early day tomorrow. I should go to my room." She hesitated.

Guilt and uncertainty seized him. He couldn't shake it. "Probably a good idea."

Disappointment crossed her face, but she hid it with a quick smile. "I'll kick George out and send him up here."

"Sounds good." What a lame thing to say. He should tell her to stay, but he couldn't—yet he didn't want her to feel bad. His wanting her to go wasn't her fault.

He was the one with the issues—the one who had to

convince himself that making love to another woman was okay. Dayna shouldn't be penalized for it. After all, he'd wanted her badly—but hadn't expected the influx of guilt afterward.

"Can I get you something before I go? A drink of water?" Dayna disappeared into his bathroom. The water turned on and Alex pushed to sit on the edge of the bed.

Well, I sure screwed that up, didn't I?

Dayna appeared wearing a towel and handed him a glass of water. She moved through the room, finding her clothes. She turned her jeans right side out and wriggled into them, then pulled on her top. She picked up her bra and underwear.

He downed the water, opened a drawer in his nightstand, and offered her a black plastic bag. "Stick your lingerie in here, so you don't have to suffer the walk of shame." His mouth twitched.

She raised her brows. "Lingerie? Fancy talk for an Alaskan guy."

"My French wife's word for undergarments."

She nodded. "I figured."

Damn, why did I have to mention Ellie?

He gave her a half smile. "I don't mind walking you to your room."

She took the plastic bag and straightened. "Nope, I'm a big girl. Get some sleep, and I'll see you in the morning." She glanced at her watch. "Which is only a few hours from now. Sorry about that."

"Don't apologize. I'm the one who invited you."

"We can sleep on the motor coach on our way to Portugal." Her eyes sparkled despite the early morning hour as she leaned to kiss him on the forehead.

She moved to the door and paused. "Alex, thanks for

a wonderful evening. You're an incredible guy." She stepped out and closed the door quietly behind her.

"Good night—" he said to the closed door, his head filling with stuffing he couldn't sort.

He'd gotten what he'd wanted, hadn't he? Conflicted didn't describe what rolled around inside him now. He hadn't made love to anyone since Ellie.

He'd been so in love with Ellie. Part of him had died with her. His phoenix had indeed risen along with another part of his anatomy, which hadn't happened in a long time. Not by walking the El Camino trail, but by Dayna Benning.

He had to get himself sorted in short order.

Making love to Dayna had exhilarated him. They'd clearly crossed a boundary tonight.

But…he had to figure out how to love two women.

Chapter 16

Dayna

Mariko poured coffee into a cup the next morning at breakfast. "Sorry about last night. I should have told you."

"Don't apologize," said Dayna, pouring cream into hers. "I'm happy you were finally with someone."

Mariko blushed. "Me too. He suggested it, then I'm all, 'yeah, let's go to my room,' and before I knew it, we were in bed. He's a hippie from Montana. He left early this morning to fly back to the States. I have his contact info in Missoula."

Dayna laughed. "That's great! About time you discovered men again."

"I had to cross the Atlantic to get laid." Mariko's grin turned into a chuckle. "After scattering Harv's ashes, I felt like I had his approval to move on with other people. And I like George." She thought for a minute. "You didn't stay with Alex. It surprised me when you tapped on the door."

"He was tired, so thought it best to stay in our room." Dayna made a dismissive gesture.

"Tired? Yeah. Right." Mariko stirred her coffee with an inquisitive grin. "What'd you do to him?"

"Nothing." Dayna's traitorous cheeks heated.

"Liar. Don't give me that." Mariko wiggled her

brows. "Come on. Spill."

"We stayed up late, talking. That's all." Dayna couldn't stop the corners of her mouth from turning up.

Mariko smirked. "And I have an island in the Mediterranean to sell you."

Rachel waved and called up to them. "It's time to go, ladies and gents."

Mariko pointed at her. "You're off the hook for now, but I want details later. Got it?"

Dayna artfully evaded her. "Come on, let's get our bags and get on the motor coach. Portugal is waiting." She rose from the table.

"Right where you met your hot Alaskan pilot," murmured Mariko.

The sound of it warmed Dayna's heart. She had no regrets about last night and was glad she'd gone to Alex's room.

Their intimacy had rejuvenated her battered spirit.

Her sense of calm and contentment had been a long time coming.

****

Alex

Alex took the elevator to the hotel lobby. His knee bothered him despite his icing it. He'd wrapped it and popped a few ibuprofen caplets in his mouth before going to sleep. Last night's rigorous activity had aggravated it, but the sex had been out of this world, thanks to their shared accumulation of celibacy.

He'd grappled with his guilt after having sex with a woman other than his wife. But after deliberating, he decided not to let it consume him. He enjoyed Dayna, and his attraction to her was too visceral to ignore. Her hold on him intensified with each passing day.

115

The elevator opened, and he stepped out to the lobby. Dayna's eyes sparkled as she came toward him. "Good morning, Hot Stuff," she said in a low voice.

"Back atcha," he drawled. Simply seeing her lifted his spirits. She'd become his elixir, his happy pill.

They boarded the motor coach and left for Portugal. Alex conked out as soon as he settled into his seat for the day's ride to Fatima, the next stop on the tour. He'd wakened for lunch, wolfed down a sandwich, then slept the rest of the way until they pulled in front of their next hotel, in the quaint, sleepy town of Fatima, about eighty-eight miles from their final Lisbon destination.

Alex stepped off the motor coach and waited for Dayna and Mariko.

Dayna sluggishly stepped down, disheveled and groggy. He liked how her face lit up at seeing him.

"Hey, Alex. Would you mind terribly if we waited until tomorrow morning to do things? I'm still maxed out." Dayna yawned as the three of them straggled into the hotel.

"We all need a good night's sleep," agreed Alex, relieved that Dayna thought along the same lines. He felt his fifty-two years after his friskiness last night.

****

Alex felt like a new man by the next morning. He appreciated the lengthy rest and had slept like a rock. His knee felt a thousand times better, having stayed off it the day before.

While waiting for Dayna in the hotel lobby after breakfast, he enjoyed chatting with others in the tour group. The ladies flocked to him, but a couple of husbands and boyfriends wandered over to chat with him about flying and airplanes.

Dayna appeared and hung back, laughing and talking with Mariko and Rachel. After Rachel made announcements to the group for the day's activities, Dayna approached, beaming at him. "You seem rested, Captain Mendes. Are you game to explore?"

"Raring to go. Lead the way."

He was more than happy to let Dayna steer them around. She seemed to take pride in scouting out places off the beaten path. He'd read about the Shrine of Fatima and how it was an important pilgrimage site for Christians from all over the world.

They strolled leisurely to the center of an enormous, paved pedestrian mall, with museums, shrines, and churches surrounding it. Alex tried to minimize his limp with his knee in its brace.

Dayna studied her brochure, then pointed. "There's the basilica, with the bell tower decorated with bronze. It says this is the second largest colonnade next to St. Peter's Basilica in Rome."

"What's a colonnade?" asked Alex, taking in the architecture's wonder.

"It's a sequence of columns linked by porticos and archways, like a gigantic outdoor walkway," explained Dayna.

She pointed to the right. "Let's go this way. My brochure says there's an exhibit of a piece of the Berlin Wall." She steered them toward it.

"Not to change the subject, but—feel like talking about the other night?" Alex wanted to know what she thought about their newfound intimacy.

"Which other night?" She slowed her pace and gave him an innocent look.

He gently bumped her shoulder with his forearm.

"You know what I mean. The night of our little workout. The one where you almost crippled me."

Her eyes widened. "Oh no, did we hurt your knee?"

"I like how you say 'we.' " He snaked his arm around her shoulder. "I'm kidding. Cripple me anytime you like."

"I didn't think of your knee." She slipped an arm around his waist. "I was focused on *other* parts of your anatomy. By the way, thanks for delivering on your promise of altitude," she said shyly.

"Not too shabby for a couple of mid-lifers who hadn't hooked up in a while." Relieved by her lighthearted attitude, he liked how he could talk freely with her and not have to tiptoe around sex.

Midlife had its advantages.

They'd strolled to the far side of the mall, arriving at a round, glass-encased outdoor exhibit. A sign to the left of it read: *Muro de Berlum*. Berlin Wall.

Alex interpreted the Portuguese for Dayna. *"Thank you, heavenly shepherdess, for having guided the people with maternal carnality for freedom."*

"Beautiful," said Dayna softly. "I had no idea this was here."

"I'd heard about it back in 1991 when it arrived here but hadn't seen it. My grandparents lived in Portugal during the war with the Germans. Portugal stayed a neutral country. After they'd emigrated to the States, my dad fought for America in World War II. He survived but came home without a leg. Happened before I was born, but I grew up with his emotion about it."

Dayna studied him with those clear blue eyes. "That must have been hard."

A group of elementary school girls had appeared at

the exhibit, laughing and talking in French. Alex guessed them to be in the fourth or fifth grade. A nun he figured was their teacher granted him permission to answer their questions about the Berlin Wall. The girls stared wide-eyed as he finished.

"*Merci beaucoup, monsieur*," they said in unison, reminding him of the *Madeleine* book he used to read to Zoey when she was little.

"*Pas de quoi,* you're welcome." Alex waved goodbye.

"They're so cute. What were they saying?" asked Dayna, watching the girls skip down the steps and continue their tour.

"They wanted to know why this was here." He gestured toward the chunk of concrete.

They stood side-by-side in silence, staring at part of the defunct Berlin Wall. Now was as good a time as any. He *had* to tell her.

He took a deep breath. "My wife's name was Abrielle. We called her Ellie. She died of ovarian cancer three years ago this month. I timed my walk on the El Camino trail with the anniversary of her death. I needed to figure out how to put it all behind me."

There. He said it. They'd been intimate and Dayna should know.

He gave her a sidelong glance.

She stayed still, with a neutral expression, her eyes fixed on the wall.

He continued. "I met her in Paris, during one of our crew stopovers when I flew for Unified Airways. One of our flight attendants introduced us. Ellie restored art for galleries all over France. She was pretty good at it. When we married and had Zoey, I didn't want to fly long-hauls anymore, so I took a job with Alaska Airlines, flying domestic routes. I'd grown up in Anchorage, so I moved us back there. I'd retired two years before Ellie died."

His words hung in the air. He sighed in relief having said them and felt lighter than he had in years.

She turned to him, concern on her lovely face. "That was difficult for you to say, wasn't it?" Dayna said quietly. To her credit, she'd sensed it.

"Yeah." He resolved never to underestimate her.

She took his hand and twined her fingers around his. "I'm so sorry. Truly I am. Grief is a selfish monster. Robs us of who we are. Forces us on desolate journeys we'd rather not take. I can't imagine losing a spouse, even if—" She looked away.

He waited for her to finish. She didn't.

"I'm still wrestling with it. I thought time would heal the pain, but it hasn't," he trailed off, shaking his head. "Speaking French to those girls and seeing this brought it all back, I guess. The Germans killed Ellie's grandfather in France. We shared each other's histories. But my history died with her."

Dayna rubbed his forearm. "I'm honored you trust me enough to tell me. The pain of losing someone is a scar you'll have for the rest of your life. Hopefully, the pain fades as you heal."

He appreciated Dayna's understanding. "I haven't even talked about Ellie's death with my daughter. Like robots, we've gone through the motions of pretending to move on. But we haven't. Not really. We put on false fronts for each other."

He shifted his gaze to find her studying him.

"We aren't always ready to talk about our pain. Maybe you can talk to her when you get home." She took a step, tugging his hand to follow. "Come on, let's walk around."

He didn't move. "Dayna, wait."

She turned to him.

He took her in his arms and hugged her, then kissed her forehead. "Thank you."

She lifted her face to him. "For what?"

"For listening. And being here with me." He meant it. She'd become an oasis in his maelstrom of relentless grief. He'd take things one moment at a time. It's all he could manage for now.

Because he knew their time together was ending.

Chapter 17

Dayna

Dayna stepped onto the main portico outside of the basilica.

Alex followed, and she turned to face him, forcing out the words. "Here's the thing. I'm working on forgiveness. Long story, but I'm working on it. Ever since Lourdes, whenever we tour a cathedral, I'm reminded of it."

"Is that why you jumped my case on the bus when I mentioned the Door of Forgiveness?" he asked.

What would she lose by telling him? She looked him in the eye and took a deep breath. "Since we're baring our souls, here it is. First, please understand I'm not a religious person. Mariko talked me into this pilgrimage tour, thinking I needed a break—plus she wanted me to help her scatter Harv."

She glanced up with a teasing smile. "We both know my petal scattering expertise."

Alex laughed, and it emboldened her to continue.

"My editor thought it would make a good story for our travel magazine." She hesitated. "The surprising thing is, I've learned a thing or two about myself."

Alex nodded. "Travel does that. Opens our eyes, gives us new perspectives."

"Why I love my job. You, of all people, get that."

She glanced at him, then looked away. "My ex-husband Paul left me for a younger model. Literally. A young supermodel named Genevieve. I know it's cliché, but it's true. When I tell people, they think I'm making it up." She surprised herself by sharing this so readily.

She watched the steady stream of people entering the beautiful cathedral.

"Tell me about Lourdes," said Alex.

She turned back to him. "Mariko persuaded me to do the holy baths because they had healing powers."

"What did you want to heal?"

"Nothing other than my high blood pressure." Her mouth quirked up, recalling the experience. "After skinny-dipping in that frigid water, I felt warmer. And calmer. My blood pressure lowered."

"Whoa, back up…skinny-dipped?" His brows raised in surprise.

She laughed. "I panicked and tried to bail when I found out I had to go in naked."

Realization crossed his face. "Wow, all those nude women? Wish I could have been a fly on the wall."

Dayna laughed. "What guy wouldn't?"

"So, your blood pressure lowered?" His brows lifted, and he nodded. "Maybe there is something to the healing powers of the water."

Dayna chose not to counter his conclusion. She believed the real reason her blood pressure had gone down was…*him*. All right, she'd take a chance and trust him.

"The little nun who took me into the bath told me to open my heart to forgiveness and let the water wash away my bitterness and anger. Like she read my mind." She still marveled at how the nun knew.

Dayna flicked her eyes up at Alex. "Do I seem angry or resentful to you?"

"I've not sensed that about you. You're a fun, adventurous person."

"How'd the little nun know that? I'd never seen her before."

"Who do you need to forgive?"

"My ex-husband. And the woman who stole him from me."

Alex shrugged. "Think of the thousands of people the nun has immersed and prayed for. Don't you think she could read people by now?"

A corner of Dayna's mouth lifted. "Or maybe she had a Ouija board, or a tarot card reader hidden behind those curtains."

Alex smiled, then sobered. "Why didn't you leave your husband when you found out he'd been cheating on you?"

She figured he would ask. "I was a good Catholic girl, determined to work it out. I kept giving him another chance. And another…and another, until he left for good. I refused to be the one who ended our marriage."

"Must have been hard to do," said Alex.

"Now I detest myself for sticking it out. All this time I've wondered—did Paul fall in love with Genevieve, or did he fall out of love with me?"

"Did you ever ask him?"

She shook her head. "I was afraid of the truth."

Alex blew out a breath. "Here's what I know about forgiveness. We only harm ourselves when we cling to resentment and bitterness, when people rip our hearts out. Forgiving them is the best thing we can do for ourselves. Forgive your ex, then forget him. He'll face his own demons for hurting you."

She looked at Alex the way an infamous wannabe fighter had beheld his master when learning the ways of the galaxy. "You've summed up in seconds what I've paid three hundred bucks an hour for a therapist to say."

He shrugged. "Life kicks all of us around. You aren't the only one who's had heartbreak. People break your heart when they die."

"We're both walking wounded, aren't we? Must be why we get along so well." She blew out air. "It's crazy. The bullshit things people do to hurt us, and what we do to hurt them back..." She shook her head, forcing back the water wanting out of her eyes.

"You're in the land of miracles, so give yourself over to them. Everyone thinks forgiveness is for the offender's sake when it's really for our own. Unless you forgive yourself first, how can you forgive your ex? Let go of your relationship with him, so you can move forward. Accept the apology from him you never received and call it good."

She shrugged. "I thought I had let go the minute he walked out on me."

"Doesn't sound like it."

"What do you mean, I should forgive myself first? For what?"

"Maybe you think something happened in your marriage that caused him to—I don't know, seek another relationship?"

Defensiveness seized her. "Are you suggesting I'm the one who messed up? That it's my fault he had affairs and chose infidelity over our twenty-eight-year marriage?"

"I'm not suggesting it was your fault. *You* believe it

was your fault."

Dayna stared at him. He'd never inquired about her history. It seemed like he knew her situation better than she did.

"I was always faithful." Her voice tremored more than she would have liked.

"Just because your marriage failed doesn't mean *you* failed."

She watched people mill around the main portico to the basilica. "I couldn't measure up. He graduated from law school, and I graduated in journalism. We married, and he wanted me to stay home. I raised our son while he partnered in a law firm. When he had the affairs, I blamed myself. Thinking if I lost weight, took cooking classes, became smarter, learned more about law. And these—"

She lifted her breasts. "These were a gift to him for our twenty-eighth wedding anniversary. That's when..."

She gripped the railing to collect herself. She refused to break down in front of Alex. "That's when he told me he'd filed for divorce."

"I'm so sorry, Dayna." Alex reached out and rubbed her arm.

He leaned back on the marble railing. "I did some thinking on the El Camino trail. No matter how hard we try to hang onto those we love, it's not in our control. We can't blame ourselves when they leave, like we could have prevented it. Forgive yourself for believing it was your fault your ex walked out. He left the marriage long before he ended it. You did nothing wrong. Turn the next page. You owe it to yourself."

His words unlocked the trunk of self-blame she'd borne since Paul had first cheated on her. It was as if a courtroom judge had slammed his gavel in a 'not guilty' verdict.

"The weirdest thing is, we used to think the sun rose and set on each other and we were the luckiest two people on earth. Then we talked less and less until there was only silence." Dayna stared off into the distance. "One day I woke up, and the silence turned into his walking out the door for good. Neither of us had what the other needed or wanted anymore."

Alex nodded. "People change. You both must have changed."

"That didn't happen to you, did it? Sounds like you and your wife were in love until the end."

He raised his brows at her spot-on insight. "Yeah."

She swallowed hard. "I got sucked in by the fairy tale, the illusion that when I fell in love, it would last forever. I signed on the dotted line, mumbling gibberish about sickness and health until death do us part. Those vows were nothing but empty words—husbands leave anyway."

His gaze locked on hers. "Some of us stay."

He understood, and it's all she wanted. Someone to listen and understand, without judging. She had so much more she wanted to share, but this was enough for now. "We still don't know each other very well."

"It's time we do something about that." His mouth curved up; his eyes soft on her.

She spoke haltingly. "We're still on the friends with benefits option, right? No strings attached?"

He thought for a moment. "I know I said that. But I haven't wanted to know a woman—I mean really know a woman. Until you."

Dayna couldn't hold back any longer. She slid her

arms around his neck. Tears rushed out and she let them fall. This was someone she could trust. He held her while she buried her face in his chest, releasing the torrent of emotion like a broken dam.

"I've got you, Dayna," he soothed, gently rocking her. "I've got you."

Time stood still. She had no clue how much time had passed. She became oblivious to everything except him. For the first in a long time, she felt understood. Appreciated. Listened to. Desired.

Her quiet weeping slowed, and she lifted her head, involuntarily sucking in quick, jagged breaths. Alex stroked her hair and tucked one side behind her ear. Resting her head on his chest, his warm heartbeat reassured her.

Not her therapist, nor an army of girlfriends bearing bottles of wine, had done for her what Alex did just now. She took a deep breath and swiped at her cheeks.

He loosened his embrace. "Everything will be okay."

"I'm scared."

"About what?"

"What happens next with you and me."

He lifted her chin. "Don't be. We'll take it one moment at a time." He pulled out a small square of soft fabric and offered it to her.

She took the cloth with *Alyeska Eye Care* printed in black. A corner of her mouth lifted. "I don't want to goober up your lens cleaner."

"It's all I have, sorry."

"I'll get you a new one." She wiped her eyes.

"Not a problem. I have more." His profile in the archway's shadow caused her breath to hitch. A breeze teased his hair as if nature conspired to make him even more striking.

"Alex, I can't tolerate being abandoned again. Can you understand that?"

"Honey, you're preaching to the choir." Alex pulled her to him. "We deal the best we can, but we can't blame ourselves for other people's actions. Death, divorce, or otherwise."

She stepped back and took in his hypnotic, tempest eyes. They weren't as sad as before. She wished he would kiss her.

Instead, he motioned to the cathedral door. "Let's go in. Feel better?"

She took his hand and jiggled it. "Best I've been in years. Thanks, Little Green Wisdom Giver."

"Welcome, you are." He grinned and held the door open for her.

She should have known there would be no stopping the dam from holding back their real lives. There it all was. Every pound of baggage they'd shared with each other. It exhilarated her—felt good to air her pain with someone who was brand new to her life and didn't judge her by her past.

Alex took her hand, and they walked down the center aisle, where she stopped in front of the tall, marbled altar, with long white steps leading up to it.

This trip *had* changed her. She wanted to believe again. Trust again. Love again. She let go of Alex's hand, and he stepped back to give her space, which she appreciated.

Maybe she could force herself to forgive Paul. It would be a stretch, but she'd give it a shot to let go of her anger and resentment from the divorce. Alex was right.

She should forgive Paul for her own sake. She'd always had it backward. Thinking to forgive someone meant you did it for *them*, to make *them* feel better.

She must heal her own heart first—not an ocean of holy water could do it for her. Not something she could do overnight. She wasn't a miracle worker.

Dayna gazed up at the altar and folded her hands. Instead of asking for something as she'd always done, she gave thanks for this terrific guy who'd entered her life. But she had something to ask of herself.

Help me forgive myself for believing it was my fault my marriage ended. And please help me forgive Paul for not loving me anymore.

She made a quick sign of the cross, then turned to find Alex gazing at her in such a way...it took her breath away.

Chapter 18

Dayna

When the tour reached their final destination in Lisbon, Dayna steeled herself to say goodbye to Alex. She stayed calm and casual, after rehearsing what she'd say...*I had such a good time...you were so much fun...the sex was fantastic...!*

"Would you consider staying a few days longer in Lisbon?" Alex's gray eyes twinkled at her from across the table on their last tour dinner at the Lisbon hotel.

"Seriously?" Dayna's insides left her body and ping-ponged around the room. Uncertainty made her stall for time. "I have to think about it."

He sported his light-up-the-room smile. "What's there to think about?"

She duck-paddled. "Well, I have to talk to my editor." She did, and she didn't. Tessa wouldn't care, long as Dayna submitted her piece on time. But Alex didn't know that.

"I'll help you write your magazine story." His mouth edged up.

She flirted unabashedly. "I'll bet you will."

Wanting to stay longer to spend more time with Alex was one thing. Whether she should do it was the question of the year. This was uncharted territory.

"Tell you what. I'll let you know in the morning."

Alex motioned to her phone on the table. "Check your texts later." He rose and stepped close to squeeze her shoulder. "I hope you stay." He crossed the room, stopping to talk to a table of tour group ladies, who begged him to sit. Instead, he shook their hands and nodded good night.

Dayna had the urge to run after him with a resounding *Yes, I'll stay!*

To her dismay, she stayed glued to her chair, sifting through logic and practicality, which were boring as hell and no fun at all.

He wanted to spend more time with her.

An electric current had ripped through her like a voltage regulator when he'd asked. Her adventurous side thumped her heart, while the uncertain side made her hesitate. They'd become good friends in a short amount of time, sharing their painful pasts along with fantastic sex.

If she didn't stay, she'd have that same missing-out feeling the day she'd met Alex, and he'd waved goodbye as her bus left Nazaré. What if she were to fall head over heels for him, and he'd leave her like Paul had?

Do mid-lifers even fall head over heels? Weren't they a little *old* for that?

So many questions and no sure answers.

She snatched her phone and did a quick online scan of her credit card damage. If she was frugal, she could squeeze in a few more days before maxing her card. The lure of an exotic—or rather, an *erotic*—Mediterranean fling with an incredible American guy was too good to pass up. After all, she couldn't ignore all those signs that had led to their serendipitous meeting in O Cebreiro.

She whipped out her notebook to jot down the pros

and cons of her staying longer:

> *For starters, no guy has made me feel so wanted or desired. (I can't ignore that)*
> *I'm not as broken as when I left California. (Alex had a lot to do with that).*
> *He'd awakened a passion in me I thought was long gone.*
> *I haven't finished interviewing him for my story about the El Camino trail. (I'll stop here and go with this one).*

Dayna didn't bother listing the cons.

Instead, she called Tessa to say she wouldn't be back for another week. Tessa cautioned about slipping her magazine deadline and Dayna assured her the submission would be on time. She texted Tessa a photo of Alex, with a pitch to write up his interview of having walked the El Camino. Tessa's reaction was an enthusiastic thumbs-up, and she texted:

—You'd be insane not to spend more time with this guy! Not bad for a silver fox. Just make sure you submit on time.—

Dayna knew her submission deadline would be tight, even before leaving California, but she hadn't sweated it. She was confident she could meet it with no problem.

But all of that was before Alexander Mendes.

****

Dayna stood in the hotel lobby to say goodbye to Mariko. "Safe travels to San Francisco. Thanks for talking me into coming with you on this tour."

She hugged her beloved friend. "It's been an honor

to help you scatter Harvey."

"Thank you, my dear. Have fun with Alex. He's good people." She let go of Dayna and cupped her face. "I know this goes without saying, but don't get hurt. Take things slowly. This one is fragile." She tapped Dayna's cheek.

Mariko was anything if not cryptic.

Dayna's heart skipped a beat. "What do you mean, 'fragile'?"

"He is. You are. Open your heart but tread softly." Mariko gave her a slow wink. "Call me when you get back."

She picked up her bag and walked out to her transfer to Lisbon Airport.

Dayna stared after her. Mariko had a way of making her point with few words. Most of the time she was dead-on accurate.

Dayna scrolled through the photos Alex had texted last night—images of an impressive stucco villa—perched on a high bluff, overlooking the Atlantic. Another showed a spacious pool and jacuzzi, surrounded by palms and flowers.

Alex texted:

—*I promise to give you something to write about. Smiley face*—

After chilling her girl parts, she'd texted:

—*In that case, I'll stay. Smiley face*—

Who was she kidding? She'd decided to stay the minute his question had rolled off that sensual tongue of his. But she hadn't wanted to seem overly enthusiastic. Anticipation had her tossing and turning all night.

The hottest guy in the lobby swooped in on her, grinning. "Ready for Lisbon? Our rental car is waiting."

"I was born ready," she flirted, lifting the handle of her carry-on and rolling it out of the hotel.

Alex led, and she happily followed. When they reached the sidewalk, a smartly dressed man held up a sign: *Mendes.* Alex stepped toward the man, who clicked a key fob to unlock the doors of a sporty royal blue Tesla.

Dayna gaped slack-jawed at the sleek windshield, which stretched to the trunk of the car. The lustrous vehicle glimmered as if to say, *this is the coolest thing on the road.*

"This is your rental?"

"Zero to sixty in one-point-nine seconds. She does two hundred-fifty miles per hour."

"That's great—for an airplane." She laughed. "You jet pilots are seriously out of control."

"What can I say? I'm used to moving at seven hundred miles per hour." He stepped to the man who'd delivered the car and scribbled on the guy's phone, then lifted Dayna's bag and settled it in the trunk.

Alex opened the passenger door and motioned her in. His grin couldn't get any wider. *"Entre, meu doce."*

Dayna widened her eyes, her heart zooming a zillion miles an hour as she stepped into the luxurious car. "I'm thinking you'll tell me what *meu doce* means?"

"I'll show you later." He raised a brow and took the driver's seat.

She watched him get situated, adjusting his seat and fine-tuning the mirrors. He was meticulous and procedural, the way she'd envisioned him preparing to fly a 747.

"I hope this isn't costing your entire 401k."

"That's what it's for." Alex maneuvered the Tesla like a pro, weaving in and out of traffic. He pressed a

135

button on the dash and a portion of the roof retracted, mangling Dayna's carefully styled hair.

Once out of the city, Alex turned onto a winding road that climbed a high bluff, sprinkled with eucalyptus and olive trees. He downshifted as the Tesla hummed up a steep hill, and he brought it to a stop at a tall cast-iron gate. Pulling plastic from his wallet, he scanned it and the gate opened.

"You've got to be kidding me." Dayna's jaw dropped as if he'd driven them to the moon.

He shot her a confident smile and shot the car through the gate on smooth asphalt. They drove along a lane bordered by soaring bougainvillea, so thick the fiery pink brilliance shone like neon. The car rolled to a stop in front of the pale pink stucco building in the photo he'd texted her last night.

"Welcome to *Mendes Villas do Santa Maria*," said Alex, cutting the engine. His seat belt slid back automatically, and he glanced at her.

"Named after your family?" Her mouth hung open, her seat belt also releasing.

"This has been in my family for generations. Let's go." They both climbed out.

Dayna turned in a circle, still gaping. "This is surreal. Mind if I take photos for the magazine?"

"Click away. The PR staff would love it." Alex reached in the back of the Tesla to retrieve their gear, and Dayna found her digital camera and set to work taking photos.

"I'll be right back," Alex called out, walking up wide, cobalt-tiled steps to the main office.

"Okay." She admired the landscaping, palm fronds and kaleidoscopic flowers she couldn't identify. In the distance, someone bounced from a diving board into a pool. The mighty Atlantic made itself heard in its relentless pounding on the rocks below.

Alex appeared, dangling keys. "We're all set. Let's get our bags."

She helped him retrieve their carry-ons, then followed him along a narrow concrete walkway bordered by a colorful array of exotic plants.

He stepped up to a separate building set back in a grove of trees and tapped up the wide steps, flanked by lofty potted palms. After unlocking an outside security door with a key, he typed a code on ornate double doors. He swung the door open to a large foyer with a far wall of towering windows presenting a panorama of the blue ocean. Ceilings elevated so high she stopped guessing—thirty-five, forty-five feet?

The foyer opened onto a great room that led to a spacious teal and white marbled kitchen with an island so large, Dayna figured it had its own GPS.

"You own this?" She couldn't keep the awe from her voice.

"Aunt Mara and myself. My grandparents owned this acreage back when it was a vineyard. Dad and his sister Mara inherited it and built high-end villas to lease to the wealthy. When Dad died, his share went to me. This villa had a one-week opening, so I reserved it."

He set their bags to the side and stepped to her as she stood in front of the floor-to-ceiling glass, taking in the spectacular view.

"This is indescribable," she breathed, shyly sliding her arm around his waist.

"Hmm, that could be problematic for a travel writer." He regarded her with those tempest eyes that rushed warmth through her veins. "At the time I reserved it, I didn't know I'd be sharing it." Alex took her hand. "Come up and check out the view."

He led her upstairs to the second floor. They walked into an enormous master bedroom with a larger than king-size bed and enough walk-in closets to accommodate several shoe collections—which she'd have no problem filling, if given a choice.

Dayna poked her head into a generous bathroom with a long walk-in shower that had multiple nozzles mounted on all four walls. Everything about this place reminded her of the posh villas in Beverly Hills she'd written about for Ziggurat Digest.

Alex opened a tall sliding glass door to a veranda and motioned outside. "Get a load of this."

The California king bed, with its own zip code, enthralled her. Silk, peacock-blue sheets beckoned as if to say, *come check us out.* A tingle ran up her spine in anticipation.

Alex stepped out to the tiled veranda, and Dayna followed. A pool stretched to the left and a large, tiled, oval hot tub on the right. She stepped down wide stone stairs in the center leading to a lower deck cantilevered over a beach. A two-person cabana occupied the deck. She rested her palms on the deck railing.

"There are no words for this. I feel like I won a game show prize."

"I'm happy to be your game show host." Alex came up behind her and slipped his arms around her waist. "I know one thing. No one will bother us here."

"This is paradise." She twisted in his arms to kiss him.

Dayna wanted to share every available, delicious minute with Alex for whatever time they had left.

Here and now was all that mattered.

Chapter 19

Alex

After considerable thought, Alex had invited Dayna, intending to spend time with her without the distraction of forty other tour people. He desperately needed to put things into perspective and hoped Dayna could help him do it. He wouldn't ask more from her than she wanted to give.

One step at a time. One day at a time.

How to date, when to have sex—these things mystified him. The dating world had changed since he'd been out there the first time. There were no manuals for being older *and* single. At least his aviation manuals specified procedure.

He flew by the seat of his pants now.

He'd taken Dayna to dinner at his favorite restaurant, serving authentic Portuguese food. She'd reveled at the splendid homes along the coast next to their expansive compound. He wanted her to see the sunset on the Atlantic, so he'd made sure they were back at the villa in time.

He poured each of them a Port. "Take your pick: pool, hot tub, or cabana on the deck."

She sparkled at him. "Cabana."

He studied her slightly swaying ass in her swimsuit cover-up, as he followed her down to the cantilevered deck.

Balancing her wine glass, Dayna sank down and swung her muscular legs onto a side of the two-person chaise lounge in the partially covered cabana. She patted the spot next to her. "Take a load off."

Alex settled in next to her, taking care not to spill his wine.

She leaned back, folding an arm behind her head. "I can't believe how calm the ocean is. The Atlantic always seems angry, like it was at Cape Finisterre."

"That was fun, despite the storm." He took in the glimmering ocean, happy that Dayna had agreed to stay longer with him. "And those wild-assed goats."

She laughed. "You perfected the art of kissing in a hurricane." Her hand found his. "Thank you for inviting me here."

He studied her, the blonde streaks in her brown hair glinting in the setting sun. "Glad you stayed."

She raised her glass. "Here's to O Cebreiro in Spain, where we happened into each other."

"What were the odds?" He clinked her glass and sipped, remembering something. "What did Mariko mean on the motor coach when she said, 'you found him after all?' I've been meaning to ask you."

Dayna paused and removed her sunglasses. "After I first met you on the beach, I had all these signs, like seeing you on the news and talking to the bartender in Burgos. I even had a dream about you."

"Bartender?"

"In Burgos, I saw a sign for San Miguel beer on a bar window, so I went in. Spotted an Alaskan Amber beer decal on the wall and mentioned it to the bartender. He said an Alaskan pilot had been in for a beer and gave

141

it to him. I knew it had to be you. It was one of those serendipity things…like I was supposed to find you."

His eyes bugged out. "I've carried those decals for years and leave them in places I visit. Wow, what were the chances of you finding the one I left in Burgos? Woman, you've just goose-bumped the shit out of me." And she had. He couldn't believe it.

He rubbed his wineglass with his thumb, then lifted his gaze to hers.

"So, when you dreamed about me, was it a sexy one?"

"No. It was scary, actually. You sank underwater, and I couldn't reach you to pull you up. We kept reaching for each other, but you sank too fast." She looked at him. "I woke up and couldn't get back to sleep. I went down to the hotel lobby and saw you on TV."

He grimaced. "Weird. Wonder why you dreamed it." He shifted his glass to his other hand and reached for hers. "No matter. I'm glad we found each other again."

She threaded her fingers with his. "Why did you ask me to stay?"

It seemed an obvious question, and he wasn't sure how to answer. So, he'd give her his truth. "I wanted to spend time with you without sharing you with forty other people."

She laughed. "We have fun together, don't you think? I feel like I can tell you anything."

"Let's have more fun together." He set down his glass and pulled her into him, kissing her. And kissing her.

And kissing her.

Chapter 20

Dayna

Alone at long last.

Nothing and no one to hold them back.

This turned Dayna on in ways she hadn't imagined. Her perpetual high of being desired and appreciated soared her heart like a petrel over the ocean.

Alex had her cover-up and swimsuit off so fast she swore they evaporated. She leaned back on the plush cabana bed, and he moved over her, propped on his elbows. She took in the sun, flirting with the straight line of the Atlantic, sending flashes of color like shooting stars across the horizon.

Soon, a blanket of starlight would twinkle over them.

"Thank you for all this," she purred up at him, rubbing his flexing biceps on either side of her. She cradled his face to kiss him. No guy she'd ever kissed came within a million miles of measuring up to Alex Mendes. He was surprisingly gentle.

And wouldn't an airplane pilot have to be?

He slid his hands along her sides, pausing at her waist and hips, while a warm ocean breeze goose-bumped her wet skin after he glazed it with his tongue. He was sensual and far more patient than she was.

She reached down and fumbled with the waistband

of his jeans. His hand collided with hers and together they laughed.

"Teamwork," she murmured, as they tugged off his jeans. She loved his warm skin touching hers. His masculinity intoxicated her.

"You pilots make great lovers." She tugged his face to hers, shoving her tongue into his mouth so deep he gripped her tighter.

"Lift your leg over my shoulder and prepare for liftoff," he murmured.

"If I do that, I won't walk for a week," she panted.

"Yes, you will. Here, let me help." Alex eased her leg over his shoulder and held it there as he entered her.

Oh! That made a delicious difference! She was more flexible than she thought. All those yoga classes paid off.

"Whoa, where did you learn to do this? It feels…it feels…Alex, oh gawd…" She didn't know where she went, but wherever it was, he'd made her feel so good she swore she had an out-of-body experience.

As Alex made love to her, Dayna took in the glow of orange, pink, and purple from the setting sun reflected on the water. When he pushed deeper, she couldn't tell where the sky ended and the water began. She peaked and cried out his name.

He filled her, then rested on her as they spiraled down.

"I'd been waiting for this ever since that first night in my hotel room," he said, his voice gravelly.

"Me too." She tugged him in closer. "Stay inside. I love you there."

"I'm squishing you."

"No, you aren't. Stay where you are." She hadn't felt this level of physical intimacy in so long she'd forgotten what it felt like.

He stayed a while longer, then rolled off and settled beside her.

She snuggled into him, and they shared a comfortable silence as the twilight surrendered to starlight. She could love this guy.

But should she?

She studied his face and stroked his hair. It had grown since she'd first met him, and she liked the wild in it.

His eyes sparkled like they'd absorbed the stars. "Making love to you is like flying a plane. You're both sensitive to touch." He slid his fingers down low, lightly massaging her.

She shivered and arched her back. His touch ignited her like a flame starter. "Ooh…except you can't give a plane an orgasm."

"Want to make a bet?"

"Is there an ETA for an orgasm?" Her breathing became ragged as he continued touching her.

His responding belly laugh tickled her insides. "I don't know, but it sure doesn't take *you* long."

"Either you're fantastic or I'm super easy," she squeaked out, clutching his shoulder when he hit her mark again. "Oh God, Alex."

He grinned, obviously enjoying that he'd given her another orgasm.

She breathed hard. "I want you inside me again."

"Now, don't get greedy," he teased. "Besides, I can't yet. Have to wait a while to recharge."

"Recharge? As in, take those little blue pills?" Dayna had spent her younger, married days where she and Paul's reproductive equipment worked like clockwork. When they'd stopped having sex, she didn't give a flip about the frequency of his stiffies.

"Funny you should mention it. My buddies back home advised me to get some, but I had no reason to bother with it." His slow smile warmed her. "Think I better visit a pharmacy. My aunt's doctor can arrange it for me."

"Your aunt?"

"Aunt Mara. She lives here in Lisbon."

"Oh, you mentioned her. Were you planning to visit her?"

He nodded. "Wanted to spend time with you first."

She rested her palm on his chest and grinned. "I'm honored."

"I'll take care of things. Don't worry."

"I'm not worried." She gave him a playful smile. "Come on, let's go for a swim."

She rose and headed for the dimly lit pool, reveling how comfortable she was walking naked in front of Alex—so long as it was dark. She'd not felt this relaxed and uninhibited in a long time. She made a shallow dive, then breast-stroked her way back. The water caressed her nude body, rejuvenating her…allowing her the freedom to move, to be anything she wanted, without judgment or criticism.

To be herself again…with *him*.

Alex stepped into the shallow end.

She swam up to him, swirling her arms in a butterfly motion. "Are you recharged enough to break in the pool?"

His hands framed her face, his touch amping her. "I like the way you think." The tone of his voice told her he was hers for the taking.

And take him, she did, losing herself in a sensory universe of passion and desire.

As much as mid-life anatomy would allow.

Chapter 21

Dayna

The next morning, Dayna figured they had made up for years of celibacy in one night. She liked that neither of them had enjoyed this kind of intimacy since their spouses. It leveled the playing field. She rolled over, luxuriating in the soft, silk sheets, then sat up, lifting the turquoise sheet to cover herself in the bright light of day.

Alex entered the master bedroom, carrying two tall glasses of iced coffee. "Why are you covering those beauties? I know what they look like—and feel like." He raised a brow and offered her an iced mocha coffee. "Your body is beautiful. Don't hide it."

"It's *old*. Tell me you haven't noticed the stretch marks, C-section scar, and my poufy muffin top."

"Seriously? As if I'd notice when there's these." He peeled away the sheet to reveal her six-thousand-dollar breasts in all their round, perky glory. "I rest my case."

She laughed. He made her feel good about herself.

"What's today's agenda?"

"I thought we'd do some sightseeing, hit up the pharmacy, then go to the market for fresh seafood. I'm cooking tonight." He gave her a wink.

"Love a guy who cooks." She sipped her coffee with a coy look. "You wore me out last night."

"Ha, you wore *me* out. Haven't made love like that

since Ellie." It slipped out so naturally, she could tell he hadn't intended it to, by his astonished expression.

"Sorry, I didn't mean…" He glanced away, shaking his head.

"No worries." The mention of his wife jarred her, but she did her best to glaze over it. "We'd better go easy on each other, or we won't be able to walk."

"I could stay in bed with you all day."

She believed him.

She only wished he hadn't compared her to his ghost of a wife.

****

The next morning, Dayna photographed famous Lisbon sites, including *The Monument to the Discoverers* sculpture, Portugal's tribute to the main characters of the Portuguese discovery age, Lisbon Cathedral, and São Jorge Castle, for her travel article. She tapped out notes about each on her phone for her travel story.

A kind couple took photos of Dayna and Alex posing in front of the Discoverers sculpture and one of Alex kissing her, which she loved.

On their way back to the villa, Dayna shopped at a neighborhood market for fresh vegetables and seafood, while Alex went next door to the pharmacy for his "blue perky pills." He'd made some phone calls, and it surprised Dayna how fast his prescription had been prepared.

Back at the villa, Dayna helped Alex prepare dinner. She tossed a light olive salad and carried the bowl out to the veranda, placing it on a glass table with elaborate turquoise legs. She found a tall, mosaic-glass candle burner and lit it for their centerpiece.

149

Enjoying the colorful flicker, she poured herself a Portuguese red blend, welcoming the sound of wine tumbling into her stem glass. Letting the wine breathe, she sank into an overstuffed deck chair and leaned back, hugging her knees to her chest and curling her toes around the edge.

Through the window, she saw Alex move around the kitchen, and it hit her they were doing the cute domestic thing. What a welcome departure from the restaurant routine of the past few weeks.

Another painted sunset was the backdrop for their seafood dinner. Alex presented his *Cataplanta de Marisco*, a seafood stew he'd prepared with shellfish, prawns, and clams, with a special garlic wine sauce. He served it with a *Vinho Verde*, a green wine, light-bodied and slightly sweet.

After they cleaned up and put everything away, they went for a relaxing swim and Dayna showered. When she stepped into the luxurious, rectangular shower, smooth jazz played. As she glanced around for speakers, Alex's arms came around her.

He pressed his chest against her back. "I'm here to wash your back. And other lovely things." He soaped the front of her and when his hands moved from her midriff to her abdomen, she made a sharp intake of breath and sucked in her stomach.

"No need to do that," he murmured against the side of her neck, making her feel like a goddess.

She twisted to face him, resting her palms on his slick chest, while he shampooed her hair, massaging her scalp. His fingertips were strong, and her head lolled in any direction he worked his hands. He turned her around and worked his thumbs up and down her neck, then massaged her shoulders.

She moaned so loud he laughed.

"Where did you learn to do that?" she croaked out.

"From years of airport massages."

Eager to return the favor, she lathered him with soap and pushed him to sit on the tiled bench. She massaged his neck, and he leaned back and closed his eyes.

"What do you say we lie in bed and watch a movie— *Casa Blanca* in Portuguese? We need a break from ravishing each other," suggested Dayna.

He opened his eyes. "That's what you call it?"

"What would you call it?" She stepped out of the shower and reached for a towel.

He cleared his throat. "I'm a guy. We refer to it in blunt terms, like—"

"I know. I have a son," she blurted, surprising herself with her real-life admission. It jarred her like that movie where the time traveler guy pulled a modern-day coin from his pocket, yanking him from the past.

Her real-life reference felt like an uninvited intrusion.

Alex turned off the shower. "You've not mentioned him. Tell me about him."

He stepped out of the shower, and she handed him a bath towel, annoyed with herself.

She hesitated. "Josh is in his mid-twenties. He's in the Navy SEAL program in Coronado." She bent to twist a towel around her head, then straightened.

Alex's eyes widened. "That's impressive. It's a rigorous process to get in. I'd thought about it when I was a Navy pilot, but I loved flying too much. My knee injury kept me from applying."

"Is that where you learned to fly?" She'd never

151

thought to ask him.

"Learned to fly as a teen in Anchorage. Had a good GPA when I graduated high school, so Dad had me apply to the Naval Academy, where I got an aerospace engineering degree."

She blew out air. "You have a helluva resume. You were a Navy pilot? No wonder you drive fast. The rest of us must seem like sloths compared to your fondness for Mach One."

How she loved making him laugh. "Get over here, Funny Writer."

She kicked herself for allowing her real life to invade their romantic bliss. It was enough they'd each unpacked their baggage.

Alex dried himself off and stood, in all his naked glory, with veined arms, muscled legs, and the rest of his muscled parts.

She stepped to him, inhaling his fresh shower smell and running her hands over his chest and stomach.

He pulled the towel from around her, led her from the bathroom, and tugged her down to the silky sheets. They made love, then fell asleep with damp hair and clean skin, wound around each other like pretzels. In her wildest dreams, Dayna couldn't have imagined anything more glorious than this.

Never in a million years.

Chapter 22

Alex

On their fourth day at the villa, Alex woke to his vibrating cell phone. Glancing at Dayna still asleep, he took his phone and eased out of bed, walking out to the veranda. The sun glimmered the lazy waves of the Atlantic, breaking on the beach below.

Alex tapped his phone. "*Olá*, Aunt Mara."

"*Meu querido sobrinho*, I received your message about your visit. When can I expect you?" said Aunt Mara in her thick Portuguese accent.

"Tomorrow. I have a friend with me. I met her on my trip."

"Ooh, a lady friend?" Aunt Mara didn't miss a trick.

Alex laughed. "Her name is Dayna Benning."

"American?"

"A writer from California. I was thinking we'd come for a visit tomorrow afternoon. By the way, thanks for asking your doctor to call me. I'd forgotten my—sinus medicine back in the States." He almost said little blue pills.

"Of course. I hope he got you all fixed up." She hesitated. "Tell me about this writer, *querido*." She'd always referred to him as 'nephew.'

"I'll fill you in when we get there, Auntie."

"How did you do on your El Camino walk?"

"I made it most of the way. Had to call it quits in O Cebreiro, in Spain. The knee gave out. Dayna's tour group offered me a ride to Santiago de Compostela, then to Lisbon."

"Ah, I see. The writer."

She may as well have said, *Ooh-la-la.*

"Yes." He swore he could hear Auntie's brain whir at a million miles an hour. "I'll tell you all about it when we get there."

"All right. See you soon, *querido.*"

"Love you, Auntie."

Alex tapped his phone off and turned to see Dayna in her short silk kimono with the cobalt dragon wrapped around it. Her robe hung open, and she reminded him of a centerfold. His gaze raked her shapely legs and came to rest on her partially exposed breasts as she leaned against the doorjamb.

"Don't mind me. I'm admiring the view." He grinned.

She arched her brows, raking him right back.

He ambled over and slid his arms under her robe.

"Aunt Mara called. She wants to know when I'll be visiting. I told her we'd drive up tomorrow. Okay with you?" He pushed her hair back to kiss the side of her neck.

Dayna tilted her head to allow him unfettered access. "I'd love to meet her."

"I'll find us another nice place near Aunt Mara's for the rest of our time." He kissed his way up her neck and eased his lips over hers. "Kiss me, Cali-Girl. I can't get enough of you."

He liked that Dayna wanted to meet his aunt. Tonight would be their last night at the villa and he

looked forward to an evening of 'ravishing.'
And he was sure Dayna was, too.

Chapter 23

Dayna

Dayna's eyelids fluttered open, and it took a moment to remember where she was. Her lips curved up, and she sighed a hum of contentment. Alex's arm rested over her. She'd missed the ecstasy of warmth from another human being. His rhythmic breathing comforted her.

Gently, she lifted his arm and twisted around to face him.

This was the fifth morning in a row she'd wakened beside him. She could get used to this comfort of warm masculinity curved around her body. She watched him sleep, appreciating he didn't snore.

She spotted a few rogue eyebrow hairs poking up like a wizard's brow. Instinctively, she lifted a hand to smooth them into place, but she didn't want to wake him, so she pressed her lips to his morning stubble instead.

He stirred, lifting his arm over her. His eyes opened, and he gave her a lazy smile. He palmed her derriere, pulling her close to his morning erection. The pills had sure done their job—last night had been an erotic and energetic round of lovemaking.

She let out a contented sigh. "Good morning. You feel happy to see me."

"I'd be happy to show you how happy I am."

"Please do."

He slowly rolled her under him, parted her lips with his tongue, and made love to her. They moved slower than their first few days of urgent, frenetic sex. She loved their morning wake-up ritual of relaxed lovemaking, then coffee and almond cake on the veranda to decide their day.

She wished she could freeze-frame this time forever—suspend themselves in a limbo of no responsibility other than to be with one another.

Today would be different. She'd be meeting a member of his family. It wasn't as if she was his girlfriend. Still, she couldn't figure out why she was uneasy about it.

They packed up, and Alex returned the keys and keycard to the main office. After loading their bags into the Tesla, Alex drove them north of Lisbon along a coastal highway. He pointed at a grandiose home perched on a high point, like a sentinel overlooking the ocean. "That's where the filmmaker, Albert Broccoli, lives. He made the *James Bond* movies."

Dayna thought the Hearst Castle in her part of the world was impressive, but these properties were even more magnificent.

"Thanks for coming with me to visit my Aunt Mara." He glanced at her.

"Ever since you've mentioned her, I've been curious to meet her. She sounds wonderful. How do you plan to introduce me?" Dayna gave him a sly look.

"Thought maybe I'd tell her your name." He squinted at the windshield. "How would you like me to introduce you?"

She hadn't thought about it. "How about, 'this is my

writer friend from California?'"

"Writer friend." He wiggled his brows. "A very *good* writer friend."

"But don't say we're friends with benefits. It would be embarrassing."

"Actually, I think I'll say, 'this is Dayna Benning, my good writer friend from California. We've been fornicating like rabbits, and that's why I needed the little blue pills.'"

She sent him a horrified look. "Don't you dare!"

Their relationship still hurtled along at Mach One speed, and she didn't want to take the time to define it right now. *I'm living in the moment, thank you very much.*

He laughed. "I love razzing you."

"Tell me about Aunt Mara. What's she like?"

He considered for a moment. "For starters, what you see is what you get with Mara. She reads people better than most. Don't be shocked if she nails you down straight off. She's a shrewd businesswoman and deals with a well-heeled clientele. She's bought and sold multi-million-dollar mansions for Hollywood elite and heads of state around the world."

Dayna swallowed. "Oh. No pressure there."

Alex squeezed her thigh. "Don't worry, she'll like you because I do."

He exited the highway and turned onto a long lane ending at a tall wrought-iron gate. He slid down his window and tapped numbers on a digital lock.

"My guess is, you two will get on well because you're both straight shooters."

His comment warmed her heart. But while she was apprehensive about meeting his aunt, she had no stake in impressing her since she was only having a steamy vacay fling with her hot nephew.

Alex pulled into a large roundabout leading to an imposing, three-story mansion. "Welcome to *Quinta do Santa Maria*." He cut the engine.

A well-dressed gentleman appeared and had Dayna's door open before she'd reached for the handle.

"Good afternoon," he said in impeccable English, his posture rigid.

Alex climbed out and swung around the front of the car to shake his hand. "Hey Arsenio, good to see you."

"Welcome back, Mr. Mendes," said Arsenio, shaking his hand. "I'll take care of your bags and the car. Your aunt is waiting on the terrace." He stepped back to let Alex help Dayna out of the car.

"Thanks, Arsenio." Alex offered his hand and Dayna grinned as she took it, thinking of the first time she'd taken his hand that first day on the beach in Nazaré.

"Dayna, this is Arsenio, Auntie's personal assistant. Arsenio, Dayna, a travel writer from California."

"Pleased, *senhora*." Arsenio dipped his chin, then hoisted her carry-on from the car as if it were empty.

"Likewise." Dayna straightened and noted his fine physique for a guy who must be well into his seventies. He resembled a bodybuilder, and she figured he must double as a bodyguard.

"Arsenio is Portuguese and educated in the States. Let's go see Auntie," said Alex, leading the way up a set of terra-cotta steps to the portico, at the grand entrance.

Dayna thought it charming that a middle-aged man referred to his aunt as Auntie. She peered into the Tesla side mirror to apply a light lip color, then tried tugging a brush through her wind-snarled hair. She ditched the brush in her purse and rummaged for a hair clip. Combing her hair back with her fingers, she fashioned it into a French twist and clipped it in place. She hurried up the steps, smoothing her form-fitting, mauve tank top and white capris pants.

"You're a knockout." Alex held out his hand.

"Thanks, Captain." She took his hand, feeling like a movie star, voltage whipping through her as it always did when he touched her.

He guided her through the intimidating double doors into a large, marbled foyer.

The place resembled an art museum with sizable paintings, sculptures, and extravagant furniture. Alex strode to the rear of the home and opened a French door to a spacious terra-cotta-tiled veranda. A bright turquoise pool with a round yellow and navy sunburst in the center stretched away from the steps.

"You've arrived, *querido*." A cheerful, sophisticated voice called out to their left.

A tall, slender woman in a lime-green, glittery caftan sat at a round glass table sipping iced tea. Dayna guessed her to be in her 70s. A well-dressed, svelte woman sat opposite, peering over her glasses as her fingers feverishly tapped her laptop.

"Auntie, you look wonderful, as always," Alex called out to her.

"So good to see you," said Aunt Mara, rising and walking briskly to Alex. She removed her white, wide-brimmed hat to bestow a light kiss over each of his shoulders. "*Bem vinda, bem vinda.* Welcome."

Dayna remembered the Portuguese greeting from her tour. She noticed an immediate family resemblance. Height, the same widow's peak with a streak of dark in the middle, and they both shared the charming family smile.

Aunt Mara stepped back to address Dayna. "And this must be your friend."

"Auntie, this is Dayna Benning, a travel writer from California."

She stared at Dayna. "*Bem-vindo ao Quinta do Santa Maria. Você fala português?*"

Alex quickly responded. "Dayna doesn't speak Portuguese."

He turned to Dayna. "Auntie said welcome to *Quinta do Santa Maria*, the name of her estate."

"*Obrigada*." Dayna extended her hand. She thought of Alex's earlier remark about fornicating like rabbits, and she broke out in a smile.

Aunt Mara lifted Dayna's chin with familiar violet-gray eyes boring into hers. "I have a good feeling about you, my dear."

"Thank you. The feeling is mutual." Dayna didn't know she'd been holding her breath.

"Of course, you'll stay here at the guest house. I won't hear of a hotel. You'll have plenty of privacy." His aunt winked at Alex.

Alex shot Dayna a questioning look.

She nodded at him, then turned to Aunt Mara. "I am delighted to stay, so kind of you. Right, Alex?"

He seemed taken aback and hesitated. "Sounds good, Auntie. Thank you."

Dayna sensed he'd wanted to discuss it first. Maybe she'd spoken too soon.

Aunt Mara turned to the woman furiously typing. "Eva, please ensure the guest house is prepared. And have Arsenio transport their bags."

161

Aunt Mara laid manicured fingers on Alex's shoulder. "Why don't the two of you settle in, then come to dinner in an hour? We'll eat on the veranda."

"Thanks, Auntie," said Alex, motioning Dayna toward the guest house.

The veranda led them around the side of the house to a quaint walkway surrounded by exotic flowers and palms leading to a single front door.

Dayna stopped abruptly, staring at large clusters of blue-and-white striped flowers on either side of the entrance.

"Alex, check these out! Blue Dragon roses, like I grow in my garden!" This discovery delighted Dayna, seeing them growing so far from home.

"Harvey's favorite flowers. See, I remember." Alex tapped his temple. "They match your silk robe. You have good taste." He tugged her to his side, kissing her neck.

"Ooh, don't stop," purred Dayna, her palm caressing his cheek.

He let go of her and opened the door to an elegantly decorated suite, welcoming and cozy. All shades of ocean and beach colors complemented walls and overstuffed furniture.

"When we used to stay with Aunt Mara, this guest house wasn't here. It's brand new."

Dayna didn't miss his 'we' reference, but she ignored it. "I love this, so kind of your aunt," said Dayna, hoisting her carry-on up on a side table.

"You sure it's okay if we stay here?" asked Alex. "We can stay at another villa, if you like."

"Of course, it's okay. Your aunt is wonderful. Why don't you go visit with her, and I'll see you at dinner? I need to freshen up." Dayna didn't want to impose on their time together. Plus, she welcomed the time to herself.

Alex moved to her and kissed her forehead. "You're incredible. I'll see you on the veranda for dinner." He left, closing the door quietly after him.

He'd left his heavy backpack where Arsenio had placed it on another side table. His wallet was next to it. Until now, Dayna had paid little attention to his personal stuff. They'd been too busy sightseeing when they weren't fixing meals or mauling each other. Get two people together who'd been celibate for as long as they had been—and *yowzah.*

Now that she had a moment to catch her breath, she was curious. Like a kid who shouldn't open a forbidden book, she stepped to the table and picked up his wallet. She peeked inside, noting the usual credit cards, an Alaska Airlines retired pilot ID card, and his driver's license.

Her breath caught seeing a much younger and hotter Alex in his airline uniform. *Oh, my God.* She pulled it out and squinted. His hair appeared darker in the photo, but otherwise, he had the same toothy grin and gorgeous eyes.

His driver's license photo was more recent. Yes, he was fifty-two. Not that she hadn't believed him. But mostly she wanted to see his street address.

Who knew whether they'd keep in touch once back in the States?

On impulse, she took out her cell phone and took a photo to capture his Anchorage address. She took a photo of his airline ID to drool on...hating to admit she hoped to see him once they were back in the States. They hadn't discussed it yet, but she knew they would, eventually.

As she slipped his license back into the pocket of his wallet, she noticed a worn photo sticking out of another pocket. Her heart pounded.

Maybe it was his daughter. She eased it out.

No. Not his daughter.

It was Abrielle.

Chapter 24

Dayna

On one side of the plastic photo holder was the gorgeous headshot of Alex's wife, Abrielle, and on the other was a photo of Alex kissing her cheek.

A sharp pang pierced Dayna's chest, and she dropped the photo. It fluttered to the floor, and she stared at it.

She stooped to pick it up. Someone had taken this photo in a portrait studio.

Abrielle had dark brown hair with auburn highlights that flowed past her shoulders. She'd combed it to one side. She had tantalizing brown cat-eyes, outlined in black. Her lips were parted, exposing flawless front teeth, her lower lip fuller than the perfect twin peaks of her upper lip. Carefully sculpted auburn brows topped a lovely, olive complexion. She wore a strapless black top with a gold and diamond choker and one hand to her right ear.

Dayna tried to find a flaw and couldn't. The woman was drop-dead gorgeous. No doubt she'd turned heads wherever she'd gone, men and women alike.

Dayna couldn't bear to look at Alex kissing her.

Hand shaking, she eased the photo into his wallet when she spotted another.

She pulled out a memorial card with a different

headshot and turned it over. A flying gull graced the other side with handwritten cursive: *Fly to heaven, my love. I'll always and forever be yours. Alex.*

"Oh," Dayna choked out.

Her face heated, having invaded Alex's privacy. But more than that, she was heartsick with a twinge of jealousy—she'd give the universe for someone to be so in love with her he'd write something like this. She returned the card to Alex's wallet, her gut churning.

Oh, gawd, I'm jealous of his dead wife.

She hated jealousy—that traitorous green monster who'd destroyed her marriage. She'd had her fill of jealousy, and it had no place in her life. Her heart sped with the wild impulse to run. Her eyes darted around the room, searching for the keys to the Tesla, but it wasn't her rental car. She wanted to escape—get on a flight and go home.

Tears gathered, and she fought like hell to stop them.

Calm down, she ordered herself. She paced, trying to force the photo images from her mind. She kicked herself for her nosiness and should have left well enough alone.

Time to get ready for dinner. She pawed through her carry-on for a clean change of clothes. She'd washed them at the villa, although they'd wrinkled from being rolled up inside her bag.

Dayna splashed water on her face to calm herself. Her hand shook uncontrollably as she freshened her makeup. She stopped to stare at her mid-life face in the mirror. No way could she measure up to Abrielle. She shouldn't compare her forty-nine-year-old self to the twenty-something raging beauty in the photo.

Dayna finished up and let herself out the door. As

she approached the veranda, Eva busied herself setting the table for dinner. Dayna stepped inside the house, looking for Alex and Mara. She followed a long corridor with a tall, ornate ceiling leading to an extensive, high-ceilinged library. She wandered in and examined the room, admiring the bookcases.

She glanced up and froze.

A six-foot-tall portrait of Alex's wife hung on a wall over the glassed-in fireplace. It was a painting of her sitting and restoring a piece of art. She faced out of the painting, brush raised, with a thoughtful expression.

Even more beautiful than the wallet photo. Dayna couldn't help noticing the perfectly sculpted breasts peeking over a lacy top.

She stepped forward and squinted. Were they original? Since having her own augmentation, Dayna couldn't help scrutinizing other women to see if their breasts were real or fake.

The painting itself was exquisite—like Alex's wife.

Am I deluding myself? Dayna suddenly felt old and inadequate, as if the past few weeks with Alex had no consequence. Unease seeped through her as she stood gaping at the love of Alex's life.

I can't compete with this.

Heart thudding, Dayna bolted from the room and nearly collided with Aunt Mara. "My dear, Alex is looking for you. We figured you must have gone for a walk."

"I apologize. I was exploring your beautiful home." Dayna forced a smile.

She sensed Mara saw through her when she poked her head inside the library, glanced up at the portrait, and swiftly closed the double doors.

Did I make a mistake coming here with Alex? Butterflies pinged her gut, and her mind raced to figure out what to do.

Now what?

Chapter 25

Alex

Alex noticed Dayna was unusually quiet during dinner instead of her cheerful, chatty self. She mostly listened to the conversation, instead of joining in as she normally did. He didn't blame her, though, as his discussion with Aunt Mara revolved around their lucrative property management business.

Dayna seemed interested and amused by Auntie's colorful stories about the wealthy clientele from America, Europe, Scandinavia, and Saudi Arabia. She dropped names that made Dayna's eyes grow round, with tongue-in-cheek accounts of what these people were really like.

During a lull in the after-dinner conversation, Dayna politely excused herself to go work on her travel article. Alex hoped nothing was wrong. Maybe he should have stuck with his original plan to stay at another villa or a hotel.

Alex rose with her. "I'll walk with you." He glanced at Aunt Mara. "Be right back."

He put his arm around Dayna as they strolled toward the guesthouse. "Everything okay? You were quiet at dinner."

Was it sadness that crossed her face?

"I'm tired. We got little sleep last night, remember?"

She smiled at him.

He squeezed her waist. "It was well worth being tired."

When they reached the door of the guest house, Alex drew her close and wrapped hs arms around her. "We should go easy on each other tonight, huh?"

She avoided looking at him. "I must work on my magazine story. Go spend time with your aunt. I can tell she's dying to talk to you."

She pulled away as he leaned in to kiss her.

Something was wrong. Maybe she doesn't feel well?

"I'll talk to you later, okay?" He gently rubbed her shoulder.

"Sure." She gave him a quick smile, pushed open the door, and went inside.

He hesitated, wanting to talk, but she probably needed time to herself. They'd been on the go and together twenty-four-seven, and she most likely needed space. He left the guest house and walked back to Mara's mansion.

His chest felt heavy, and he knew why.

Tomorrow will be the third anniversary of Ellie's death. He'd planned to spend it finishing his walk on the El Camino trail. But after meeting Dayna and all that had happened since, he thought spending the day with her tomorrow would help him get through it.

Aunt Mara occupied her customary spot in the library. Alex went in and closed both doors behind him. She was the only family he had left besides Zoey, and their late-night talks had become a tradition whenever he'd visited. They had catching up to do.

"Hi, Auntie." He stepped over and kissed her cheek as she sat with legs crossed in her favorite wing chair in front of her grand fireplace.

"Been reviewing these spreadsheets." She peered over her glasses at him. "We've done well this year. Outside of inflation and maintenance items, our profit margin far exceeded operating costs."

"Fantastic, Aunt Mara." Auntie had kept him informed, and he'd helped long-distance with the books and taxes each year.

She held out a sheet of paper. "This is yours for the past six months. I deposited it electronically into your account, as usual. Here's your receipt."

He took it and settled in another wing chair, raising his brows at the nice round numbers and multiple zeros. "We did well, didn't we?" He folded the paper and stuck it in his shirt pocket. "So good to see you, Auntie. I've missed you."

"I've missed you, too. Must have been rough these past few years without Ellie. I understand why you haven't visited as often. I presumed you wouldn't want to stay in the bedroom suite that you and Ellie had always occupied. That's why I offered the new guest house. I had it built last year, as you know. Arsenio looks after it."

Alex nodded and glanced at Ellie's portrait. A sick feeling washed over him, and his stomach twisted at the beautiful woman who no longer shared his life. He tore his gaze away and turned to his aunt.

"Arsenio has been with you for a long time now, hasn't he?"

Her face softened at the mention of his name. "He takes good care of me."

Alex swore she blushed, despite the rosy glow on her face from the flickering fireplace. She smiled at the paperwork in her lap.

"I can see he's more than your head of household, Auntie. It's obvious the two of you love each other."

"Never could put one past you, *querido*. You know me well." Her face brightened. "Tell me about Dayna. I loved the story at dinner, how you two met in Nazaré. And how she covered you with Blue Dragon rose petals, one of my favorite flowers. How quaint and romantic."

He gave his aunt a surprised look. "They're Dayna's favorite, too. Yes, it was an experience, for sure."

"Do you love her?"

Aunt Mara's directness didn't surprise him, but he hadn't expected this question. He stared at the fireplace. "Too soon to tell. We hardly know each other."

"Don't kid a kidder, as you Americans say. I saw it on your face during dinner. And I saw it on hers, too. Alex, it's been three years. It is time you moved on."

"We've only known each other a few weeks."

"Doesn't matter. When you know, you know. We don't get to choose who we love. Love finds *us* and forces us to choose."

A gentle knock sounded, and Arsenio peeked around the door. "Anything else you need, Mara?"

Her face brightened upon seeing him. "No, my dear. Go on to bed. I'll be there momentarily."

They love each other. And they shared a bed, which made Alex smile. Good for Mara. Well played. She deserved a good, loyal man.

Mara spoke plaintively. "Tomorrow will be a bad day for you. I loved Abrielle like a daughter, and you as the son I never had. But she's gone now. Focus on Dayna and allow the day to pass. She's good for you, Alexander. I love people who make me laugh." Her eyes warmed him.

"I'd planned to be walking the El Camino tomorrow. That was the point of going to Spain in the first place until I injured my knee. Didn't expect to be here tomorrow with all the extra reminders of Ellie."

She shrugged. "So, your plans changed. Go with the flow." She paused a moment. "Will you continue to see Dayna once you're back in the States?"

He stared at her. "We haven't talked about it."

"Why not? Time is running out, don't you think?" Mara had a point.

Alex's eyes drifted up to Ellie's gorgeous face, frozen in time. He remembered the day she'd posed for this painting. He'd hated the artist's flirtation with her. Everything rushed at him like an ocean wave, thinking of all the good times they'd had in this house.

"Aunt Mara, I can't help feeling I'm betraying my wedding vows to Ellie. It's something I can't seem to shake."

"When your uncle died, I felt that way for maybe an hour." She sighed. "We both know he shared many beds. My love for him had withered by the time he passed. Infidelity does that to a marriage. It was easy for me to move on. Unlike you. You were so in love with Abrielle."

His chest tightened in the familiar way. "I can't stop loving her. If I do, I'll lose her forever, along with my past."

"My boy, you're a different person now. We're different with each person we love. You were someone else with Ellie, just as I was someone else with your uncle. And now I'm someone different with Arsenio. My love is different." Aunt Mara removed her reading glasses, letting them dangle from the gold chain around her neck. "If you choose to love someone else, it is not a betrayal."

"I want to believe that, Auntie."

"You will always love Abrielle and remember her. Because another love enters your life doesn't mean your wife no longer matters. There's always room in our hearts for another love. Dayna has entered your life for a reason. She's made you come alive. I see it on your face." Aunt Mara always had a way of putting things.

"Dayna makes me laugh. She's intelligent and passionate about things. I feel good when I'm with her." His heart lifted, admitting this out loud.

"There's your answer." Mara looked thoughtful. "Your writer friend has an inner strength that doesn't lessen her femininity. I like that."

"Now that you mention it, yes, she does." Alex had always marveled at Aunt Mara's talent for reading people. It had helped her become a successful businessperson.

"You need a woman with such strength. I know men don't like admitting that." She lightly dipped her chin. "Abrielle would want you to get on with your life and be happy, Alexander."

"I know, Auntie. I know." And he did. But putting it into practice presented its own challenges.

"By the way, Zoey called earlier. Give your daughter a call. Tomorrow will be a rough day for her as well."

"I will." Alex's throat tightened, and he needed fresh air. "Think I'll turn in now." He rose and gave her a peck on the cheek. "Thank you, Auntie, you've always had my back. I appreciate it."

"Life is short. Grab onto love, take hold of it and give it all you have. You owe it to yourself."

He stood with a lingering gaze at the first love of his life, then turned to Mara. "Auntie, how do you know when you're on the other side of grief?"

She gave him a slow smile. "When your memory of a person brings you peace instead of pain."

Alex nodded, studying the intricate designs of the Persian rug under his feet. "Okay. I'll hold you to it."

"You're a good man. Your mother and father would be proud. Good night, dear one. Sleep well." She lifted her reading glasses to resume her paperwork.

Confusion squeezed him like a vise. Had he been clinging to the sadness of losing Ellie like a loyal obligation? Aunt Mara was a wise old bird, and he knew she was right.

He hated to admit he'd had a selfish motive for wanting Dayna to come with him to Aunt Mara's estate. By inviting her, he'd figured she'd keep his mind from wandering to that dark, sorrowful place he'd inhabited for the past few years.

His memories still plagued him, and his mind always reverted to the Anchorage hospital room when hours had become weeks of staying at Ellie's bedside. And the merciless guilt when he'd returned from getting coffee to find the monitors had flatlined. His precious wife had slipped away while he'd stepped out—not even five minutes.

He'd never forgiven himself. Not being there when she died had destroyed him. The self-blame had been excruciating.

Alex took his time walking back to the guest house. A light glimmered. Dayna must still be awake.

His cell phone vibrated, and he fished it from his pocket. "Hello, Zoey, I was about to call you."

"Hey, Dad. Haven't heard from you since you left a message saying you had to quit the trail. I've called and left messages on your cell, haven't you gotten them? I called Aunt Mara, and she said you and a friend were staying with her."

Damn. Aunt Mara must have told Zoey about Dayna. He'd wanted to tell her himself. "Had my phone turned off."

"You know what tomorrow is, right Dad? Did you see my text?"

"Of course, I know what tomorrow is. No, haven't read my texts."

"Aunt Mara said you had a woman with you. Who is she?" Zoey sounded accusatory.

He didn't need this right now. "A writer friend I met."

"Why is she staying with you at Aunt Mara's?"

He didn't know how to answer. "Because—Aunt Mara invited her."

Silence.

"When are you coming home?" She spoke so quietly, he barely heard her.

"After I go through the books with Aunt Mara. I'll see you soon."

"You won't have your friend with you?"

He hesitated. "No."

More silence.

"Honey, I'm tired right now. I'll let you know when I'll be home."

"Okay. I got flowers for Mom's grave. Remember how she loved fireweed and forget-me-nots?" His heart lifted at her lighter tone.

He smiled at his memory of the chic, cultured woman from France who loved Alaskan flowers. "Yes, I remember. Put some on her grave for me…since I'm not there."

"Weren't you planning to be on the El Camino for this?"

"Yes." He paused. "Things changed."

"For the better, I hope." His daughter's words hung in the miles between them.

"Honey, please don't concern yourself with me. I'm fine. Love you, sweetheart. I'll call you tomorrow." He wanted his daughter to believe him.

"Good night, Dad. Please don't forget about Mom. Love you, too."

He ended the call, then tapped Zoey's text. The gull from Ellie's memorial card filled his screen. His chest tightened, and he powered off his phone.

Alex stood staring at rippling moonbeams on the pool, wishing he could skip tomorrow…wishing he'd timed everything better…wishing he wasn't here with the memories. He and Dayna should have stayed longer at the villa. He'd been so preoccupied with her, he'd lost track of time.

And time had knocked him for a loop.

Chapter 26

Dayna

Dayna had gone for a walk after dinner last night because she needed to think. She'd followed a narrow walkway leading to the edge of the bluff, where she'd found a wrought-iron bench chair and sat, staring at the ocean rolling in, wave after wave.

It had become crystal clear: she was competing with Alex's dead wife. She understood Alex's grief. Anyone who has lost a spouse mourns their loss. She thought of Mariko's five years since Harv died. Mariko hadn't been with anyone else Dayna knew of until George.

So how could she judge Alex, still grieving for his wife in the same amount of time?

Divorce grief was different. With divorce, there was a legal end of things, unlike death, with no emotional end. Hell, no one arrived at their age without baggage.

On her way back to the guesthouse from her perch on the bluff, she'd heard Alex's voice by the pool. She hadn't intended to eavesdrop but had hesitated upon hearing his voice around the corner of the veranda. She knew by his fatherly tone it must have been his daughter—and Dayna sensed his daughter wasn't pleased about her.

When he'd ended the call, Dayna had bolted to the guest house. She'd expected Alex to come in right away, but he hadn't. Dayna fell asleep waiting for him.

She'd awakened when he'd crawled into bed, and she'd rolled over to him. He'd kissed her lightly on the lips, then rolled over with his back to her. She fell asleep, wondering why he'd not wanted to snuggle or make love.

Dayna woke the next morning to find herself alone in bed. Instead of Alex's head on the pillow next to her, she found a bouquet of colorful flowers and a handwritten note: *Mimosas for breakfast! Come join us. Alex.*

She dressed and hurried out the door, spotting Alex and Aunt Mara eating breakfast on the veranda.

Alex's face lit. "About time you got up, sleepyhead."

Aunt Mara had adorned herself in another colorful caftan, rainbow-colored this time. "Good morning. I suggested to Alex that you and I will go shopping, while he reviews property business. What do you say?" Aunt Mara looked at her expectantly.

Her words caught Dayna by surprise. She'd assumed she'd be spending the day with Alex. He didn't seem himself. In fact, he appeared downright despondent.

"Go ahead, don't worry about me. I need to go over some financial records with Aunt Mara's accountant," he said.

Dayna noticed he wasn't his usual smiling self. "Are you sure?"

She wanted to ask him about his phone conversation last night. She should have walked up to him as he'd finished his call and asked him about it right then.

What had bothered him to the point where he hadn't come to bed right away?

179

She gave Aunt Mara a polite smile. "Okay, sounds fun."

"Finish breakfast and I'll meet you in the foyer in an hour." Aunt Mara rose and whisked herself away into the house.

"She wants to get you alone to interrogate you." A corner of Alex's mouth lifted, but his eyes held the sadness she'd observed the first time she met him.

"Sure it's okay?"

He nodded with a half-smile.

Dayna suddenly felt awkward with him in a way she hadn't before. What she'd overheard him say to his daughter had concerned her. Seeing photos and paintings of his wife hadn't helped, either. She felt guarded now and hated the feeling.

"Go enjoy yourself, so you don't tire of me," he teased, his mouth twitching.

"Like that would happen." She smiled but sensed he wasn't being honest with her right now. He was distant and removed. His blank, heavy look unsettled her.

Dayna set down her fork, leaving the eggs benedict cooling on her plate. She leaned over to him and laid her hand on his. "Thank you for the flowers you left me this morning. You're so sweet. Something's bothering you. Care to talk about it?"

He stared at her for a long moment, then leaned back in his chair. "I'm tired. Didn't sleep well. After I review Mara's financial records, I may take a nap."

She squeezed his hand. "I missed you last night," she said softly.

"I know. I took a walk." He looked past her out at the ocean.

Dayna waited for him to say why, but he didn't. She

didn't want to press. Instead, she patted his hand and stood. "I'm here if you want to talk later, okay? I'll take you for a drive in the Tesla, and we'll park somewhere so we can make out like horny teenagers. Show these Lisbonites how Americans get it on back home." She raised her brows with an impish grin.

His laugh warmed her. "Yeah. I could go for that. Have fun with Auntie."

She blew him a kiss and ambled back to the guest house to get ready, her gut flip-flopping. All she could figure was his being back here with the family memories had gotten to him. Dayna sensed Abrielle everywhere in this house. Not only her striking likeness on the wall in the library, but other family photos she'd noticed as she'd wandered around. Her spirit seemed to permeate the place—and permeate Alex.

Her heart fell because she was powerless to do anything about it.

Chapter 27

Dayna

"Let us out here, Arsenio," said Aunt Mara, as he pulled her BMW sedan up to a sprawling building in downtown Lisbon, the Fashion Boutique. She clutched Dayna's arm. "You're going to love this, my dear. If you can't find it here, you don't need it."

Mara was a touchy-feely person, and Dayna wasn't used to someone grabbing her arm to punctuate every other comment.

Arsenio was out and had the door open to the back seat before Dayna could gather herself.

"Enjoy, ladies," he said, dipping his chin in a close-mouthed smile. His gaze rested on Mara, and he offered her his hand. "I'll wait for your call."

Mara winked a response.

Dayna's heart twinged at their subtle exchange and the way they gazed at one another. This was their love language. Had she and Alex looked at each other that way?

"*Obrigado*, my sweet," purred Aunt Mara at the brawny man who'd captured her heart.

Mara climbed out, her silk, loosely flowing pants outfit billowing around her as the breeze caught it. She'd fit right in with the Beverly Hills crowd, thought Dayna, bemused with Mara's floppy hat and scarf breezing behind her as she walked.

Arsenio offered his hand to Dayna, and she climbed out to the busy sidewalk with people on determined missions. She eyed a woman in white patent leather from head to toe, with a wide black belt and stilettos to match, clicking past Dayna with an air of importance.

"The shoe department is magnificent. Americans simply *love* it," Mara tossed over her shoulder as she click-clicked briskly into the store with an oversized clutch tucked under her arm.

Dayna hurried into the store behind her and beheld the impeccably dressed salespeople swarming Mara. "I'm a tad under-dressed, wouldn't you say?"

"Not for long, you won't be," chirped Mara. "What are your preferences?" She made a grand gesture, once inside the spacious store.

"I vote for shoes," said Dayna.

"Excellent choice." Mara pivoted on her low, pointy heels, leading the way to a series of round rooms with mirrors on the walls and ceiling. Each room featured a designer. Plush, rust-colored ottomans occupied the center of each. The absence of price tags reminded Dayna of Rodeo Drive in Beverly Hills.

Dayna browsed while the sales staff fawned over Mara. To Dayna's amusement, Mara ate it up. Three pairs of shoes later for Mara, they moved on to browse clothing. Dayna breezed by a room displaying only cocktail dresses.

"Oh, no you don't! Get back here," Mara called out behind her.

Dayna lurched to a stop and turned to find Mara holding a dress in each hand, flashing her Alex's dazzling smile. "Try these." She wiggled the dresses.

Dayna eyeballed a designer tag far beyond her price range. "I don't think so," she said, shaking her head.

"Everyone needs a sexy cocktail dress. Don't they dress up in America anymore?"

"Yes, but—" Dayna didn't have room in her carry-on for a dress like this.

"Isabelle!" Mara called out to the salesperson in a tight sheath. "Find the perfect cocktail dress for this young lady."

The woman stepped back to size Dayna up. She sailed around the room, grabbing dresses from racks and handing them to her assistant, who rushed them into a dressing room the size of Dayna's living room back home.

"But I don't need a cocktail dress," Dayna protested. She'd stopped wearing dresses like these when her ex stopped paying attention to her.

"I won't take no for an answer." Mara shot her a crafty look. "Trust me."

"All right," shrugged Dayna, following the dresses into the room. Red, royal blue, burgundy, pink, green, every color and style hung on wall hooks around the room. She stood, deciding which to try first. She gravitated toward the black and plucked its hanger off the hook, holding it up to scrutinize it.

"No, my dear. This one." Mara breezed over to a dark green dress with an elegant, metallic sheen and held it out. "The color of the Atlantic at night. I simply must see it on."

Dayna wondered how the heck she'd fit into it, but Mara insisted, so she took it to try on. She stripped out of her capris and tank top. She pulled the dress from the hanger and wriggled into it. The comfortable fabric

184

stretched with her figure. She worked it over her hips and stuffed her chest into it, then tried to figure out how to wrangle the sleeves. She tugged them up onto her shoulders, but it didn't feel right.

"Madam, do you need help?" The sales assistant called through the velvet curtain.

"Yes, please." Dayna shoved the curtain aside and stepped out.

The woman chuckled. "No, like this."

She slid each narrow sleeve off Dayna's shoulders, so each hugged her biceps. Then she motioned at the three-way mirror and Dayna stepped over to it.

Mara whisked in behind her and gasped. "Striking, simply striking! *Tout à fait magnifique.*" Mara stepped back critically, as Dayna assessed herself in the dress, feeling transformed.

It fit perfectly, and her usual concerns about bulges were a nonissue. The dress hugged her form to the knee, with a partial slit up the front of one leg. But that wasn't the striking part. It was the way the dress framed her breasts. The neckline plunged in a gentle V, exposing her full décolletage.

"Giotelli created this design for you. It's exquisite," marveled Mara. "Wrap it up, we'll take it," she said to the elegant salesperson with a grand gesture.

"But—Mara—where will I wear this?"

Mara's eyes pierced hers. "We'll discuss it over lunch."

Before Dayna could bat an eyelash, Mara had whipped out a credit card and paid for the dress.

"No, no, I'll pay—"

Mara cut her off and cupped her cheek. "This is my gift to you. It's an investment." She turned to the saleswoman. "Stilettos. Have them dyed to match. Get her shoe size."

The woman grabbed a foot sizer and had Dayna step into it. She measured it and barked Portuguese to her assistant, who scurried off. Soon she returned with six shoe boxes and lifted a shoe from each and set it on each box. Dayna at once zeroed in on the pair she liked. A simple, elegant peep-toe stiletto with beading on the top.

"I'm paying for these. Put away your card," Dayna pulled out her credit card. She gulped at the sticker price of €650 euros but played it cool as if she bought big-name designer shoes on an hourly basis.

With packages in hand, Mara announced they would lunch at the bistro next door. She knew the chefs and raved about the place. Dayna wholeheartedly agreed. Alex's aunt was full of pizzazz and boundless energy.

Once settled at their table, Mara ordered a bottle of white Portuguese wine, and they placed their orders for salads. Mara inhaled her first glass, then leaned forward and folded her arms on the table. "We need to talk, my dear."

Uh-oh. While Dayna waited for the axe to fall, she took a healthy sip of wine.

Mara took a deep breath and let it out slow. "Are you aware of what today is?"

Dayna stared at her a moment, then slowly shook her head.

"September…uh, I've lost track of the days."

Mara looked at her directly. "No, my dear. That's not what I mean. Today is the anniversary of Abrielle's passing."

"Oh."

"You are aware Abrielle was Alexander's wife,

right?"

Dayna nodded as sudden understanding avalanched her. That's why Alex had been out of sorts. She flashed back to Fatima, when he'd said he had planned to time his walk on the El Camino trail with the anniversary of his wife's death. He'd be on the trail right now, had he not injured his knee—and if he and Dayna hadn't run into each other in Spain.

Her chest clenched with mixed emotion—sympathy for Alex, yet self-pity to find she played second fiddle to his deceased wife.

"My dear, I didn't tell you to make you feel bad."

"It's all right, Mara. He'd mentioned it, but I didn't realize it was today."

"Alex has not had an easy time. He and their daughter Zoey have suffered immeasurably since her death. The three were extremely close. He and I have always been close as well. We talk often, though his visits have become less frequent. He hasn't been with any women that I know of. Until you." Mara poured herself another glass of wine and topped off Dayna's.

"Thanks, Mara." Dayna took a sip.

"The minute I saw how you were with each other, I knew. You're the first one he's taken an interest in. I want you to know how delicate this is."

Dayna reeled, thinking of Mariko's parting words to her before she'd flown home. Mariko had used the word fragile for both her and Alex.

Mara deserved her honesty.

Dayna fiddled with her wineglass. "I realize now how much Alex loved Abrielle. I sensed his sadness the day I met him. When we met again in O Cebreiro, I had enchanted myself with the notion we could have a brief fling, a vacation romance. Nothing serious. Then we'd walk away to our respective lives. Now, I'm not so sure."

And she wasn't. She searched Mara's face for understanding.

Dayna continued. "I can't compete with Abrielle. I've felt her presence since arriving here. How painful this must be for Alex. Maybe it wasn't a good idea my coming here."

"My dear, quite the contrary. You're the best thing for him right now. Alex wants you here. He loves you. I see it in the way he looks at you, like he adores you." Mara sipped her wine as the server brought their salads.

Her words caught Dayna off guard, and she back-pedaled. "We haven't talked about love. We've been enjoying each other, but…" She stared into her glass, swirling it.

"Have you had sex?"

Dayna's eyes widened and heat crept into her cheeks. She couldn't help the corners of her mouth lifting.

"I thought so." Mara winked and poured herself another glass. She'd downed almost the entire bottle. "Alex wouldn't have sex with anyone he didn't love. This is no casual fling on his part. Not from what I've observed."

"These past few weeks have been the best of my life. Your nephew is a kind, generous person. A romantic at heart and fun to be with." Dayna thought back to his ability in several surprising areas she'd observed these past several days.

Mara placed her hand on Dayna's wrist. "Then help him get beyond this grief he can't seem to shake on his own. Grief is insufferable when shouldered alone."

"Not sure I know how." Dayna shook her head, picking at her lettuce.

"Were you married?"

"Yes. He was unfaithful. Left me for a younger version."

Mara blew out air. "Bastard! My husband wasn't faithful. I know your pain. Fortunately, I pushed through. I'm sure you have, too."

"I hadn't completely. But oddly enough, Alex helped me with it." Dayna stunned herself with this realization.

"Perhaps you can return the favor. No one escapes a marriage without pain and suffering, be it death or divorce. You and Alex are clinging to people who are gone. The past is over. Alex's wife is dead, and your husband left you. You both must let go of the past and embrace the present." Mara made it sound easy.

"Do you think Alex would rather be alone today?"

Mara shook her head. "You need to be with him." She downed the rest of her wine.

"I'm not sure what I could say that would help him."

"Wear the dress and take him on a date tonight. Have dinner, go dancing. Get him away from this place of memory. Fill his heart with your own."

Dayna rested her hand on Mara's. "Thank you so much for your hospitality and generosity. I want to pay you for the dress—"

"I won't hear of it. The dress is a gift—my investment in you. You make my nephew happy. Love him, and you won't be sorry. You must give each other the chance." Mara's eyes bored into hers.

Dayna hadn't expected counsel about her love life. But she understood Mara's love and concern for Alex's well-being. Mara was right. Dayna had been lying to herself that their relationship was a casual affair. But what if she allowed herself to love him and he didn't love her back? Would he abandon her as Paul had? She couldn't endure such pain again. And what would happen once back in the States? Her thoughts muddied.

They finished lunch and stepped out to the curb to find Arsenio leaning against the car, waiting.

All the way back, Dayna wondered what she'd say to Alex.

Chapter 28

Alex

Alex sat in the library, staring at Ellie's portrait. He'd brooded for the better part of the day, wishing to hell he wasn't here, hating that he was. He loved visiting Aunt Mara, but the timing couldn't have been worse. Instead of moving forward from losing Ellie, he'd moved backward, as if someone had dumped him in an undercurrent, drifting him further from shore.

He was drowning, but no one could save him but himself. He recalled Dayna's dream she'd had with him sinking through water and she couldn't reach him. His neck hairs raised. She'd dreamed that before they got to know each other.

Dayna had his mind occupied so much in the last few weeks, he'd all but shoved Ellie from his mind. He kicked himself for not paying closer attention to the timing. He'd missed Ellie so much it had gutted him. He'd battled his own anger and resentment at her for abandoning him. Who was he to lecture Dayna about forgiveness when he hadn't forgiven Ellie for dying?

He wanted to feel like himself again, get back to who he was before grief had seized him by the balls and turned him into a pile of goo. Thank God for Dayna. But he didn't want to make her his crutch. He didn't want to depend on her or anyone else to help him back to normalcy. He had to find his own way back.

A pair of lively voices let him know Dayna and Mara were home from their shopping excursion. Dayna's lilting laughs lifted his spirits.

"Alex, where are you?" called out Auntie.

He rose and stepped into the hallway that led to the grand foyer.

Mara stood, surrounded by shopping bags. Eva hurried upstairs with a Fashion Boutique clothes bag draped over her arm. Her other hand gripped a shoe box.

"Hi, Alex!" Dayna waved at him as she followed Eva upstairs.

"*Querido*, have you eaten? I instructed Eva to have lunch prepared for you."

"Yes, Auntie, she made a delicious meal," he said, giving her a peck on the cheek.

"I hope you don't think I've ignored you. I know what day this is. But we have a surprise for you. And promise me you'll do whatever Dayna wants you to." She winked at him.

"Sure, Auntie." He would humor her. What were they up to?

"That's my boy. Now chin up and go sit in my receiving room. Wait for your woman."

"My woman?" Alex raised his brows and chuckled. Aunt Mara's bluntness amused him.

He did as he was told and wandered to the large living room to peruse a familiar stack of aviation magazines left from his past visits. Choosing one, he flipped it open to read about trans-oceanic crossings in small planes.

He was well into a second article when a melodic, sultry voice floated into his space. "Hey there, Cap'n."

Alex glanced up and did a double-take.

Dayna stood at the entrance to the room. He'd not seen her in a dress. Naked, yes. In a hot dress, no. Heat seared him like a lightning bolt, his thrusters firing every nerve ending. Exactly the medicine he needed on this difficult day.

"I have instructions to take you to dinner at *Feitoria*, in the Altis Belem Hotel, overlooking the Tagus River," she said, moving toward him. "Aunt Mara reserved us the best table."

"You're—you're—wow," he breathed, lifting from the overstuffed chair he'd been lounging in. He zeroed in on her breasts and the way the dress showcased them as the featured attraction. His eyes roved south to the slit, revealing a tanned, muscular leg.

"This is quite the dress."

"Mara talked me into it." She grinned, one hand on her waist, shifting her weight so her hip moved to the side in a movie star stance.

"I'm glad she did." He took in her ruby lips, wanting to kiss them.

Her hair was elegantly up off her shoulders and neck, with a sexy sweep draped over one eye, hugging her cheek. He loved the way her ankles curved, and her feet arched in those come-do-me heels.

She was damn hot; so hot he couldn't wait to get her out of the dress. What was it younger guys said about older women?

MILF. Dayna is most definitely one of those.

He stumbled on the coffee table as he crossed the room, wanting his hands on her. She chuckled as he placed his palms on her shoulders. He wanted to stick his hand under the slit on her leg but restrained himself.

He'd rather skip dinner and go straight to the guest house. Until then, he'd enjoy the splendid view.

Her face turned up to him. Long lashes, and there seemed to be more of them. He kissed her, inhaling an exotic cologne he hadn't smelled on her before.

They mutually ended the kiss, and she chuckled and wiped her thumb across his bottom lip. "Got lipstick on you."

He grinned. "It's my private badge of honor."

She stepped back, heavy-lidded, her lips parted. "Hand over the keys to the Tesla," she said in a husky voice.

Like a robot, he reached into his back pocket and tossed the key fob at her. He'd do anything she wanted right now.

Damn.

She caught it nimbly, like a *Giants* catcher at home plate. His lips curved up at the thought of being at a baseball game with her. He envisioned sitting in the stands with her, pulling on a beer, hotdog in hand, yelling at the batter.

Mara entered the room. "Tell her she's a sight to behold. Then clean yourself up, and she'll take you out on the town, as you Americans say."

Alex regarded Dayna like a ravenous lion. "You *are* a sight to behold."

He winked at her, then scurried to the guest house. While shaving, his eye caught clothes laid out on the bed. Eva must have delivered them from the bedroom he normally stayed in.

Mara had sent over a light blue oxford shirt, a navy-blue suit jacket, and a pair of khakis. He chuckled at his aunt's nudge for a night out and appreciated her good intentions. Like most people, she'd taken to Dayna's charms. Both of them had indeed saved him from drowning in his sorrows today. And he was grateful for it.

He finished shaving and splashed on a men's cologne Arsenio must have deposited in the bathroom. He checked himself out in the mirror.

"You aren't getting any younger," he mumbled to his aging image.

On his way out the door, he used his pocketknife to whack the stem of a Blue Dragon rose.

Dayna was a natural in the driver's seat, ready to command the quietly idling Tesla. As he stepped from the portico to the circular driveway, she leaned forward, squinting at the dash, impatiently tapping the GPS.

Amused, Alex opened the door and folded himself into the passenger seat. His seat belt automatically encircled him as he settled in.

"It's the technology age. Talk to it."

She shot him a look. "Did you talk to your 747s, telling them where to go? I don't trust these devices. They record us. Still don't know what companies do with all those monitored and recorded phone calls," she muttered, digging through her purse. She produced her cheaters. "And what the heck is quality assurance, anyway?"

He laughed, amused by her quirkiness. He offered her the rose.

She lit up. "Aw, thanks, Captain Mendes. Ever the gentleman." She took the flower and held it to her nose. Her cat-eyed look went straight to his crotch.

Down, boy, no need to rise to the occasion. Yet.

He leaned toward her. "You're the captain of this

195

mission, so do it your way. Didn't know you were averse to technology. And we're across the pond from the CIA."

She grinned at the windshield, shifting smoothly into gear. "You pilots and your black boxes. How can you work when being recorded all the time? Now get your seat in its upright and locked position."

She sent him a sultry wink and teasingly ran her tongue slowly over her bottom lip as she maneuvered the Tesla down the long lane to the coastal highway. She gave it gas and hummed the car along like a racing pro.

He admired how deftly she handled the car. Her hot dress framed her breasts like a Da Vinci painting. He eyed the muscled definition of her leg peeking through the slit and ending in those sexy heels. He blew out air and leaned back, thinking how his pants would bulge the rest of the evening—no little blue pill needed.

"Watching you drive a hot car in that scorching dress drives me wild. I can't wait to get *you* in an upright and locked position."

"Good." She lowered her shades and peeked over them. "I have orders to cheer you up."

"You already have." He'd do whatever she wanted; he was putty in her hands tonight.

She followed the GPS directions to the Altis Belem Hotel, pulled in front, and the valet opened their doors. She handed him the key fob.

As Alex waited on the curb for her to round the front of the car, he noticed how the evening light cast a sexy glow on her skin. They made their way through the hotel to the *Feitoria* restaurant. Dayna fit right in with this upscale Mediterranean crowd. Heads turned as she passed, sending a wave of delight through him.

Like Ellie used to whenever she walked through a room. He shoved aside that notion.

You're here with Dayna now. Stop comparing.

Chapter 29

Dayna

Dayna sat upright at the dinner table so she wouldn't slouch. Mara had given her strict orders to keep correct posture.

"Throw your shoulders back, stick those ladies out!" she'd whispered into Dayna's ear as she headed out to the Tesla.

After a delicious seafood meal, Dayna fiddled with her crystal of Port. "I'm sorry. This has been a tough day for you."

"It no longer is." Alex smiled at her across the cozy table, looking good enough to eat—reminding her of that first day on the beach, when she saw him for the first time.

"You clean up real sexy, Cap'n." She eyed him like prey as she sipped her Port.

He eyed her back the same way, and she'd loved how his eyes traveled over her. Mara and Eva had teamed up to give her a makeover upstairs in Mara's bedroom. Mara had helped her wriggle into the dress, and Eva fixed her hair in an up-do and did her make-up. Their enthusiasm amused Dayna that she'd become their personal *Pygmalion* project. She hadn't minded. She needed every advantage for her discussion with Alex.

The problem was, she didn't quite know what to say.

I hope the words magically come to me when I need them.

Now was as good of a time as any to segue into it. She scooted her chair forward and rested her forearms on the table. "Thank you for spending time with me on the tour and inviting me to stay longer. I can't remember when I've felt so relaxed and happy. It's been glorious."

He gave her a warm look. "Yes, it has. I've had a fantastic time."

"I admit, I did try to track you down." She melted into his eyes. "After we met. Even though I thought you were married. Felt like a homewrecker."

"You saw me on TV and talked to a bartender in Burgos. Then we bumped into each other in O Cebreiro in Spain." He tilted his head, studying her. "Coincidence or fate?"

She shook her head. "Not coincidence. Because I dreamed about you. Couldn't figure out why the universe clobbered me with signs to track down a married man."

She lowered her arms from the table and leaned back. "Tell me something. Why do you still wear your wedding band?"

He lifted his hand and stared at it for a moment. "Fear, I guess."

She waited, remembering how Mara had cautioned her to be patient. "Fear of?"

"Losing Ellie forever. Forgetting her as if she never existed. Our marriage hung unfinished. Didn't feel right taking off the ring."

Dayna tried hard as she could to understand. "And now?"

"Now...I still don't know."

She swallowed hard. "Why?"

199

"It's still hard. Suddenly, I was without the woman who'd been my best friend for twenty years. The one I'd made love to, shared my innermost self with, and who gave birth to my daughter. When death stole her, I felt stripped of everything. Nothing made sense after that." He fingered his ring. "This is my last genuine connection."

She let out a long sigh. "I understand. More than you think I do."

He looked up at her. "Loss is loss, right?"

"Even if the person is still alive." She sipped her Port and watched a guy at the next table lift a woman's hand and kiss it. "People are never really gone. They live in the hearts of those who loved them, like they sing about in songs and movies."

He stared off. "It's not only that they're gone, but they also take our history with them. They knew the skeletons in our closets, knew how we changed through the years. They knew what brought us to our knees and what made us happy. When they leave, a chunk of our lives goes with them."

"You and I have that in common." Dayna let out a long sigh. "Mine and Paul's shared history lives on cassettes, VHS tapes, CDs, DVDs, photos, and mp3 videos. Couldn't bear to chuck it all. Throwing it away would erase twenty-eight years of my life. It's still sitting in a box gathering dust. I'm in no position to judge you for wearing your ring."

He leaned forward, his eyes piercing hers. "After she died, I struggled with the changes in the order of things. Death disrupts your world order. It spins you into a continuous chaos, like a Cessna in a cat-five hurricane. You crave a logical explanation, but no one can give you one. Some try to comfort you with, 'They're in a better place now,' or 'God has a reason for everything.'" Alex emptied his wineglass. "There is no reason. Shit just happens."

"I know." And she *did* know. Only she'd blamed herself for her loss.

A muscle jerked in his jaw. "I talk to her now and then, like we're still married," he confessed. "We said goodbye, but it felt more like she was going on a trip, and we'd see each other again. A never-ending goodbye."

Dayna knew he had to get this off his chest, so she stayed quiet.

Alex shook his head. "What kind of God creates us, makes us love each other, then tears us apart forever? What kind of God does that?"

"I don't know. But I don't think it's forever." Her heart went out to him. She wanted him to be happy and wished she could wave a magic wand to make his grief go away.

Dayna took a deep breath. "Moving on doesn't mean you'll forget her. It means you're willing to accept she's gone, and you still have a life ahead of you."

She nodded at his hand. "Someday you'll take off this ring, thinking it's only a ring. You'll melt it down for a salmon lure or toss it in the ocean, like I did. If it stays on your finger, you might miss out on the love you could have had." She reached across and covered his hand with her own. "That's not living life."

He lifted his chin. "You're right. It isn't."

"I know what else I'm right about." She flashed him a seductive smile. "Both of us should blow this pop-stand for some bone-busting, lusty sex. What do you say,

Captain Mendes?" She wiggled her brows at him.

He threw his head back and laughed. "I like how you get right to the point."

She breathed in relief at getting him to laugh, so she channeled her inner Texan. "Let's go, y'all, we're burnin' daylight, and we ain't gittin' any younger."

He chortled again with a surprised look. "I said that to myself earlier."

The server brought the bill, and Alex reached for his wallet.

"Nope. Put that away. This is my treat."

Dayna handed the server her credit card, and he swished it through his smart phone. She scribbled her name with her forefinger on the phone screen, and the server emailed her receipt.

"See? I manage technology just fine." She took pride in her ability to keep up with it.

"Thanks, Cali-Girl." The sparkle in Alex's eyes let her know he appreciated it. He stood and waited to help her from her seat.

Dayna loved the feel of his hand on her as they walked outside. While waiting for the valet, she turned to him and wrapped her arms around his neck. He needed loving right now, and she was determined to give it to him. She tugged him to her and pressed her lips to his in a vigorous kiss.

He slid his fingertips along her arms and pulled her close, kissing her deep, the way he had back at the villa.

The valet rolled the Tesla to a stop, and the doors swung open. Dayna and Alex continued kissing. She didn't care. She'd arrived at a decision.

She would risk loving Alex Mendes.

And maybe, just maybe…he could risk loving *her*.

Chapter 30

Alex

Alex had spent the evening figuring out how to get Dayna out of that enticing dress. He had a feverish desperation to get back to the guest house. Maybe it was the wine buzz. Or maybe it was to shove Ellie from his head. Whatever the reason, he didn't care.

Throughout dinner, he'd noticed how the flush on Dayna's cheek reminded him of the blush of the sunset as it dipped behind the sea. It occurred to him to tell her this, but he didn't.

When they stepped inside, he tried to close the door but missed. He was intent on getting Dayna out of her dress and heels. Or at least out of the dress. A naked woman in high heels would be a bigger turn-on.

Dayna laughed at his lame attempt to shut the door. She moved to close it. When she turned back, he'd wriggled from his jacket and jettisoned it to the closest chair. He was all over her, kissing the neck he'd been ogling all night, moving his hands over her, fingering down the narrow sleeves around her arms, tugging the dress down below her breasts.

As he tugged, she unbuttoned his shirt and undid his pants.

"Buckle in, Fly Boy, I'm the one taking *you* to altitude tonight."

When he had her out of the dress, he was shocked to find she hadn't worn her intimates. Had he known, they wouldn't have made it through dinner…or the ride home. He would have done her in the hotel parking lot.

His need was primitive and forceful—he had to have her. *Now.*

Absorbing her delicious scent, he led her by the hand into the bedroom. He considered picking her up, but his sore knee niggled. Once there, his gaze raked her from top to bottom. She turned off the light, and it didn't bother him this time. She pushed his shirt back from his shoulders, then scooted back on the bed to lie down, her arms reaching for him.

****

Dayna

Dayna couldn't believe how fast they had their clothes off. Alex moved over her, his weight on propped elbows on either side of her. She eased his head toward hers, and he covered her mouth, hungry for her. His touch seemed rougher and more aggressive. She wasn't alarmed; she figured the dress had him all fired up.

She hoped that's what it was.

He reached down to see if she was ready for him, then he broke the kiss and abruptly pushed into her. He seemed like he was on an urgent mission, instead of their leisurely lovemaking ritual they'd enjoyed back at the villa.

"Oh, Alex," she breathed, taking him in. "You feel so good—"

He pushed down on her and then shuddered as his boys swam out.

"Ahh, Ellie."

Dayna was too stunned to move. Every sexual part

of her flattened, as if by a steamroller. Her world slammed shut at the abrupt realization Alex hadn't made love to *her*.

He'd made love to his wife. Dayna was a vessel for a ghost. She fought tears. His rapid heartbeats now angered her.

Does he know what he said?

Obviously not. Should she point it out, make him feel terrible for saying it? She knew he would. Today was the anniversary of his wife's death, so of course, she was on his mind. Aunt Mara could have bought a thousand sexy dresses, and it wouldn't have mattered.

"You're heavy. Can you please get off?" She couldn't control the tremor in her voice.

"Are you okay?" He kissed her forehead, then withdrew and rolled onto his back, his forearm over his face.

Instead of reaching for him, she stayed rigid while her insides slammed. Her mind numbed, staring at the slow-turning ceiling fan. *Round and round. Round and round.*

If she pointed out what he'd said, he'd suffer humiliation and remorse. It wasn't his fault; he didn't deserve it. She couldn't do that to him—she loved him, after all.

Summoning her willpower, she rolled onto her side to face him. "I'm willing to risk loving you. Are you willing to do the same?"

She felt him tense. He hesitated. "What if I said I need time to think about it?"

Not what she'd expected. She summoned more courage. "What if I said I'd be willing to wait until you did?"

"How would we work that?"

"With patience. I think you're worth it."

"I have to figure out how not to feel like I'm betraying my wife."

So, there it was. She would have to fight for him. Time for tough love. She sat up. "*Was* your wife, Alex. She's gone. You're not married anymore." Her no-nonsense tone sounded abrupt.

What does it take to get through to him, dammit!

She rose and put on her robe, then stood looking down at him. "Saying the 'L' word was not a simple decision for me. After my divorce, I'd reached the point where I'd found myself again and loved my independence. Then you came along, and I fell down a rabbit hole, and now I can't climb out. Believe me, I've tried. But each day I discover one more reason to love you."

He took her hand and kissed It. She wished he would say something.

His silence was deafening.

****

Alex

Alex worked hard not to panic. "I care deeply for you, Dayna." It was all he could manage right now.

"But not enough to love me." The flat disappointment in her voice stabbed him. "Then, here's my proposition. If I can overcome my fear of loving again after being big time dumped, you can overcome your feelings of betrayal to your former wife. Deal?" She'd emphasized the word former.

"Dayna, I…" He trailed off with muddled thoughts. What could he say that made sense and not hurt her? "I've loved these past few weeks, getting to know you."

She slowly nodded. "I know we agreed to keep this a vacation fling. But somewhere along the line, our lusty romp morphed into the good friend's realm somewhere after Fatima. Then, when you asked me to stay longer in Lisbon, our friendship status changed for me. I kept telling myself not to fall for you—I tried to keep things on a neutral level—but failed. So here we are. Me, scared as hell, willing to love you—asking you to give us a chance. I'd say we've accomplished a lot in a few weeks. Wouldn't you?"

"We have." He forced a smile, his mind spinning.

"Then what's holding you back?" She reached for his hand and pinched his wedding band between her thumb and forefinger. "Is it this?"

He glanced at the ring, then at her. *What should I say?*

She took a deep breath. "If I were to love you—not that I'm committing to right now, mind you, but if I were—there would be two conditions. The first…I wouldn't tolerate a guy walking out on me again. The second, in equal standing with the first…I'd refuse to compete with a ghost."

"I wouldn't expect you to. I just—I don't know if I'm ready—"

She plopped down on the bed. "What the hell does ready mean? I'm willing to wait for you, Alex, but not for years on end. My time on the planet is getting shorter. So is yours. We could both have coronaries tomorrow. But at least we'd have each other."

He regarded her with exasperation. "I have to work this thing out in my head."

"Then get professional help." She threw her hands up. "No widow or widower I know of has trotted around

207

with a big red 'A' slapped on their chest for having relationships after their spouse died. Surely, they have therapists in Alaska. It's not *that* primitive up there, is it?"

"I had grief counseling for a while."

"No offense, but it didn't take." She rubbed her hand on his chest, then patted it. "I love your company. You're fun, adventurous, and your badass body stops me dead in my tracks. You make me feel valued. Special. Desired. In a way, I've not known since…" Water gathered in her eyes, stabbing his heart.

He didn't want her to cry—didn't want to cause her pain. She'd had enough. He pushed himself to sit and put an arm around her. "Dayna, I don't want to hurt you."

"But you'll always compare me to her, won't you?" She pulled away and clicked on a lamp. "If we don't seize this opportunity, we'll never know. Is the hell not knowing? Or is it the knowing, and the hell comes later? That's why they call it risk. Every time we love someone, it's a risk. Didn't they teach you that in flight school?"

He avoided her gaze, and she gripped his shoulders, daring him to look away.

"What do we have to lose other than regrets on our deathbeds? Where we'd say, 'Oh gosh, wish we'd have taken that chance to love each other.'"

She cradled his face. "I don't know about you, but I won't live a life of regret—not taking a chance on love. I'd rather risk everything and fail, rather than live a life like an empty coward with a hollow soul."

He chose his words carefully. "Dayna, I care for you deeply. Beyond measure."

"I know you do. But…" She shook her head. "I can't be your friend. In the beginning, sure. I thought I could have a friends-with-benefits fling with you. But my heart wouldn't stay there. I told it to, but it seems I don't have a choice in the matter."

Her words stunned him as he thought of Aunt Mara's remark about having no choice in who we love. His heart picked up with the panic of not knowing what the hell to say, much less do.

Not looking at her, he rose to get a drink of water from the bathroom. He gripped the sink and stared into the mirror.

What the hell are you doing? Tell her you love her. Why can't you tell her you love her? What about Ellie? I can't...I need time.

He wiped his mouth with the back of his hand and wrapped a towel around his waist. Suddenly, he felt awkward and at odds with himself, his tension suffocating him. He walked out to see her sitting on the edge of the bed, staring at her lap.

He pulled her to her feet. "The last thing I want is to hurt you. Please believe me." He pulled her close and rubbed the back of her head, his fingers in her hair. "I need a little time."

She stepped back, grasped his hands, and caressed them. "Alex Mendes, I'm willing to fight for you. I can wait. How long, I don't know, but I'll give it my best shot. The rest depends on you."

"You're willing to fight for me?"

Dayna lifted his hands, squeezing them. "A good friend told me once...no matter how hard we try to hang onto the people we love, it's not in our control. We can't blame ourselves when they leave us, like we could have prevented it."

He flicked his eyes up at her, recalling when he'd

said these words to her.

She spoke softly. "Forgive yourself, Alex. Forgive yourself for wanting to love again after the love of your life left you. Forgive Abrielle for leaving you. Until you do, you won't turn the next page in your life. A dear friend also gave me that advice."

Dayna had him reeling at turning his own advice on its head. He couldn't think of what to say…because deep down, he knew every word was true. He'd come to these conclusions on the El Camino trail walk. If only he could make himself put all these words into action.

Alex pulled her to him and hugged her tight for the longest time. He needed time to think and sort through it all.

When you avoid things for so long, it doesn't happen overnight…it just doesn't.

"I understand what you're saying." He lifted her chin and looked deep into her eyes. "I want you to know I've had a fantastic time with you. Especially tonight. Thanks, Dayna, you've helped me more than you know."

"You're welcome. I've had a wonderful time, too," she whispered.

He needed to buy time. "How about we sleep on it?"

"Okay." She tugged him to her and kissed him. "Remember what I said."

"I will." He kissed her deeply, with all the passion in his heart and all the fiber of his being…knowing what he had to do. "Good night, my Cali-Girl."

"Good night, Captain Mendes."

They crawled into bed, and she spooned into him. He held her tight. She felt so good, and he felt so bad…he didn't deserve her.

He didn't deserve anyone.

Chapter 31

Dayna

Dayna awakened, anxious and unsettled. Reaching for Alex, she found his side of the bed empty. She propped herself on her elbows.

Something was off. Something was wrong.

"Alex? Alex?" She flung the covers off and stumbled from the bedroom. No sign of him, his duffle, or his backpack. It was as if he'd evaporated.

She zeroed in on a fresh bouquet of Blue Dragon roses in a vase on the dining room table, when a rapid knock at the door startled her.

Did Alex get locked out?

She flung the door open and launched herself at the person standing there.

It wasn't Alex.

"Aunt Mara! Good morning." She backed up, noticing Mara's red eyes. Had she been crying?

"What's wrong? Where's Alex?" Dayna sensed something was off kilter.

Aunt Mara pulled Dayna close in an abrupt embrace.

Dayna pushed her back. "What is it? Did something happen to Alex?" Alarm permeated her chest. Especially when his things had vanished into a black hole.

"Alex asked me to tell you—well, to explain—"

Dayna cut in. "Why can't *he* tell me? Where is he?"

Her lungs thickened with a fear she couldn't grasp yet knew it to be real. Her heart escalated into a thumping that further alarmed her.

Aunt Mara's face displayed pain. "He flew home. To Alaska."

"Um, what?" The words wouldn't deposit into her brain. "Alaska?"

Her face wrinkled, not understanding.

Aunt Mara held out a folded piece of paper. "He asked me to give you this."

Comprehension not yet in her wheelhouse, Dayna's eyes locked onto the note in Mara's hand.

"He asked me to tell you he had to get home to his daughter—and he needs time to think."

Dayna stared at her as if she'd skittered down a wonky rainbow. She shook herself from confusion. "Why didn't he tell me himself?"

Mara's face fell again. "He was upset—confused— he said he needed time to think." She raised her arms and dropped them to her sides, exasperated.

"Dayna," she said, shaking her head. "There's so much you don't know…"

"Oh, trust me, I know." Dayna's tone turned to ice, as her heart's survival instincts froze over once more into bitter realization.

Oh yes, I know this scenario. Should have seen it coming.

Dayna didn't know what to say. Nothing seemed appropriate.

Mara pressed Alex's note into her hand. Dayna stared at it, shaking her head. "Why couldn't he tell me himself last night?" She searched Mara's face.

"He didn't plan to leave until early this morning. He

woke me to tell me and seemed panicked. What did you say to him last night?"

Dayna stared at her, astonished. "What did *I* say? It was more like what *he* said." She didn't care to elaborate on how Alex had cried out the name of his deceased wife when he released inside of her.

Too damn humiliating.

Mara shook her head. "He's still in anguish. His bereavement has eaten his soul. He asked me not to wake you until this morning."

"How considerate." Dayna tried to sympathize but came up short. "Oh, I get it. So, he'd appear valiant in your eyes, while ghosting me at the same time. Go, Alex." Her sarcasm didn't play well with Mara.

"Alex needs time." Mara declared it like the world should stop to consider.

Dayna nodded slowly as reluctant understanding crept through her. She accepted Alex's note from Mara, as if it held acid.

"Thank you. I should probably get ready to go home." She fought tears as she gave Mara an obligatory hug.

Mara looked like Dayna felt—pathetic. Not that it made anything easier for Dayna.

Mara glanced around, appearing perplexed. "Let me know if you need anything. Arsenio will drive you to the airport." She whirled around, her ever-present caftan billowing behind her like a persistent breeze.

Dayna stared at the folded piece of paper in her hand. She retreated inside and lowered herself to sit on the end of the bed—what she'd regarded as her love nest with Alex. It took all of her will power not to spit on it.

Alex's cursive on the outside of the note looped her

name, like an artist's rendering. Her fingers stilled for a moment before she unfolded it, dreading his perfectly written message.

Blinking, the walls zoomed in and back out again as she clawed her purse for her cheaters. She shoved them on, not caring how crooked they perched on her nose.

She read the handwritten note twice, unable to comprehend it the first time—not wanting to believe it the second time.

My Sweet Cali-Girl,

I laid awake all night, thinking. I decided it was best for both of us if I returned home to Alaska. You're right about what you said. I still have to work out some things. But most of all, I don't want to hurt you or cause you pain because I can't let go of my wife. It's not fair to you, Dayna. You deserve better. Our time together was fantastic, but it's best for both of us if I bow out now. Safe travels home. Your airfare to California has been taken care of. All you need to do is choose your flight and check in with Unified Airways. Arsenio will take you to the airport. I'll never forget our time together.

Love, Alex

He couldn't say it to her *face?*

His note slipped from her fingers and floated to the floor. She stepped to the table and grabbed the vase of roses and heaved it, not caring where it landed. After the resounding crash, she stood staring in disbelief.

"Love, Alex?" she screamed. "LOVE? Bullshit! You liar! If you loved me, you wouldn't have gone!" She snatched the note, tore it in half, and stomped on it. "Why did you do this to me after everything? You phony! You poser! I never ever EVER want to see you again! Do you hear me, Mendes? NEVER!"

214

She wanted to call him more names. Scream what an absolute, low-down, dirty jerk he was. But she couldn't. He wasn't a low-down dirty jerk. Just a man still in love with his wife. In love with a memory. In love with the past. This is how it will always be for him. How sad. If she didn't hate him so much right now, she might feel sorry for him.

Her eyes brimmed so full of tears, the blue-and-white Dragon roses blurred, lying scattered on the floor.

She fell to her knees, sobbing.

"They always leave. No matter what they say, they always, always leave."

How nice of him to inform Aunt Mara he was leaving. But not *her*.

That alone spoke volumes.

****

Arsenio sped the BMW along the highway toward the Lisbon airport. As far as Dayna was concerned, he couldn't get there fast enough. Aunt Mara rode in the back with Dayna, clutching her lacy hanky with a loopy M embroidered on the corner.

She held Dayna's hand with the other, squeezing it periodically as if donating blood.

Dayna struggled for composure against an emotion she had no words for—and here she was, a writer.

"I'll buy you another vase. I'm sorry it shattered when I attacked the wall in your guesthouse," mumbled Dayna, her eyes red and puffy. "I'm not normally violent."

Alex's pity bouquet steamed her. As if Blue Dragon roses were a consolation prize. *Here, you can't have me, so have your favorite flowers instead.*

She wanted to scream out the window, but it might

upset Aunt Mara. Alex might be on Dayna's shit list, but his aunt had a heart of gold.

"No need. Ming vases are inconsequential, my dear," sniffed Aunt Mara. She squeezed Dayna's hand again. "Didn't things go well last night? I hoped the dress would have done the trick."

"Apparently, the dress wasn't enough—and I'm not enough," Dayna said dully, watching buildings and landscape zoom by.

"I'm so sorry." Mara continued squeezing her hand. Dayna wished her empathy helped, but it was an empty consolation.

"I said I was willing to love him. Told him I'd wait for him when he decided he could love me back. He doesn't love me. He loves *her*." The words rolled out in a flat monotone.

"He needs time." That's all Mara could offer.

Dayna appreciated it, but it wasn't enough to fend off the daggers piercing her chest. "He loves a ghost. I'm alive. I'm the one who is here. But he'd rather love someone he can no longer have."

Aunt Mara sniffled, touching the tissue to her nose. "He's grieved for so long. I thought he might love you enough to move on."

Dayna's scowl deepened. "You can't make love with a ghost. Well. Unless you're an incubus. Or *they're* an incubus. Whichever way it works…" She trailed away with an off-handed gesture and watched blurry buildings whiz by, without focusing on any of it.

She continued her wallowing. "There's a reality show on TV where people claim they make love with ghosts. Be sure to tell Alex about it next time you talk to him. He'll need some tips."

Now she'd gone and done it with her smart-assed remarks…she made Aunt Mara cry harder.

Dayna managed a fake smile and patted her arm. "That was mean. I'm sorry, I know you're upset, too."

Aunt Mara blew her nose and wiped it with her monogrammed hanky. She squeezed Dayna's hand. "Please don't give up on Alexander. He's a good person. Go after him, my dear."

Dayna caught herself before saying, *Yeah, that'll happen.* She glanced at Mara and patted her arm. "I'm sorry. You've done so much for me."

"But I saw how he—"

"—how he looked at me?" interrupted Dayna. She pursed her lips. "It was only for sex. He's a guy. They like the sex. Of course, he looked at me like that. I had my boobs done." Her voice had the same bitter tone she'd used after the divorce.

Here I am, back to square one. Abandoned again.

"He loves you. I could see it." Aunt Mara would say anything so her precious nephew would be happy.

God love her. I wish I had an auntie like her.

Dayna shook her head and frowned. Anyone can tell anyone anything. If Alex told his aunt he loved Dayna, it meant nothing. Meaningless words to placate her.

Blah blah blah.

Actions speak louder than words, huh Mendes?

He'd left her. The same as Paul had. Same as they all do.

Arsenio glanced back at Aunt Mara as he pulled up to the airport drop-off. Dayna envied that kind of caring and loyalty, the way they were with each other, watched out for each other, respected each other.

Alex had respected her, hadn't he? He seemed to.

Then why did he go?

Anvils had once again taken up residence inside Dayna's heart, but it shouldn't change how she treated people. "Mara, thank you so much for your gracious hospitality and all you did for Alex and me…" Her eyes watered.

Mara leaned across the seat to hug her. "You are welcome back anytime, my dear. As for Alex, he will indeed hear from me. Please find it in your heart to forgive him. I know I'll have to work on it."

Not likely. If one more person harped to Dayna about forgiveness, she would scream. Now she had two men to forgive?

Forget it. Hell will freeze first.

Dayna kissed her on the cheek. "Goodbye, Mara."

"Keep in touch, my dear."

She numbly nodded, knowing she wouldn't. Not without Alex.

Arsenio already had her carry-on out of the car and lifted it effortlessly up on the curb.

Dayna shook his hand. "Thanks, Arsenio. Take good care of Mara."

"Safe travels, Miss Benning." He dipped his chin at her, then inserted himself back in the driver's seat.

Mara got out and sat in the front seat, blowing kisses to Dayna, her face contorting as Arsenio drove away.

Chapter 32

Dayna

Dayna cruised along at 35,000 feet, vaguely remembering going through security and checking in for her direct flight to San Francisco. Her body tingled from Alex imploding her heart, and the damn thing still ached in her chest.

She'd had an out-of-body sensation ever since, like a bomb had detonated and she was a dazed bystander, staring back at herself in a billion scattered pieces.

I'll never forget our time together.

That's all Alex could say about the past several weeks? It had been a short time frame, but the intensity of their time together certainly hadn't been. If he couldn't let go of his wife, then why did he ask Dayna to stay longer with him in Lisbon?

None of it made any sense.

She should have politely declined his invitation. It wasn't as if her gut hadn't warned her of emotional involvement. Served her right, thinking she could have a romantic screw-a-thon and then disappear into the mist, like in that 1950s Scottish movie musical.

Dayna oscillated in the familiar revolving door between hurt and anger. Flashing back to the hotel in Santiago, she recalled the first night in his room when she'd had doubts. Should have followed her gut—

shouldn't have fallen for him.

The red flag warning of his inability to let go of his deceased wife was something she should have heeded.

Now she would cut her losses and not waste any more time competing with a ghost—because the ghost would always win.

She berated herself for allowing Alex's incredible looks to suck her in. Next time—if ever there was a next time—she'd choose the worst-looking, down-and-out guy she could find at the DMV. Snag a hunched-over, aging hippie and ask if he'd be up for a good time. BYOV—Bring Your Own Viagra.

She made a long face at the cotton-ball clouds floating past the oval window.

First thing she'd do at home would be to mail Alex a check for the airfare. The last thing she wanted was to be indebted to him. Oh no, she didn't have his address. Wait, a minute—yes, she did. She whipped out her phone and swiped her photos to the one she'd taken of his driver's license.

She should have kept pieces of the Dragon Roses bouquet and the shattered vase. She'd mail those too, all busted and withered, like her feelings for him now.

Blowing out another heavy sigh, she made a resolution. Never on this side of the grave did she want to see Alex Mendes again. And on the other side of the grave, she'd haunt him forever for abandoning her.

She'd make sure he'd pay…just like Paul.

Chapter 33

Alex

Alex swung into his driveway near the top of the hill overlooking Potter Marsh, at the base of the Chugach Mountains, south of Anchorage. It felt good to be back home. He welcomed the crisp September air and the mountains across the glimmering tidewaters of Turnagain Arm.

The eighteen-hour flight from Lisbon had fatigued him. He'd left Aunt Mara's at 2 a.m. to catch the last seat on a 5 a.m. flight after returning the Tesla.

He'd taken a cab from the Anchorage airport, dragged his gear in the house, then collapsed into bed. He slept most of the next day and woke around dinnertime.

The sun hovered above the horizon, shooting all colors of red and orange across the sky, reflected by the waters of Cook Inlet. He watched the spectacular display from his living room and thought of Dayna and how they'd loved watching the sun sink into the ocean.

Heaviness took hold, the same as it had after he left her. It had been a shitty thing to do. Now he hated himself for having done it.

The worst of it was, Dayna told him that was the one condition if she were to commit to him. Her words rang in his ears—she wouldn't tolerate any guy who would abandon her again. He'd burned that bridge. Not deliberately, not from any kind of malice.

But because he loved her.

Loved her so much he couldn't bear to hurt her, because he couldn't let go of Ellie. He'd panicked at Dayna's admission of love for him. He'd deluded himself into thinking their relationship would stay a wonderful friendship with fantastic sex—a good time, fun companionship, more sex—not a *love* commitment.

Right. Who was he kidding? He'd fallen for Dayna from the get-go. He'd wanted her the minute she'd turned around after tossing the rose petals on him. First thing he'd done was look for a wedding band, and it had delighted him not to see one. He should have removed his. What a mistake.

He knew that now.

He hadn't known what else to do with his screwed-up state of mind. He'd always felt a strong love connection to Ellie. She'd come to him in his dreams, and he'd taken comfort that her spirit was with him, and their marriage vows still bonded them.

What the hell else was I to believe?

Since Ellie had passed, her presence had stayed with him, and when things got tough to deal with—like right now—he felt her helping him and urging him to move on.

But he couldn't.

His cell phone sounded—a landing jet for his ringtone, as he stared at his empty fridge. He tapped it. "Hey, Ben."

"You're back. Want to shoot pool? It's Marc's birthday, and his wife is in Juneau on a business trip."

"Sure, I'd be up for that." Alex grabbed a bottle of Arctic Glacier water and closed the fridge.

"Good, see you at Play-It-Again Billiards around eight then," said Ben.

"Yeah. Later." Alex ended the call, unscrewing the water bottle and sipping. He stepped to the floor-to-ceiling windows, staring at Cook Inlet, unable to tell the difference between sky and water during the spectacular ocean sunset.

Dayna had mentioned that during one of her orgasms.

His mouth curved up. He missed her. And he missed giving her orgasms.

There was a light knock on the front door. Zoey opened it and poked her head in. Her blonde hair was in its usual messy bun.

"Welcome home, Dad! I'm on my way home from my yoga class in Girdwood." She was all smiles and flung her arms around him.

He hugged her back. "Good to see you, honey."

"You look tired. Didn't you sleep on the flight?"

"Hard to sleep when someone else flies the plane." He took a sip from a water bottle.

"You can take the pilot out of the cockpit, but..." Zoey took a seat at the granite counter separating the kitchen from the dining room.

"I've been worried about you since talking to you at Aunt Mara's. So, what have you been doing since leaving the El Camino trail?"

He'd been thinking all the way back about how he would dance around this with his daughter. He met her head-on. "I met a woman, a writer from California, and we spent some time together."

223

"Aunt Mara mentioned her. You were with her on the anniversary of Mom's death. How could you do that?" Her accusatory tone had a sharp edge to it. "Way to forget about Mom." Her words dangled in the air.

"Zo, we need to talk about my seeing other women."

"Dad, it's only been three years."

"Exactly, but I haven't let go. And neither have you."

"You aren't ready to let go, Dad. You still wear Mom's ring." Her jab of guilt always hit the target. She pointed at photos around the room. "You keep Mom's photos in every room of the house. And you haven't deleted her voice on that old answering machine."

"Zo, I know you mean well, but this is my life. I want to choose what I do with the rest of it." He looked up at her as she braced, defensive whenever this subject came up. Each time, their argument ended with each stomping off to lick their wounds.

"You can't replace Mom. You can't erase her." She began sobbing, which ripped his gut to pieces.

"I know. I won't try to do that. But I don't want to spend the rest of my life alone—with Ben and Marc for company."

"I want her back, Dad. I need her now more than ever." Her sobbing increased. "I'm pregnant. And Mom will never see—" Her words stuck in her throat. "She'll never see her grandchild."

Oh, shit.

Alex moved to Zoey and put his arms around her. "Congratulations, honey, I'm so happy for you." He fought for calm, trying not to sound stunned. "All of us will love your baby. And she'll have a guardian angel, your mother, watching over her." He grabbed at straws to calm her.

Zoey buried her head in his chest. "I don't want a stranger taking Mom's place." She lifted her head. "How serious are you with this woman?"

Alex stared at her a moment, then gazed past her out the window at the lingering Alaskan sunset over the water. An avalanche of emotion hit him like a bore tide. "I care deeply about her. That's why I came home."

Zoey raised her tear-filled eyes. "Please. Not when I'm having Mom's grandchild. I couldn't deal with it, Dad. Please don't bring someone into our family who won't know me or my baby."

"I have made no decisions like that."

"Dad, no one will ever take Mom's place. You know how special she was, how everyone loved her. She had the kindest, most generous heart of anyone I'd ever known." Zoey's voice had risen to a high level that made Alex uneasy.

Alex knew better than to reason with her right now.

He led her to the couch and urged her to lie down. She sobbed so hard she had the jags. He comforted and consoled her as best he could, then offered her his water bottle.

As she gulped water, a knock sounded at the door. Alex moved to open it.

"Hi, is Zoey here?" Her husband, Ethan, stood in his Carhartt's.

Alex smelled fish. "She stopped by on her way home. Congratulations on becoming a father." He smiled at his son-in-law. "What were you fishing for?"

"Steelhead. Yeah, I'm going to be a dad. Pretty cool, huh?" Ethan looked around him for his wife.

Alex gestured toward the couch, and Ethan moved

to Zoey and leaned to kiss her. He was thankful his daughter had Ethan. He'd helped her cope with her mother's death over the past few years. Ellie had attended their wedding in a wheelchair shortly before she'd passed away. He recalled how she'd been so shrunken and feeble. Withering away and dying before his eyes.

Alex had a sudden urge to escape from the house. The elevated chaos of emotion overwhelmed him after leaving Dayna.

I've done the one thing she said she wouldn't tolerate...I abandoned her.

He bent over his daughter. "Now that Ethan is here, I have to go out for a bit. We'll talk later, okay?"

He shot a look at Ethan that said, *comfort your wife, buddy.*

Alex reached for his leather jacket and headed to the garage. He tapped the automatic door opener, climbed into his dark gray pickup, and backed it out. He needed space. Fresh air. Jet lag piled on top of his twice-broken heart and worry about his daughter, now pregnant—he had to get away and think.

Once he hit the Seward Highway to Anchorage, he opened the engine for a speed rush. He was antsy to get in the air again. Maybe he'd take his Beechcraft Bonanza up tomorrow, fly up around Denali Mountain. Clear his head.

He pulled into the Play-It-Again Billiards parking lot and went inside. His buddies, Ben and Marc, hollered at him from a corner pool table. "Mendes, over here! Hey Jenny, bring Alex his usual."

The server deposited a bottle of Alaskan Amber into his hand. Alex wished it was a San Miguel, which made him think of Dayna. The sunset made him think of Dayna. Doing nothing made him think of Dayna. His brain fogged, and he took a pull on the bottle.

" 'Bout time you got back," said Ben, slapping his shoulder. "How was the El Camino?"

Alex filled them in on what he'd hiked, why he quit, and what happened afterward with the enchanting, animated writer from California.

Ben rested the pool cue on his boot. "Let me get this straight. You go all the way to Spain and Portugal to meet a California cutie. Wouldn't it have been easier to fly to California and hang out at Venice Beach?"

Alex opened his mouth to respond but didn't get far when Ben held up his hand.

"Am I correct in saying you met this beautiful woman, then let her go? What a mother-effing, lame-brained thing to do!" He shook his head and pointed his pool cue at Alex. "Lucky for you, she shows up in a backwater mountain town in the middle of bumscrew, Spain."

Marc burned a fast pitch into Alex's gut. "You didn't deserve that stroke of luck after letting her go." He made a what-the-hell-were-you-thinking face. "Then you went and left her at your aunt's house in Portugal? Are we missing something?"

Ben made an "L" with his thumb and forefinger and held it out to Alex. "Loser! Hello!"

Alex took a distressed pull on his beer and heaved out a sigh. "Yeah. I'm an idiot."

"Ya *think*?" Marc smacked his own forehead with the heel of his hand. "Let's see how much of an idiot. Show me this hottie. Got photos?" He waggled impatient fingers at Alex.

LoLo Paige

Alex gave him a sour look and swiped his thumb on his phone. A sexy dress caught his eye. Aunt Mara took their photo before he and Dayna had gone to dinner—what, two nights ago? He pointed the phone at Ben and Marc.

"Holy *freaking* hell!" Ben's exuberance at seeing Dayna in her bodacious, dark green dress lit him like a firecracker. He snatched the phone, nearly dropping it. "That's her? Nice rack. Way to rob the cradle, dude."

Alex scratched his nose. "She's forty-nine."

Marc snatched the phone and studied it. "No effing way. She's just as gorgeous as Ellie." He glanced at Alex. "How do you land these knockout women? Why the hell aren't you with her?"

"I don't know. I messed up. Ran scared of commitment." Now that Alex was thousands of miles away with a distanced perspective, it had increasingly dawned on him he'd made a gigantic mistake. And that was putting it mildly.

Marc looked up at him. "Listen, pal. That wasn't chance, that was destiny. I know what a hard time you've had without Ellie. But it's time, bro. Been telling you that for the past year." Marc held Alex's phone out to him. "Look how happy you are. Haven't seen you like that in years. You belong with her."

Ben put his hand on Alex's shoulder. "When Ellie died, you said your life was broken. Well, bro, here's how to fix it. Back when we tried getting you to date, you said you could only love one woman at a time. You'll always love Ellie." He gave Alex's shoulder a shake. "It's time to let go, buddy."

Marc bent to line up a shot, resting his cue stick between thumb and forefinger. He flicked his eyes at

228

Alex. "Does this beauty love you?"

"If she did, she doesn't anymore. I blew it." Alex pressed his lips together.

Marc sent a ball into each corner pocket, then shook his head. "Then what the hell are you doing here? Take that fancy-assed plane of yours and fly down to California. You need to fix it with her."

Ben pointed his forefinger at him. "You'll regret it if you don't."

Chapter 34

Alex

Alex closed the door behind him, surprised to see Zoey asleep on the couch. She hadn't gone home with Ethan. He tiptoed down the hall to his bedroom. He took off his jacket, then relieved himself and came out of his bathroom.

"Dad." Zoey stood in his bedroom doorway. "I stayed to talk to you. I'm so sorry." She moved to hug him. "I have no right to say who you can have in your life." She stepped back and held up her phone with a photo of him and Dayna, laughing.

"Aunt Mara texted this to me. She called, and we talked for quite a while. She told me about Dayna and said you two loved each other. And she said you left Dayna there. Dad, even I have to agree that was a terrible thing to do." Zoey gave him a rueful smile and sat on his bed.

Alex sat next to her. "You and I have never talked about Mom's death."

"I know, Dad, but whenever I'd bring it up, you'd get angry and shut down on me."

He took her hand and stroked it. "Couldn't get beyond my own broken heart to help you with the loss of your mother. I'm so sorry, Zo. I haven't been a good father that way. We should have talked years ago."

Lying side-by-side on Alex's bed, they talked through the night about Ellie and how her death had affected each of them. He told his daughter how special Dayna was, how she'd made him feel alive again. And since being out of touch with her, he felt like part of him was missing. He talked about her positivity, how funny she was, and her blunt honesty.

Zoey lifted her phone. "It's five-thirty a.m. and all you've talked about in the last hour was Dayna. Don't you think it's time you did something about it?"

"Ben and Marc think I should fly down to see her."

Zoey let out a sigh. "Then you should go. But from a girl's perspective, I must warn you that groveling will be in order. You ran out on her and that's the absolute worst. Call or text her first. We ladies hate the sudden pop-in. If Dayna is who you want, go get her." She kissed him on the cheek. "Love you, but I need sleep."

"Thanks, honey, love you too."

She rolled over and soon little snores told him she was in dreamland.

He covered his daughter with a comforter and let out a long breath of relief that they'd finally reached catharsis after all this time.

Load. Off. *Thank God.*

But he couldn't sleep. *Fix this with her,* Marc said. After staring at the ceiling, he lifted from the bed and fired up his laptop. Typed "Sunrise Magazine" in the search engine, then he scanned the masthead. He damn near got a hard-on when he spotted Dayna's email address. He sent her an email—apologized and groveled. Then sent another. More groveling. Then he texted the same.

And sent another with hearts and emojis.

He climbed back onto his bed and rolled to his side. Father and daughter had begun to heal at long last. Gratitude and relief flooded him, and an enormous weight floated up to the heavens. Away to Ellie, who'd been the love of his life. Alex could let go of her now. And put his marriage vows to rest along with her.

It was okay. He'd be okay. Zoey would be, too.

Now he had another love in his life. He'd made room in his heart for her.

He prayed it wasn't too late.

Chapter 35

Dayna

Dayna sat back and closed her eyes after clicking 'submit.' She'd finished her travel feature for Sunrise Magazine, and it was on its way to Tessa. She'd ignored her email and turned off her phone to rid herself of distractions to write and meet her deadline.

Now she was exhausted.

As a sidebar to her travel piece, she'd written about the El Camino de Santiago trail. Tessa made her include Alex's interview about his pilgrimage, since she'd pitched the idea to her back when she was all gaga over Alex and had texted Tessa his photo.

"I'm sorry he broke your heart, but he's too hot not to include. Write it up and submit," Tessa had ordered her.

It had gutted her to write about Alex, so she'd distanced herself behind her narrative to stay neutral about the El Camino *peregrino* who had shattered her heart. Her own fault. She shouldn't have fallen for him.

Excluding personal details, Dayna wrote about the reasons Alex had undertaken his journey. She gave readers an understanding of why people from around the world made this pilgrimage—from the personal to the spiritual—or simply escape the din, the rat race, the obligations. She talked about healing, reconciliation, and renewal. Then wrapped it up with a tidy little bow at the end and sent it to Tessa.

On impulse, she pulled up a blank screen to write a short humor story to send off to *Cosmo* as a listicle: Five Ways to Have a Romantic Fling on Vacation. They'd probably reject it, but so what? She wanted Alex out of her system, and the one way she knew to do that was to write him out.

She bled on the page while gobbling mouthfuls of chocolate-chip cookie-dough ice cream. Screw weight loss. After multiple rounds of edits, she clicked 'Submit' and sent it off. She poured herself a glass of California merlot and hit the power button on her voice-activated portable speaker.

"Play Queen. Loud," she said flatly, shoving a spoon-load of ice cream in her mouth, remembering her remark to Alex about talking to devices. *Another One Bites the Dust* charged out, the pulsing beat filling her ears. *Ain't that the truth*, she thought sourly, listening to the words. She scraped the bottom of the pint, then shoveled in the last spoonful.

She pushed away from her computer and snatched her wineglass to wander out the front door of her cottage house.

The gardener she'd hired did a terrific job while she'd been gone. She stepped along the paved-stone walkway in her front yard, her eyes drawn to the sapphire waters of the Pacific Ocean in the distance.

Pacific Ocean Blue.

A pang stabbed her chest at the painful reminder. Her gaze fell to the hibiscus, hydrangeas, and her prized Blue Dragon roses. Their fresh scent jerked her back to Lisbon when she'd admired Aunt Mara's stunning display. The same colors as the blue-and-white curtains at the holy baths in Lourdes…and in Alex's consolation bouquet.

Screw you, buddy. You did the one and only thing I feared you would do.

She shook her head, tempted to rip the petals apart. Her eyes brimmed with tears, recalling how she'd hurled the vase after reading her 'Dear John' note.

Reminders. Everywhere she looked were reminders. The ocean, the beaches, the sunsets, the wine. The roses. Planes flying over.

She couldn't get away from reminders of Alexander Mendes.

Out of the corner of her eye, she saw her next-door neighbor. He'd moved in a few months ago. Rumor had it, he was a fused glass artist. She thought about asking him over for dinner. She squinted at him mowing his lawn. He stood at her same height, and he was balding. Had a bit of a paunch, but outside of that, not too bad. Easier than trolling the DMV for a date.

She slurped her wine, then downed the whole thing.

Letting out a sigh, she wandered back into the house as Freddie Mercury crooned *Love of My Life*. She sank into a teal wicker chair, listening to the lyrics. He sang about hurt, a broken heart, and desertion. She rolled her eyes upward, then a chill shot up her spine when he said *obrigado* at the end of the song.

The one Portuguese word she'd memorized.

A sign? No, only stupid coincidence.

All of it with Alex had been dumb, stupid coincidence.

Chapter 36

Alex

The next morning, Alex stared at his laptop screen, now and then checking his phone. No emails or texts from Dayna. This may prove harder than he thought.

Surprised as hell, he zeroed in on an email from Mariko, and he clicked it open. She said little other than "READ THIS!"

When he clicked on the attachment, up popped Dayna's travel piece in *Sunrise Magazine,* "Finding Your Way on the El Camino." He lifted the laptop from the table, rested it in his lap, and leaned back in his chair.

Alex devoured each word, a beautifully written segment about his trek on the El Camino. Her words impressed him, about the pilgrimages people made and the countless reasons for walking this famous trail. Her descriptions of Spain, Portugal, and France were spot on.

She was a terrific writer. He was proud of her and wanted to tell her.

Damn.

His stomach roiled. *You idiot, you let the wrong woman go.*

Up popped a second email from Mariko, with a "READ THIS TOO!" note and an attached article Dayna wrote for *Cosmopolitan*, "Five Ways to Have a Romantic Fling on Vacation."

He couldn't read it fast enough.

Dayna wrote about how they'd met. He noted with amusement she'd changed his name to Harry. He laughed out loud at her comical take on sprinkling rose petals on him like a flower girl in a wedding—and how she'd thought he was married. Then discovered he was single after bumping into him in a quaint Spanish mountain town. Then he read the last sentence:

"Maybe someday I'll forgive that fabulous guy for breaking my heart in Portugal."

Her words smacked him like a 747. He'd hurt her deeply—deeply enough for her to write this. He grimaced and grabbed his mouse to scroll through Mariko's email, thinking he'd seen her phone number. There, at the end.

He snatched his cell and tapped Mariko's number.

She answered on the second ring. "What took you so long, Mendes?" she quipped.

"I'm a slow reader." He smiled into the phone. "How are you doing down there in San Francisco?"

"Great. But I know someone who isn't, and she happens to be my best friend. Why the dickens did you leave her like that, Alex? Shame on you!"

He heaved out a long sigh. "I know. I messed up. Please help me fix it, Mariko. She won't answer my texts or emails."

"She goes dark when she's on a writing deadline, so she probably hasn't seen them, anyway." She paused a moment. "She never wants to see you again. She must say it twenty times a day."

"Well, at least she's thinking of me."

"And not in a good way," Mariko said dryly. "Don't get delusions of grandeur."

"Did she really say she never wants to see me again?" His heart dripped to his shoes. "What if I were to fly down? I can be there in a day or two."

"You can try, but I doubt if she'll see you. She's devastated, not to mention severely pissed at you." Mariko sighed. "Why do you think she resisted getting involved? She didn't want the pain and trauma of being abandoned again. Like *you did*, by the way." Mariko made it clear she was not happy with him either.

Alex hesitated. "After losing my wife, I was a train wreck that lasted three years. Then along came Dayna, who helped me see things clearly. Now that I'm back home, I realize how badly I screwed up. I let the wrong woman go."

"Shouldn't you be saying this to Dayna?" Mariko said quietly, letting out a sigh.

"How can I get her to see me?"

Another sigh. "Well, we could trick her into it. Maybe arrange a fake meeting. Her editor might set it up…she knows about you and Dayna after the Sunrise article. Will you be flying commercially?"

"No, I'll fly my own plane down. Takes longer, but I'll need that time to figure out what to say to her."

"It better be good, that's all I can say. The nearest airport to Cambria is San Luis Obispo."

"Think it'll work?" He sounded desperate, then remembered his daughter saying groveling was in order. "I love her, Mariko."

"So do I." Another pause. "I'll see what I can do and hope I don't go to hell for lying."

"You won't be alone. I'll be doing time there as well for the same thing." He felt hopeful. "Thanks, I owe you one."

"You brought me George, so we'll call it even. He's driving down to see me next month."

He chuckled. "That's great. Let me know what you come up with. I'll be in touch."

"You better be sure about this. Please don't hurt her again, Alex. Or you'll answer to me. Good luck." Mariko ended the call.

Alex stood, holding his phone. Instead of taking a leisurely jaunt up to Denali, he'd better ready the Beechcraft for a long-haul flight south. Checklists cycled through his brain as he tugged on his leather jacket to drive into Anchorage. He had a plane to get ready.

He'd never been surer of anything in his life.

Chapter 37

Dayna

Dayna swung her Miata into the parking lot of Otter
Pier between San Luis Obispo and Pismo Beach. After
Tessa called the day before yesterday to request a
meeting at Ye Olde Crabpot restaurant at the end of Otter
Pier, Dayna had been curious why the meeting wasn't at
Tessa's high-rise office in downtown San Francisco.

Dayna loved any excuse to drive up to the city. She
had her favorite shops and haunts along the way.

Ye Olde Crabpot near San Luis Obispo was out of
character for Tessa. It was cozy and quaint, with a family
vibe instead of a business vibe. Dayna had decked herself
out in a navy-blue, form-fitting business suit and
stilettos, because dress code was a big deal to Tessa.

She hoped Tessa might offer her the Executive
Editor slot at Sunrise Magazine. That could explain why
she'd been so mysterious on the phone.

Dayna entered the restaurant at two p.m. sharp and
requested outdoor seating near the water because she
loved watching the harbor seals and sea otters. She used
to come here with He-Who-Would-Not-Be-Named. She
kicked herself for recalling this memory and gave herself
an eye roll.

The hostess led Dayna to a table in a corner of the
pier, shaded by an enormous umbrella. Sunlight tinted

the water in the tiny cove an emerald green. A sleeping sea otter rode gentle swells on its back. He was grizzled, his fur faded.

Old like me.

Dayna settled in and ordered a chilled Riesling. Finally, she could catch up with her texts and emails on her phone while waiting for Tessa. Tapping her message icon, unidentified texts from area code 907 popped up. She wrinkled her face.

Where the heck is 907? She tapped the first one.

—Dear Dayna, I screwed up. I'm so sorry. Can we talk? I miss you. Alex.—

Her eyes nearly popped from her head. She sat up straight and her heart sped as she tapped the next one.

—Dear Dayna, please call me. I want to talk to you. <3 <3 <3 smiley face. Alex.—

She stared at her phone as if it had combusted. The texts had been sent a few days ago. She'd turned her phone on in time to receive Tessa's call for a lunch invitation but hadn't bothered to read her texts or emails. She'd been so wiped out after the long flight home and scrambling to meet her magazine deadline that she'd had no energy for anything else.

A long shadow fell across the table.

"*Desculpa.* Would it help to say *desculpa* again?"

She froze, heart thundering at the bizarre possibility. Her brain had trouble registering, then when it did, she was cornered—wanting to run, not wanting to run. She raised her chin, incredulous.

There stood Alex, in his brown leather jacket, in the same handsome way he had in Portugal. Instead of his usual light-up-the-world smile, Alex's expression was more like a scolded puppy.

"You're here. In California. How did you—why are you—?" Dayna glanced around.

"Anyone sitting here?" He pulled out the chair across from her.

"Uh, well Tessa…" She pointed absently toward the pier parking lot while his sudden presence ping-ponged her like a lottery ball machine.

"I'm here to meet my editor. Why are you—wait a minute." Dayna jerked her head around, searching for her editor, groping for a logical explanation why the man of her past dreams—whom she'd wanted to strangle since abandoning her at his aunt's house on another continent—suddenly appeared in all his hot, fetching glory.

"Tessa isn't coming," he said calmly, removing his jacket and draping it over the chair. "I came here instead. You wouldn't answer my emails or texts." He sank into the chair and leaned back in that relaxed way of his that had always made her loins bounce around.

Well, she refused to let them bounce around now.

She motioned at her phone as her brain fried. "I just read—wait, is this a mother freaking set-up? How did you get Tessa to call me? You don't even know her."

"Mariko arranged it. Don't yell at her, yell at me. I asked her to. I needed to talk to you. This way, you can't ignore me." A muscle jerked near his temple.

"Did you happen to be in the neighborhood, or did you fly all the way from Alaska to talk to me?"

"I flew my plane down here to talk to you."

"All the way from Alaska?"

"I didn't Amelia Earhart this. Small planes have flown from there to here before." He matched her sarcastic tone, then softened it. "Dayna, I had to see you."

"Now you've seen me, so be on your way. I plan to keep ignoring you." She dismissed him with a flippant wave and tossed her hair in defiance.

Alex waited, as if challenging her to go through with it.

Dayna found a perverse pleasure in his challenge. "Screw you, Alex Mendes." She pushed back her chair and shot to her feet. "You get what you give." She marched off, fully aware of her dramatics.

He bolted from his chair and pressed a hand to her arm. "Dayna, please. Sit down and listen to what I have to say."

She yanked her arm away. "Why should I?" She glared at him, heat spreading in her face. He'd caught her off guard, sprung a trap, and she felt like a cornered seal. She hadn't planned on ever seeing or talking to him again.

Dammit.

"Because I'm asking you to," he said in a quiet voice.

"I have a few choice things to say as well." Her sharp tone could slice steel.

This was their first real argument, and she hated he looked so damn good in his denim shirt with the cuffs rolled back on his forearms.

Dammit again.

His mouth formed a straight line. "Let me go first."

"You don't deserve to go first. Deserter."

He grimaced. "That was a low blow."

"The only blow you're going to get," she quipped with bitter sarcasm. She sent him a rebellious look and plopped into her chair. Triumph flooded her as he winced at her words.

"Guess I deserve that." He smoothed his hair back in a nervous gesture. He hadn't cut it and she annoyed herself by noticing it was sexier than ever. Some guys aged well. *They* didn't have to get body parts lifted. Oh wait, yes, they did. She swallowed a smirk, remembering Alex's need to "recharge" with his little blue pills.

"Oh, ya think?" It wasn't her nature to be mean. She reconsidered a long, hard moment. "All right. So, talk."

"You have things to say. You go first." He shifted in his chair. "I'm listening."

Words squished around on her tongue like raw scallops. She spit out the obvious ones.

"That was a rotten thing you did, leaving me at your aunt's house. And you had Aunt Mara explain it all to me? Why couldn't you do that? God, Alex!" She shook her head, the anguish twisting her heart all over again.

"I'm sorry." He nodded agreement. "I deserve that, too."

"At least we agree on one thing. So, tell me something. When we made love the night you *abandoned* me—were you making love to me, or Ellie?"

He regarded her with surprise. "You. Of course, you."

"Bullshit. You weren't. You called out her name when your boys swam out." She waved her hand in a circle.

His jaw dropped, his vexation clear. He looked as if he'd just learned the world was ending. "Dayna…" He shook his head. "I didn't mean to—I would never—"

She cut in. "I wouldn't lie about something like that. The worst thing? You weren't even aware you'd said it. And my God. You told your aunt you were leaving but not me. Holy shit." Heat crawled into her cheeks. Her foot wiggled ninety miles an hour

"Why didn't you call me out on it? Why didn't you say something?"

"Seriously, Alex?" Dayna turned her face toward the water. "It was the anniversary of your wife's death, for crying out loud. That's all you talked about at dinner, remember?"

"Well, thanks for cutting me some slack." He had an edge to his tone.

She plunged on carelessly. "No slack now, buddy. Not after *abandoning* me in the middle of the freaking night at your aunt's house—how low can you go, by the way—why do you think I'd want to talk to you after that? Explain it to me because I'd really like to know." She folded her arms and leaned back, glaring at him from behind her sunglasses.

"I told you, I needed time. We—us happened so fast—"

Her voice increased in volume as she made a grand sweep with her arm. "It was just a fling, Alex. But you could have woken me up or told me the next morning you wanted to leave…instead of sneaking off like a ninja in the middle of the flipping night."

Heads turned in her direction, and she couldn't care less.

"Not just a fling. I had to leave because…" He trailed off.

"Because why?"

He opened his mouth to say something, but only shook his head.

"You're insane to think you can waltz down here from Alaska, farting hearts and rainbows and all will be forgiven. I told you I would tolerate *no one* to run out on me again. I told you that—and you did it, anyway. You friggin' did it anyway, Alex. How can I ever trust you again?" Her voice caught, and her hand flew to her chest. She willed the water back that wanted to fill her eyes.

She'd be damned if she'd get emotional in front of him, but her control was slipping. "That's what hurt more than anything. I wasn't enough for my husband and—and—" her voice caught as her throat constricted. "I'm still not enough." She stared at her lap.

"That's not true." His harsh tone made her look up in surprise.

She couldn't read him behind his shades. "Take off your damn sunglasses. I want to see you."

"Fair is fair. Take yours off too." He sounded like a kindergartner.

She would have laughed if she wasn't so pissed at him.

They each removed their shades. Dayna swallowed hard and boldly held his gaze. His eyes weren't any less gorgeous, and she hated him for it. Hated that he still attracted her like no other. She saw something different in his eyes. Instead of sadness, remorse.

Good.

"I didn't mean to hurt you. Please believe me." He reached across and took her hand. It was warm, like the first time he'd held it on the Portuguese beach. "That was the last thing I wanted to do."

She yanked her hand away. "Yeah, you keep saying that. But you *did*."

"Dayna, I—"

"You need to understand something. I will *not* compete with your former wife for your affection. She's gone, Alex, but you refuse to believe that. I was jealous of her, and I didn't even know her! Jealous, because even in death, she has what so many would kill to have—a devoted husband. You're still so in love with her you're willing to spend the rest of your life loving a ghost. Well, I'm not a channeler or medium with the spirit world."

Her words spilled out like a dam had broken. She sat back and shook her head at him. "God love you, Alex. I wish I had a guy like you."

"You do." He grimaced and wrinkled his face. "What the hell is a channeler?"

"A channeler, like in that nineties movie where a lady was the conduit to the guy's dead wife so he could make love to her." She saw pain in his eyes, and she didn't care. She wanted to hurt him like he'd hurt her. "Oh, come on. Don't say you haven't seen that movie."

"Yeah, I've seen it." He made a face. "That's just…twisted."

Dayna's head snapped back to look at him. "So is saying Ellie's name while we're making love!" Her words shot out like a cannon.

Heads turned their way with raised eyebrows.

She lowered her voice. "I searched the internet for widowers who can't let go. Do you know what therapists advise those who consider serious relationships with them? Don't do it! Because no matter how hard the alive-and-kicking woman tries, she'll never come first. She'll only warm his bed and be his roommate because she'll forever be compared to the deceased wife. No, Alex, I'm not up for that. Sorry."

"You believe all that because it's on the internet?" His eyes bored into hers.

She'd rattled his calm demeanor, and it gave her a

smug satisfaction. "People feel sorry for widowers. Well, guess what it's like for a divorcee? No one feels sorry for me. Instead, I have a black spot stamped on me like a Caribbean pirate, as if the divorce was all my fault. Stop playing the martyr. You need to let Ellie go, like I had to let Paul go. We were both abandoned, and we need to suck it up and get on with our lives!"

Dayna purged herself of the tension she'd accumulated since seeing Ellie's portrait in Aunt Mara's library. It felt good to have this out in the open. At last, her pent-up hurt and anger found the light of day since leaving Portugal.

Alex said nothing, only fiddled with something in his lap. He cleared his throat and shifted in his chair. His disappointment was obvious. "Well. Thanks for telling me where you stand." He stood to go.

Her heart thundered so hard it hurt.

Her hand flew to her chest, and she wondered if she was having a heart attack.

Chapter 38

Alex

Alex felt gut-punched, knowing he deserved her wrath. Knowing deep down she'd react this way. What did he expect? He stood staring down at her, vacillating.

Stay or go?

When her hand clutched her chest, she seemed in pain. His indecision switched to concern. "Are you all right?"

She took her hand away, rested it on the table, and took a deep breath. "Yes, and no."

"Is it your blood pressure? I'm sorry if I caused it to rise."

"Normally you've always lowered it. I considered you my BP medication." She gave him a cool look. "Don't worry, I'm not about to croak. Not yet, anyway."

Alex knew what he had to do.

Somehow, he had to convince Dayna that he wanted her more than anything. More than Ellie. He sat, his neck muscles tensing. "You said before you'd fight for me—fight for us. Did you mean it?"

"Yes—before you ran out on me." She fidgeted, wiggling her high-heeled foot.

She looked terrific in that suit. Hot and professional. It ached him. "I left because I feared commitment and didn't want to hurt you."

Her face contorted. "Oh baloney, don't give me that! Enough of the 'didn't want to hurt you' routine! You aren't scoring points with me. You already ripped my heart to shreds!"

"Aunt Mara filled me in on how you re-decorated her guest house with a Ming vase. I told her to subtract it from my profits."

Dayna lifted her chin. "I'll reimburse her for it. Even if it takes my entire 401k—"

"I took care of it. Don't worry, it wasn't valuable." He held up his hand. "Listen, Dayna, please. Hear me out. Give me the chance to say what I came here to say." He'd practiced all the way down from Anchorage.

She snapped her mouth closed, pushed her chair back, and crossed her legs. Her stilettoed foot wiggled so fast he thought it might be spasming.

"My daughter, Zoey, and I stayed up all night talking when I got home. We realized neither of us could let go because we'd never talked about losing Ellie. We were each spinning in our grief phases of denial and depression. Never made it to acceptance." He shifted in his chair and took another sip of water. "We've helped each other to acceptance now. We're both healing. I couldn't let go because—I hadn't realized I needed my daughter's permission."

Dayna's expression remained neutral. "You're a grown man. You don't need your daughter's permission."

"I was afraid of losing her." He cleared his throat. "All the way down here, I told myself to stop wasting time. All that mourning got me nowhere—only further away from you."

He leaned forward and rested his forearms on the

table. "Please believe me when I say the past is behind me. You're right. You shouldn't have to compete with a ghost. And from now on, you won't. I've let go of my wife. Please trust me when I say that."

"Trust you?" Pain crossed Dayna's face, and she squinted at the water. "Don't know if I can."

"Look at me, Dayna. Please. Look at me." He had to make her understand.

She swung her gaze back to him. She appeared soft and golden in the afternoon light.

He dragged his chair next to hers and took her hand. "Eventually, you must trust to have what you want. But first, you must believe you can. You've got to have faith. Can you forgive me for leaving?"

Her face tightened, and she bit her lip. She turned her head, staring at the water.

"I messed up, Dayna," he said, sighing and shaking his head. "I panicked when you said you could love me. I needed time to figure things out. And I have."

"I want to believe you. I really do. Now I'm the one who needs time..." She shook her head and her eyes watered. She turned toward the floating sea otter again, wishing she could be at peace right along with him.

Alex's chest clenched at having caused her so much pain. Resting his hand on hers, he reached in his pocket with the other and handed her his lens cloth. He liked how her mouth curved up when she took it.

"This is the same lens cloth you gave me last time I cried." She dabbed at her eyes.

"Please believe me when I say you're the person I want to talk to, wake up next to, make love with. I've not heard the end of it from Aunt Mara or Zoey. They've chewed me out and ripped me a new one. Can you find it in your heart to forgive me?" He waited, willing to do more groveling. "Please?"

She wiped a tear from her cheek, then sat still, clutching his lens cloth. His eyes tracked hers, fixed on the sleeping sea otter floating peacefully next to the pier.

"Dammit, Dayna, what do I have to do to prove it to you?" He glanced down the pier, then stood and held out his hand. "Come with me."

She stared at his hand but didn't take it. "Where?"

"Just come with me a minute. Please." He stepped along the pier.

She hesitated, then stood and followed.

He walked a short distance and stopped. Turning to her, he held up his hand, fingers spread. "See this? You said one day I'd take off this ring, thinking it's only a ring—that I'd toss it in the ocean or melt it down for a salmon lure. Well, I'm not fishing for salmon anytime soon."

He flicked his eyes at her, then tugged off his wedding band. He rolled it into his fist, stepped back in a pitcher's wind-up, and chucked it out over the water. The sun glinted it before it plunked into the ocean.

The sea otter remained oblivious, but a gull landed on the deck rail, eyeing him.

"Do you believe me *now*?"

Dayna glanced at the gull, then up at him. "I don't know…I just don't know…" She swiped at a tear.

He wanted to throw his arms around her, but he didn't think she'd want him to. "I'm flying out first thing in the morning. If you change your mind, you have my number."

He felt a numbing sense of relief as the gull lifted off and flew toward open water, the same as on Ellie's memorial card.

Goodbye, Ellie.

Remembering his jacket, he stepped back to the table to retrieve it. Without a word, he pulled it on, slid on his sunglasses, and straightened. He finally did it—cut the cord to the past. And to his relief, it felt good.

If only Dayna would smile and open her arms to him. Instead, she stood there, staring at him. "I don't know what to say."

"This might help." He pulled a folded magazine page from his pocket and with one hand snapped it open and read out loud. "Maybe someday I'll forgive that fabulous guy for breaking my heart in Portugal." He held it out to her. "Correct me if I'm wrong, but I think someday is today."

Her jaw dropped as she took her magazine article and stared at it, then glanced up at him. She opened her mouth to speak, but nothing came out.

"I hope you can walk your talk, Cali-Girl." He hesitated, then turned and strode briskly down the pier, leaving her gaping after him. Without breaking stride, he turned to face her, stepping backward.

She stood, staring at the page in her hands.

His heart tugged at her forlorn, bewildered expression, but he resisted the instinct to go to her. Instead, he called out, not caring who heard him.

"I left because I love you!" He turned and headed to Mariko's waiting Prius.

His gut twisted, and he hoped Dayna could find it in her heart to forgive him. This was the only woman he wanted; the only woman who'd made him feel good about himself. She was full of life and made him laugh. Sure, they'd both been the walking wounded. But who wasn't at this point in life?

She was good for him and helped him see things for what they were. If she couldn't find a way to forgive him for leaving her, he'd never forgive himself.

Alex climbed into the car. His vexation must have been evident, as Mariko reached over and squeezed his hand. She started the car and drove him to the San Luis Obispo airport.

Alex had told Dayna everything he'd flown all this way to say.

Chapter 39

Dayna

Dayna blinked in confusion and couldn't stop trembling. All she could do was sit and contemplate the sea otter who'd awakened and busied himself with cracking shells on his chest.

Alex tossing his wedding ring like a *Giant's* pitcher, combined with his parting words, hit her with such force a server asked if she was all right.

"May I have some ice water, please?" She inhaled deep yoga breaths to calm herself, clutching Alex's saturated lens cloth in her fist. She opened her hand and stared at it, remembering their time in Portugal, and how they'd first bared their souls to one another.

She pawed through her purse for ibuprofen. Clutching the bottle, she sat back and closed her eyes, pinching the bridge of her nose with thumb and forefinger.

Why couldn't she take him back? What had stopped her?

If Alex abandoned me once, would he do it again?
Her insides shredded.

The server set down a tall glass of ice water, and Dayna popped the ibuprofen in her mouth and chugged. Brain freeze replaced the pain jabs in her head. She sat back, watching the floating sea otter crack more shells on his chest.

After a while, footsteps sounded, and Mariko stood before her with folded arms. "I can't believe you're so damn stubborn that you won't take him back!" She yanked out a chair and plopped into it.

Dayna retaliated. "Why did you set me up like that? Can't believe you did that."

"You wouldn't have talked to him otherwise. He practically begged me to think of a way for him to see you. I called Tessa to set up a fake meeting. So, sue me. What was I supposed to do?" Mariko rarely spun herself up, and it hurled Dayna off center.

"You could have given me a heads-up," snapped Dayna, hands trembling. She clasped them to stop the shaking.

"How much groveling do you want Alex to do? You're making him bury his wife all over again. You won't have Alex or anyone else until you accept people for who they are."

Dayna leveled her tone. "I accept everyone for who they are." She wished this wasn't happening. Her heart pounded, abhorring this confrontation with her gentle, soft-spoken bestie.

Mariko groaned. "Don't hand me that crock. You don't work on it, you *do* it! What if this is your only shot at love for the rest of your life? Alex loves you. Christ, Dayna, this isn't rocket science!"

Flabbergasted at Mariko's red-faced outburst, Dayna gawked at her friend, open-mouthed like a hungry bird. She'd never heard her use JC's name in vain.

Mariko's eyes flashed. "Why else would he have flown all the way here from Alaska? You want a guarantee he won't leave you again?" She framed her mouth with her hands, same as when she'd yell at third base. "Newsflash! There are no guarantees on this model. You can't exchange him for a better one at Costco. When will you get a clue? When you're six feet under or scattered on a beach someplace?"

"No! I just—I just…" Dayna's eyes filled with tears.

"Don't you dare cry. You aren't the victim here." Mariko's eyes burned a hole into Dayna's.

To say she was angry was an understatement. For a moment, Dayna thought Mariko might get physical. She'd never seen her lose her shit, and it rattled her.

"I need some time—" Dayna squeaked out.

"Bullshit!" Mariko thundered on like a locomotive. "Alex is here *now*. He's moved mountains for you. Know how hard that is? Those of us who've lost the love of our lives to death let go when we're damn good and ready. It's taken Alex three years, and it took me five. Some spend lifetimes of never letting go. All I can say is, Alex must love the hell out of you to go to all this trouble."

"He ran out on me, Mariko!" She practically yelled it.

"So the hell what? He came all this way to make it up to you. For cripes' sakes, Dayna, give him another chance. Don't screw this up, or I'll have to listen to you whine about it for the rest of your freaking life."

Dayna's heart thumped like a scared rabbit. "I don't want to get hurt again—"

Mariko's voice rose another octave.

"He *will* hurt you again. I guarantee it. And you'll hurt him. You think Harv and I never hurt each other in all the years we were together? That's why it's called hurt. When you love each other, you hurt each other. You apologize, you fix it, and then you love each other some more. People hurt each other because, I don't know—humans are stupid shits!"

Dayna sat still as a stone, staring at her friend as if she'd morphed into an octopus. In all their years of friendship, Mariko had never raised her voice to Dayna, much less used profanity. This was a historical moment. One that would live in infamy.

"He still grieves his wife—" Dayna said in a quiet voice.

Mariko leaned forward. "Grief is complicated. Loving widows and widowers is even more complicated. Mix it together and you have one hot mess."

"No, I'm the hot mess!" Dayna mumbled.

"Well, praise the saints. We agree on something!" Mariko threw up her arms. "FYI, the fix to your hot mess is at the San Luis airport, getting ready to fly home. Let's see if you have the guts to step up to the plate."

"Alex said he wasn't leaving until morning," countered Dayna.

"He changed his mind after he couldn't change yours. He's probably gone by now."

Mariko smacked down a *Sunrise Magazine* and a *Cosmopolitan* on the table. "I sent Alex your articles. Instead of judging him for not letting go of his past, follow your *own* stinking advice and let go of your *own* past." She turned and marched off the pier.

Dayna's chest hollowed, watching her friend disappear out of sight. She stared at the magazines, then picked them up and stuck them in her purse.

She'd plunged headlong into an endless chasm, without a life preserver—lost and confused. She'd never experienced Mariko's wrath, and frankly, it scared the shit out of her. Her cheeks heated at being called out on the truth: she'd been so obsessed about avoiding the past, she'd feared living in the present.

Mariko nailed it...I'm a hypocrite, lecturing Alex about not letting go when I've done the same thing.

It pained Dayna to admit that her BFF was right.

About everything.

Chapter 40

Dayna

Dayna sped her Miata down the highway, tapping her phone for the hundredth time. Why wasn't he answering?

Pick up, Alex!

She tossed her phone onto the passenger seat and left the speed limit behind in the dust.

"It's only a guideline anyway. Highway Patrol, don't even think about pulling me over," she mumbled, peering into her rearview mirror.

Not after deciding to forgive Alex Mendes.

Finally, she spotted the sign for the airport. She slammed her brakes, tires squealing and laying rubber. She turned right onto the road leading to the airport, trying to remember where the small planes were parked. There were only two runways, but she'd always used the commercial airlines. She missed the old days when you could walk right up to the small plane hangars.

She found her way to the parking lot on the opposite side of the main terminal. Had Alex said what type of plane he flew? Had she even asked him? Her mind drew a blank. She climbed out of her tiny blue convertible and slammed the door. Stepping along a tall chain-link fence, she searched for a gate and spotted one up ahead.

A white car with an orange cherry on top cruised the

tarmac and pulled up to the gate. Airport security.

She hurried to talk to the driver as two gates automatically swung open. The driver slid down his window.

"I'm looking for a small plane pilot from Alaska. Can I go look for him?"

He pointed his shades at her. "No, ma'am, not without a specific security pass."

She gestured with her phone. "I can't get hold of him. Is there a way you can radio pilots or something?"

He shook his head.

"Can you please check to see if there's a plane from Alaska?"

"Lady, look how many planes are over there. It'll take all day." His window slid up, and he rolled his car through the gate.

A reckless thought flashed. Maybe she could sneak inside before the gate closed. She hesitated. Too late. Fingers curled around chain-link, she peered inside at planes parked across the tarmac. Who knew which one was his? Her heart trickled to the asphalt.

Positioning her shades in the bright sunlight, she squinted at her phone and tapped Alex's number. It rang forever.

"Hello?"

"Alex? It's Dayna."

"Who?"

She clicked her tongue. "You know who. Where are you?" She moved closer to the fence, peering across the tarmac.

"Right here." A voice behind her caused her to jump. She spun around and sucked in a breath. Her heart shot to her throat.

Alex stood with one hand holding the phone to his ear and the other gripping a duffle at his side. He was a vision in his brown leather jacket and blue jeans. A gentle breeze lifted his hair. "Took you long enough."

She pushed up her sunglasses and placed her hands on her hips. "Since when do you read *Cosmo*?" Joyous tears blurred him, and she blinked them back. She bit her lip to hold it together.

"Since you wrote about someday forgiving me." He gave her a playful grin. "You didn't know I was a closet *Cosmo* reader? Picked up some tips on romantic flings when traveling—from a writer friend in California."

She'd missed his gentle camaraderie and subtle wit. "Care to have another vacay fling? You're still traveling, and I know where there's a good beach."

"Hmm, let me think and get back to you." He paused. "Okay, I've thought about it." He dropped his duffle and gathered her up to kiss her.

She slid her arms around his waist and kissed him back, wrapping a stilettoed foot around his leg. Her pencil skirt protested with a loud rip.

Alex chuckled into her mouth and when he finished kissing her, he backed up, smiling. "So. You believed me."

She wiped her mouth with the back of her hand. "I only showed up because you're a good kisser." She nodded at the airfield. "Put that plane to bed. We're going to my place."

"Already have. What took you so long, anyway?"

She dropped her jaw. "Well, aren't we presumptuous? How did you know I'd even show up?"

"I know you. Once someone proves something to you, eventually you get around to believing it. But sometimes it's best to flat out trust people."

She raised her brows, joy untangling her insides. "Is that so?"

"You're fun to argue with, I'll give you that. Frankly, it turned me on—until you went for my jugular." He scratched his nose with a forefinger. "Where are you parked?"

"Why?" She sent him a coy look. "You want to do me in my tiny convertible? Your legs would dangle over the side."

He grinned. "Love how you cut to the chase. I've missed that about you."

Dayna turned and pointed. "I'm parked over there."

She practically ran to her car, stumbling in the stupid stilettoes, her heart soaring like the planes taking off. Dayna clicked open the trunk and Alex tossed in the duffel and closed it. She kicked off her torturous heels and tossed them on the floor in the passenger side.

Alex swung a leg over the passenger door and climbed in, sinking into the white leather seat. "Cute car, Cali-girl." He held up a peep-toed stiletto and lifted his brow. "You sizzle in these, by the way."

"Wore these to dinner, remember? They cost me my firstborn at the Lisbon Fashion Boutique." Beaming at him, she lowered herself to the driver's seat, intent on getting him to her bungalow as fast as she could. She wanted to get naked with him as soon as possible.

Once on the highway to Cambria, she glanced at him and yelled above the road noise, "What you said back there? Say it again."

"Which part?" he yelled back.

She lowered her shades, hair whipping around her face. "You know which part."

His smile lit up her world. "The part where I want to wake up with you for the rest of my life?"

She knew he knew what she angled for. "And the other part." She blew past a sign for Padilla Beach.

"Wait—turn in here," Alex pointed at the upcoming turnoff to the deserted beach, his hair lashing in the wind. "Just in time for the sunset."

"You're such a romantic." She flashed him a grin and pulled into a parking space and cut the engine.

"Damn right." He leaned across and kissed her. "I want make-up sex on the beach. We met on a beach, remember? We need to consummate things on your home turf." He opened the car door and turned to look at her. "Then on mine." He got out and slammed the door, rocketing her anticipation.

"You'll fly me to Alaska? Are the beaches there warm enough for—consummation?"

"In the summer, yeah." He shot her a seductive wink that fired her afterburners.

She bailed out of the driver's seat and couldn't open the trunk fast enough to pull out a beach blanket.

"Pick up the pace, woman," he called over his shoulder before disappearing behind the sand dunes.

As she stumbled after him in bare feet with the sand massaging her toes, her heart bubbled over. She thought about coincidence and fate.

Aunt Mara was right. You don't get to choose who you love. It happens, whether you like it or not. Alex was also right…believe it can happen and trust that it will.

Alex had everything off but his boxers by the time she'd reached the private spot he'd chosen behind the dunes. She laughed at the miniature puffins dotting his boxers. He turned to display his rear, with 'Stud Puffin' scrolled across his luscious ass.

Her smile deepened into laughter. "You can be my Stud Puffin any day."

Dayna spread her blanket on the sand, then her fingers flew to unbutton her suit jacket. Alex stepped behind to unzip her skirt as she pulled her silky white tank top over her head.

She tugged off his boxers and accosted him. In no time, he'd stripped her naked. She was no longer embarrassed about her body with him. She stood proud, head held high, shoulders back, offering him her six-thousand-dollar breasts because he made her feel young and beautiful.

"Tell me again what you said on the pier," she breathed as they lowered themselves to the blanket and he kissed his way to her lips.

He eased back, gazing into her soul. "You mean that thing where I said I love you?"

She decided his eyes weren't gray. They were Pacific Ocean blue. "Yes. Prove it."

"You writers are such cynics. All right. If you say so." He positioned himself to take her. As he did, lazy waves curled and broke at the shoreline in a subdued cadence, their gliding remnants smoothing the sand.

"With unlimited access to each other, we'll need to pace ourselves." She breathed hard under him, relishing every deep push. "We aren't twenty anymore."

"I still have my little blue friends from Lisbon, so I'll wear *you* out first."

"Little blue...oh!" She ascended to altitude, happy tears tracking her cheeks.

"Lay back, relax, and enjoy your flight." He pushed harder.

"We'll break in your plane. Fly me where no woman has flown before," she moaned, reaching her stratosphere as a spectacular display of pinks, purples, and reds spliced the horizon.

"Love it when you talk travel." He peaked at his own edge of space.

She had always hoped for a miracle to love like this again.

This new beginning opened Dayna up in ways she never expected. It freed her, opening her world to endless possibilities. The little French nun had been right all along. Turns out forgiveness was the golden ticket out of endless self-flagellation and blaming others for what she couldn't have.

The heavy chains she'd bound tight around her heart had dissolved. Gone.

All she had to do was click her heels three times and open her eyes to see what—and who—was in front of her. Could she love harder than before?

I already have.

She nuzzled Alex, and they held each other to the sound of gentle, breaking waves.

As twilight became starlight and the night sky reigned supreme, Dayna Benning gave herself over to the miracle of loving Alexander Mendes.

And miracle of miracles…he loved her right back.

A word about the author…

LoLo Paige is an award-winning author who has a passion for writing romantic comedies after decades of theatre experience acting in stage comedies. While comedy is her first love, she also writes the pitfalls of falling in love in the action-packed, perilous world of wildfire. As a former wildland firefighter who married her hot firefighter husband, she lives her HEA, spending glorious Alaskan summers at her oceanfront cabin on Kachemak Bay, and winters in Eagle River, with her husband and two golden retrievers.

Thank you for purchasing
this publication of The Wild Rose Press, Inc.

For questions or more information
contact us at
info@thewildrosepress.com.

The Wild Rose Press, Inc.
www.thewildrosepress.com